An excerpt from Caressa's Knees

He lifted her cello with almost tender movements. She watched, feeling some alien emotion. Fondness? Damn Denise. Caressa looked away, letting music crowd into her subconscious as she followed him off the plane. There was always music in her head and she never knew what kind it would be. Of late, it was Saint-Saëns most of the time, tormenting her and riddling her with doubts. She must have been crazy to take it on at this point in her career. Saint-Saëns' Concerto One was something cellists did at the height of their arc. After this, there will be nowhere to go but down.

Caressa sometimes suspected that she wanted to go down.

"Caressa?" Denise said her name sharply, and she yanked her gaze from Mr. Winchell's broad back. *You can call me Kyle*, he'd said on the plane, right after she asked him to call her Caressa. *Mr. Winchell* fit him better, with his perfectly-tailored dark suit and serious expression. He couldn't be much older than her, but he seemed older.

Caressa trailed after him and Denise fell in behind her. Saint-Saëns went silent in her head, replaced by thoughts of what Mr. Winchell might look like with his suit off. The idea of it made music start again. Wild, unruly arpeggios. The more she thought of it, the more her nipples tightened against the scratchy mesh of her sheer bra. She pulled her cardigan shut in front of her, lest he turn around and see. When they climbed into the limo, she placed her cello between them like some kind of shield.

God, the music was making her crazy. She just wanted some silence, just for a moment, a minute. She was going out of her mind, and Kyle Winchell wasn't going to do anything but make her crazier. Somehow, she was sure of that.

Caressa's Knees

By

Annabel Joseph

For Miri

Prologue

Bright blinding light. A sharp, rough-edged voice.

"Wake up. *Wake up!*"

Kyle came to alertness like a deep diver surfacing for air. He opened his eyes and closed them again with a groan. *Too bright.* Someone had opened the blinds, and that someone was shaking him. He wanted to throttle whoever was doing it, but he couldn't seem to move his arms. "Damn it," he muttered to no one in particular.

"Wake up, Kyle. God, you're a fucking mess."

Kyle still couldn't open his eyes, but he recognized the voice of his employer. Knew it like he knew his own face. Kyle convulsed in a cough and tried to roll over, running his fingers through his tangled hair. "What are you doing here? How did you get in?"

"The door was unlocked."

Something in the dire tone of his voice finally registered. Kyle forced his eyes open and focused them on Jeremy Gray. How many people got shaken awake on any given morning by an angry movie star? Lucky him. Jeremy, his long time employer, looked put together and suave as always. A blue-eyed, blond-haired god, and as successful as ever, despite the fact that Kyle had been a piss-poor personal assistant the last year and a half. He supposed he should count himself lucky that Jeremy hadn't fired him months ago. Jeremy wasn't even in town very often anymore, and besides that, Kyle was slowly losing his shit. Slowly? The slippery slope was actually turning into more of a freefall.

Kyle noticed Jeremy scowling at something on the floor. Damn. It had to be the coke. Had he passed out? He was still half dressed. His bed was rumpled, with a couple empty vodka bottles and a pair of fuzzy handcuffs rounding out his disgrace. Jeremy reached over him to pick up the handcuffs with a disdainful snort.

"Fur, Kyle? Really?"

Kyle frowned and tried to lever himself into a sitting position. "Yeah. They're easy to get out of. In case I pass out in the middle."

Jeremy crossed his arms over his chest. "I heard it was bad with you, but I didn't realize how bad. And it's my money paying for…this?" he asked, sweeping another look around Kyle's messy, vice-strewn apartment. His thousand-dollar wardrobe was scattered in piles on the floor, and beer and alcohol bottles were everywhere. Kyle leaned down to surreptitiously slide the mirror and coke under the bed. Jeremy's foot came down on his wrist in a press of expensive Italian leather. "I've already seen it. Leave it."

"I was at a party, Jeremy. Things got out of hand. Brought this girl home."

"Yeah, and that girl probably took your wallet home. Cocaine?"

"She brought it with her."

"Yeah, right. I heard you got blacklisted from LoveSlave last week. Something about playing while intoxicated. I didn't believe it, but now…"

"Fuck LoveSlave. I wasn't that messed up that night. That sub was just…" He screwed his eyes shut, rubbing them viciously. He *had* been messed up, chasing demons that never went away. "Who the fuck cares? There are a hundred other dungeons in L.A."

"Yeah, but LoveSlave is private and exclusive, and remind me who got you in there?"

"You did," Kyle grumbled.

"Yeah, I did. Now word's gotten around that you're a mess, that you're dangerous."

"You're the one who got me into the kinky shit in the first place."

"Oh, it's my fault?" Jeremy asked with one dangerously arched brow.

Kyle sighed and dropped his head in his hands. "What do you want, Jeremy? If you're going to fire me, fire me. It would probably be the merciful thing to do," he added under his breath.

"If I knew it would get this bad, I would have fired you long ago."

I wish you had, you fucking prick. Then I could have drank and partied myself to death that much sooner. It was getting too hard, too hard. Jeremy was like a father, brother, and best friend to him, all rolled in one, but it was getting too hard to keep up the facade anymore. It was getting too hard to maintain any facade at all. He hated himself. He hated his life and the way he lived it. He hated that Jeremy had everything, including the woman that haunted his dreams.

"How's Nell?" Kyle asked in a bitter whisper.

"Get up," Jeremy snapped. "We're going out."

* * * * *

Kyle knew Jeremy was right. He was a mess. His clothes didn't even fit him anymore, his belt cinching jeans over a dwindling waistline and his tee hanging loose on his shoulders where it used to stretch tight. He used to have a six pack. The body of an Adonis. Now he looked like shit. He felt like shit. Jeremy parked a block away from the restaurant and Kyle was sure it was so he could chuckle inwardly as Kyle squinted against the L.A. sun and labored to take each step. He had to cut out the coke. And those sleeping pills he'd started taking. That had been a huge mistake.

He could get off them though. The alcohol was the really bad thing, because he never stopped with that. He had the shakes already. When they got to the restaurant, Jeremy chose to sit outside on the patio, in the sun and stifling August air. Kyle felt shamed and dissected in the harsh morning light as he tried to hold it together in front of his boss. Damn Jeremy. It was too early to order a drink.

Kyle hunched over the menu and ordered iced coffee and toast. Jeremy ordered enough food for both of them, being the pig he was. But damn, he looked great as always. He was in his mid-forties, almost twenty years older than Kyle, and he was the picture of good health. Kyle had been drawn in by Jeremy's charisma and energy from the start.

When he'd shown up at the job interview for personal assistant to Jeremy Gray, movie star, he'd been fresh off the bus from Spur, Texas. He didn't know how he'd made the first cut, or how he'd ended up being hired after a short sit down with the megastar himself. He only knew that his life had changed, that *he* had changed irreversibly in the months and years that followed. And not for the better. He looked up at the man across from him. Honestly, Jeremy had given him so many opportunities…and the salary… It was hard to feel ungrateful, but…

"You know, I feel this is my fault," Jeremy said, as if reading his thoughts.

Jeremy's words sounded heavy, like some kind of ending. Was this an ending, right now? Kyle had known it was coming, but he still felt shocked somehow. He was flailing, about to go under the waves. Jeremy was texting on his cell, cool and collected as ever. Kyle tried to keep his voice steady. "Look, I can pull it together. I can still work for you. It was just a party that got out of hand. One party."

Jeremy glanced up from his phone with a grimace. "It wasn't just one party. We've worked together for five years. We've had our dicks in the same woman. For fuck's sake, don't lie to me."

Jeremy looked back at his phone. Text, text, text. The food arrived and Kyle's stomach clenched and turned over. Jeremy shoveled his food in and washed it down with Pellegrino. If Kyle had still been doing his job, he would have known who Jeremy was texting. He would have known exactly why he was in town, and when and where his next appointment was. With a start, he realized he hadn't actually done work for Jeremy in weeks, and yet he was still getting paychecks. Paychecks to finance the partying. Kyle picked up a piece of toast, then put it down again.

"So I guess you're here in town to fire me. Thanks for making the trip."

Jeremy put his phone down on the table with a scowl. "Fire you? I'm not giving you anything to do anyway. I only kept you on because I felt I owed you for…"

For her. Nell. The love of my life. And yours.

They never talked about Nell, by tacit agreement. Nell was ensconced back in Boston, taking classes at Harvard, being Jeremy's wife. Nell, with the fiery red hair and those eyes that never, ever looked cynical or ruthless. Kyle had found Nell, and he had delivered her to Jeremy like the good personal assistant he was. And of course she'd wanted Jeremy. Nell loved Jeremy, adored him, and Jeremy worshipped her. Kyle knew Nell was not for him, and Jeremy knew Nell was not for him. Nell knew she was not for him. They *all* knew it, so why couldn't he get over her?

He'd started the drinking and partying to dull the pain after Nell and Jeremy got married. He'd started haunting the BDSM clubs to try to find someone like her. He'd taken on a never-ending parade of willing, nubile subbies, none of whom he could recall by name. All of them poor substitutes for Nell. He'd stayed in Jeremy's employ just to have that tenuous link to her. He found he loved the alcohol, he loved dominating women, sure… Much needed distraction. But his love for Nell wasn't going away.

"Kyle, I actually hired a new personal assistant. Two months ago."

Bam. And there you go.

"You were good at your work once, but working for me just isn't the right situation for you anymore. And to be honest, I asked you to do things I probably shouldn't have."

"Yeah, and I did them."

"Anyway. Water under the bridge. I'm different now. You are too. But I'm better, and you're worse. Much worse."

Kyle swallowed hard. Jeremy was always so brutally blunt, which had its good points and bad. Kyle took a bite of dry toast, wishing he had some rum to put in his coffee. Jeremy was ignoring him again, more texting on his phone.

So he would need to find another job. He could manage it, he was sure. Even if he didn't find something right away, he had tons of money in the bank. Jeremy had overpaid him ridiculously during the time he worked for him, so he could coast for a while. Figure out what to do. He had no real skills, just a knack for organization and a Spur High School diploma, which didn't count for much in Texas, much less L.A. He'd been told many times he could work as a model. Maybe if he got back in shape. Jesus, the idea of going to the gym... He cleared his throat and ran his hand through his hair. He needed a haircut. And Jeremy needed a personal assistant who was actually capable of assisting him.

"I hope the new guy works out, Jeremy."

"Sure. But what about you?"

"What about me?"

Jeremy waved his phone. "I've been communicating with a friend in New York. Runs an agency. PAs, security, household workers. Discreet service personnel for celebrities and filthy rich people. If you still want to do this kind of work, I can get you a spot with him. The money's good in New York and he's a stand-up guy."

"You would do that for me?"

Jeremy leaned back and tapped his fingers on the table. "Yeah. When you're clean, of course. How long have you been using?"

"Using what?" Kyle tried for a smile, but didn't quite accomplish it with the sudden tightness in his throat.

Jeremy chuckled. "I see. That bad. You were totally clean a year ago. I rarely even saw you drink."

"People change."

"And they can change back." Jeremy leaned forward again, pinning Kyle with a ruthless gaze. "She's not worth it, you know. Nobody is worth what you're doing to yourself."

"Not worth it? I thought you loved her."

"I do love her. I still wouldn't let her destroy me. And she is destroying you."

Kyle laughed. "Really? Dramatic much? I haven't even seen her in months."

Jeremy didn't respond, just stared at him with those blue, piercing eyes. Those eyes that made billions, sold movie tickets to avid fans all over the world. But this wasn't a movie.

"Kyle," Jeremy said. "Nell's pregnant. We're starting a family."

"Oh." It knocked the breath right out of him, the thought of it. "You wanted that?"

"Yes. We wanted it. She's very happy. I can never thank you enough for everything you did for me. For her. For us." He smiled. "Jesus, you took a bullet for her."

"Eight centimeters from the heart," Kyle said woodenly.

"Yeah." Jeremy sighed. "Now it's time to move on. It's time for you to get better. I am guilty about enough things—I can't live with this too."

Kyle clasped his hands in front of him, resting his cheek against the back of his palm. Why were his hands so cold? It was still warm in Los Angeles. He was so cold. He felt frozen.

"I'll help you, Kyle. I know a good place you can rehab. Once you're off the stuff, you can build a new life in New York so you don't even miss it. There's a lot going on there and I think a change of scene will do you worlds of good." He paused and thought for a moment. "There are other Nells out there too, you know. Maybe not exactly the same. But they're out there."

Kyle tried for flippancy. "I'll hire a personal assistant to find one for me."

Jeremy didn't laugh, didn't even smile. "I'll do whatever I have to do to help you. I swear, Kyle. I owe you. I won't let you go down."

Chapter One:
Valuable and Fragile

Kyle headed into Ironclad's New York office in the breezy spring weather, feeling dapper in his favorite gray designer suit and tie. He liked dressing up for these meetings, shaving off the stubble and putting on the monkey suit. All of Ironclad's clients were wealthy, so its employees were well-versed in the currencies of money and power, not to mention discretion.

In his old life as Jeremy Gray's assistant, discretion had been Kyle's middle name. It had to be, and for a long time, that was okay with Kyle. But things were different now, and in a good way. Jeremy had been right, he'd just needed to sober up and find a change of scenery. Last week, when the photos of Nell and Jeremy's newborn daughter were burning up the internet and plastered all over the tabloids, he'd felt a twinge, but nothing like the despair he'd expected.

The truth was, as much as Nell moved him, he could never have made her happy. He realized that now—now that the haze of drugs and alcohol had evaporated. He'd always been the third wheel to their barreling love story. He was his own wheel now. A unicycle. He planned to stay that way for the foreseeable future.

Kyle jabbed the button for the elevator. Five minutes early. He'd get to the thirty-fifth floor right on time. He was a little curious about meeting his new client, some classical musician who made a lot of money for a lot of people and needed an assistant for an upcoming tour. *Caressa Gallo*, Walter had exclaimed, as if that should mean something to him.

Kyle wasn't a classical music kind of guy, but he could fake it. He'd worked in L.A. long enough to fake it with the best of them. The client's agent said she wanted a personal assistant and light security, which was more or less the same thing he'd done for Jeremy. As if that weren't enough, Walter named a salary that was Jeremy Gray-ish in its generosity.

Curious, Kyle had typed '*Caressa Gallo, cellist*' into a search engine, and been shocked to find so many results about a person he'd never heard of before. He'd read a short bio he found on the first page and learned that she was just twenty years old. So young to have accomplished so much in the music world. He'd clicked on the photo tab and found pages of pictures of his prospective client. A mop of outrageously unkempt hair, dark like his. Green eyes. Was he *still* a sucker for green eyes? Even now, with a singular focus and intention to forget her, he subconsciously measured all women against Nell.

But Caressa Gallo would not be a woman to him, just a client. He would do what he was paid to do and keep his emotions out of it this time. Manage her concert commitments, appearances and travel, whatever she needed. Maybe she just wanted a lackey to tote her cello around. She definitely needed someone to brush her hair, because she seemed uninterested in doing so. As long as he was getting paid, he would lend his expertise to whatever tasks necessary.

Still, Kyle felt somewhat disappointed when he got to the conference room only to be greeted by Walter and an older woman. The woman offered her hand and Walter introduced her as Denise Gallo, Caressa's aunt and manager. She had mousy brown hair and a kind of affronted manner about her. Her mouth tightened a little as Kyle shook her hand. After they sat, Walter slid a dossier across the table in Kyle's direction.

"The specs of the job. Caressa Gallo is embarking on a nationwide tour beginning the second week of May that will culminate in a series of appearances in Europe through late August. Ms. Gallo tells me they are most anxious to find an assistant who can sign on for the entire tour, rather than having to shuttle people in and out."

"I can understand that," said Kyle. "It's not a problem for me." Not with the numbers Walter had highlighted at the bottom of the first page. Kyle was sure his family would understand if he passed on the Spur Fourth of July festivities this year. "So, what exactly will your niece need in the way of services? Scheduling? Managing appearances? Personal errands?"

"We have a remote tour manager who deals with most of the day-to-day scheduling and such," Denise Gallo said.

"So it's more of a security detail?" Kyle asked.

Walter paused a moment and Ms. Gallo shifted with obvious uneasiness.

"Mr. Winchell," she said. "My niece is…how shall I say this? Very high-strung. You must understand, she has led a most unusual life. She began to play at six and started her first tour when she was ten. She recorded her first CD soon afterward. She is very passionate and talented, but she can sometimes be…difficult to handle."

Kyle regarded the woman, choosing his words carefully. "Are you saying that my job will be to 'handle' her? How involved a task will that be?"

Ms. Gallo laughed. "Don't look so alarmed. She's not mentally unbalanced or anything. She is just…different. And with me being family… Well, let me be blunt here. We both need a break from one another sometimes. I'm hoping if someone besides me is dealing with the day-to-day issues, the tour will run more smoothly."

"I understand. Family ties can complicate matters, especially with work. But what about her parents?"

She looked down with a small frown. "My brother and his wife died some years ago in a tragic accident, so it's just been me and Caressa."

"Oh, I'm sorry to hear that."

"There have been difficult times for Caressa, but music is what has always sustained us. Hopefully you can lend a professional edge to the tour and a professional outlook when things between me and my niece go awry. She has her ups and downs, like anyone."

"Artists," Kyle joked with a smirk. He meant to lighten the mood, but Walter coughed and gave him a look. Thankfully, Denise nodded and smiled.

"Precisely. But most of the time she's quite charming. It's unfortunate that you couldn't meet her today but she had prior obligations. A photo shoot, and then practice. Always practices and rehearsals. This tour is a very special event, what could very well be a highpoint of her career. She's going to be playing Saint-Saëns' *Concerto No. 1*." The woman stopped and looked at Kyle for a reaction, and seemed slightly disappointed when she didn't receive it. "*In A minor?*" she added, as if that might shake some inkling of recognition from Kyle's brain.

Kyle shrugged with an apologetic smile. "I know nothing about music. It won't affect my ability to help Miss Gallo fulfill her professional obligations."

"Of course," the older woman said. "Well, what you don't know of it now, you'll learn soon enough. It is a virtuoso piece, and it is demanding not just technically, but emotionally. Let me be perfectly clear, Mr. Winchell. My niece is not an easy person to deal with at times. She will be even less relaxed on this concert tour. What I want is for Caressa to be able to concentrate fully on her music and appearances without getting derailed by distractions, or butting heads with her stodgy old aunt over things that can't be changed. The tour manager, Paul, is adept at scheduling, and I can keep a handle on social arrangements and such, but I'm not so great at handling Caressa herself. My niece is a wonderful person and an extremely talented artist, but more and more lately, I think she needs a…firm hand."

A firm hand. For one wild moment, Kyle imagined himself pulling the talented, mysterious Miss Gallo over his lap for refusing to practice. *You naughty little prodigy.* He felt a hot flush growing behind his ears and leaned forward in his chair, willing his thoughts into submission before a tent formed in his pants.

"Ms. Gallo, I can assure you that I'm up for the job." *Both literally and figuratively.*

"And you can be firm if…well…if she is not always the easiest to manage?"

Kyle smothered a smile. "I can be firm when I need to be. And I understand exactly what you mean about focus. There are always so many annoying details and distractions when you're traveling and trying to get work done. You just want me to provide a nudge when necessary, and keep her focused when she's supposed to work. In the most professional way possible."

Ms. Gallo looked relieved, nodding. "Exactly. Yes, you understand completely. You see, I only want my niece to find success. She has worked so hard—"

She stopped, placing her fingers very carefully over her lips, and for a moment Kyle thought she might cry. But she rallied and waved her arm with a flourish. "She is an amazing musician. She works very hard, and I want to surround her with all the tools of success."

So Kyle was to be one of those *tools of success.* He could be a tool all right. "I understand, Ms. Gallo. It would be my pleasure to help your client reach her goals. I'm sure Walter has shared my references."

"Of course. That was the reason we considered you first. Glowing references, and from Jeremy Gray no less. He says you are professional, dependable, courteous. Discreet." The woman looked hard at Kyle. "Of course, professionalism and discretion will be a must. In this situation…"

Her voice died out, but Kyle kept listening. *In this situation…* What situation? Well, these types of highbrow, arty people always got their panties in a twist, thinking their "situations" were somehow more over the top than everyone else's. Kyle was sure the *situation* was nowhere near as dire as Ms. Gallo seemed to feel. He could control one wayward cellist with a hand tied behind his back. Two hands, probably.

"I'm sure I'll enjoy working with your niece, and you can count on my professionalism from day one to the last day of service. I actually can't wait to meet her, Ms. Gallo."

The woman nodded with a relieved smile and said, "Call me Denise." Then the signing of contracts began.

* * * * *

A couple weeks later Kyle was packed and ready to go. He'd made arrangements for his apartment and spoken to his family in Texas about his new assignment. He felt strangely excited about the detailed itinerary Walter had sent him, along with a thick folder of legal notices, schedules, and questionnaires about his own travel and dining preferences, assembled by the intrepid-but-absent tour manager Paul. This tour was clearly a big undertaking, something very important he'd become involved with.

Not that he was worried. The job specs were simple. Keep an eye on Caressa. Get her where she was supposed to be. Denise would tell him the schedule and he would make sure the Prodigy cooperated. *The Prodigy*. The moniker had stuck in his head after viewing some old concert footage of her online. She had been eleven or twelve maybe, an awkward pre-adolescent with a talent that overshadowed her frizzy hair and acne, and the gangly knees that poked out on either side of her cello. Kyle hoped he didn't slip up and call her The Prodigy to her face.

Just after ten, his luggage was picked up and taken for him to the airport. A separate car was due to arrive to take the three of them to their flight. Kyle, Denise Gallo, and The Prodi—er—Caressa. He was suited up again in a starched shirt, tie, and dark jacket, hoping against hope he and his new client would get along, since it would be a long three-and-a-half month assignment if they didn't.

Unfortunately, the first meeting wasn't auspicious. The limousine pulled up to the lobby of his building and he climbed in, finding it rather cramped since Caressa's cello case took up the lion's share of the space. She was huddled behind it. When her aunt introduced them, Caressa didn't even look up.

"She's stressed," Denise explained under her breath to Kyle. "She doesn't like to travel."

Kyle nodded and settled back against the seat, studying the young cellist surreptitiously. It was difficult to reconcile the belligerent, frizzy-haired brat he'd envisioned with the silent, serious beauty sitting across from him. And she was a beauty. Long, sleek spiral curls, pale skin and dark lashes. Really lovely lips turned down, at present, in a small frown.

Perhaps Aunt Denise had exaggerated her problem-child qualities. Kyle hoped so. The rest of the trip to the airport was uneventful. He and Denise small-talked about the upcoming trip, while Caressa—the reason for the trip—sat in sullen silence behind her cello. In fact, Caressa didn't say a word to him until they were getting out of the limo at the airport, and he reached to help with her instrument.

"Be careful," she snapped. "That's very valuable."

The cello case was hard-sided and, Kyle assumed, had some kind of cushioning system inside, since it was significantly larger than an actual cello. It had wheels and a built-in handle that Caressa pulled out of the wider side.

"Let me do it," he said. "It's no problem."

She looked him in the eyes then, for the first time. An assessing look from decidedly green eyes.

He dropped his voice and leaned closer. "Listen, I'm not stupid. I get it. It's valuable and fragile. You can trust me with it."

For a moment it seemed she would argue, but then she let go of the handle and let him maneuver the instrument across the pavement toward the sliding glass doors. She tripped along beside him, clutching a small handbag and biting her lip. Denise sent their bags off to be checked, but the cello stayed. At security, agents measured, opened, and scanned the case. They carefully inspected Caressa's instrument while she hovered, glowering. Forget about the threat of a concealed bomb or firearm. Kyle thought if they damaged her cello, she would do more violence than all those weapons combined.

With that done, he helped her replace the cello, noting the interior placement and fastenings. As soon as it was secure, she let him roll it to the gate. Denise was already ahead of them, leading them to a private lobby and soon afterward onto the flight. In the first class compartment, there were two seats on one side and three on the other. Denise slid into the double seat with another passenger, so Kyle was left with no choice but to help Caressa strap her cello to the window seat of the three-row.

A flight attendant hovered over them but Caressa wouldn't let her touch the case. Kyle was starting to wonder if Caressa really *wasn't* right in the head, despite Denise's assurances. By the time she flopped into the middle seat beside him with a scowl, he was wondering what he'd gotten himself into. She leaned on the armrest and bit a nail while the other passengers filed past, gawking at her cello. It was so large, it crossed into her space so she was forced even closer to him—no doubt against her will.

Kyle gestured toward the huge case. "Why don't you just check that?"

"The fact that you would even ask that tells me you know nothing about music."

"Guilty. Try not to hate me for it."

She made a small sound like a snort and flipped back her hair, only to have the thick curls fall right back in her face again. "Cellos are very delicate. This one is a Peresson. It's very rare and valuable. The tone and responsiveness—well. Whatever. It's impossible to explain to a non-musician."

"Thank you for trying though. I appreciate it." His conciliatory tone in the face of her haughtiness seemed to give her pause, and she fell silent. "So you don't put an instrument like that in the cargo hold, I suppose."

"No. You would never do that. I wouldn't put a cheap five-hundred-dollar cello in the cargo hold, much less this one."

"Five hundred dollars is cheap? What's that one worth?"

She reached out for the case, caressing it in an almost reverent manner. "I couldn't really say. It's priceless. The fact that I play it makes it even more valuable."

"That's very modest of you." Kyle stretched out his legs and relaxed back into the cushy seat.

"Well, it's true." Was she blushing? Maybe she did have some small inkling of social graces. Probably not. She dug in her bag for sunglasses while the attendant launched into the safety spiel up front. "No offense," Caressa said, "but I don't feel like talking. Despite the fact that Denise purposely trapped me here next to you."

"Trapped you?" Kyle leaned closer to her again, modulating his voice to quiet but authoritative reproach. "Miss Gallo, have I done something to offend you? Because I can honestly say I've never made the acquaintance of anyone so rude."

He couldn't see her eyes through the sunglasses, but her face was pinched and stubborn. "Why should I be happy to meet the new policeman?"

"I'm actually your assistant, not a policeman."

"Is that what she told you?" She gave a mirthless laugh. "Believe me, you're a policeman, and she'll pretty much expect you to keep me under lock and key."

"Really? I was under the impression you did all this voluntarily." He waved his hand around, indicating *all this*—the airplane, the two-inch-thick dossier of tour docs in his hip bag, the monster cello case pressing against her right knee. "If you're being made to tour the world against your will, by all means say so, and I'll whisk you to safety. I love that kind of stuff. Knight in shining armor."

She shifted away from him again with an offended sniff, a slight made less insulting and somewhat funnier but the fact that her cello prevented her from moving more than an inch or two. Her left knee was just a finger's width from his, encased in dark blue denim. He had a sudden urge to put his hand on it and order her to be still. What would she do? Throw his hand off? Curse him out? Or go quiet and docile...?

Ugh, these thoughts. His hand made a loose fist and stayed right where it was. He was determined to be ruled by propriety and not libido.

The attendant was finishing the safety lesson and preparing the cabin for takeoff. As the plane started to move, Caressa's hand came down on the armrest between them and he had to move his arm to make room for hers. His gaze moved from her knees to her fingers, long and graceful as they curled around the edge of the padded divider. He could hear her breaths growing shorter and shallower.

"Okay?" he asked.

The plane was picking up speed as it taxied down the runway. She wet her lips and then bit her lower lip, a nervous tic he already recognized.

"Are you an anxious flyer, Miss Gallo?"

She blanched as the engines roared to life and the plane surged forward. "A little."

He could have rattled off the comforting statistics, explained how unlikely a plane crash really was, but she probably wouldn't have heard him. As the plane tipped backward and took flight, her whole body tensed and she actually gritted her teeth.

"It's okay," he said. He put his hand over hers, lightly, just a reassuring brush of fingertips over her knuckles. As the wheels folded up with an audible *bump bump* and the plane banked sharply left, she turned her hand and closed her fingers on his.

Her palm was sweaty and the higher the plane climbed, the harder she gripped him. He sat very still, trying not to react to the viselike pain of her grasp. He was fairly sure she didn't even realize what she was doing. Behind her glasses her eyes were shut tight. It wasn't until the plane was righted and at cruising altitude that her grip began to ease in slow increments. Finally, she pulled her hand away without a word and hunched onto her side, her shoulder a tense barrier between them.

He left his hand where it was, on the armrest, in case she needed it again. She was silent and still for so long he thought she had fallen asleep. Then he heard her voice—just barely—over the hum of the engines.

"You don't have to call me Miss Gallo. My name is Caressa."

Kyle smiled and looked over at the clouds out the window. It was a small thing, but it was something. And God, she was so pretty. For all her aunt's warnings, he was starting to think this job would be a piece of cake.

Chapter Two:
Hands Full

Caressa uncoiled slowly as the plane taxied up to the jetway. Another flight finished. She felt half-conscious, caught between panic and alertness. She watched him handle her cello, being deliberately slow and cautious, waving off her attempts to intervene. "Let me handle it," he said. "I'm being paid to help you."

Well, she didn't know about that.

Caressa had steeled herself to dislike Kyle Winchell. After the last tour, when her aunt and she had almost killed each other, Denise had set on this idea of hiring a "helper". Caressa thought it was the stupidest idea ever, and hadn't really believed her aunt would do it until the man climbed into the limo that morning. Of course she'd chosen a man, like that would make everything okay between them. Like a man could prevail where two women couldn't find peace. Ironclad Solutions. Ridiculous.

She'd expected a suited-up, pompous gorilla to climb into the car, but the man Denise hired was more like a…panther. Oh, that was so hokey. But she couldn't really look at her new "assistant" without imagining the sleek, smooth power of a panther. He was even dark like a panther, dark-haired and bronze with eyes like dark blue pools. He was actually disgustingly handsome. Caressa knew he was from Los Angeles, which probably explained why his clothes fit so well and his fingernails looked like they'd been professionally manicured. Her own nails were short out of necessity, and she'd never had them done. No one touched her hands, not ever. Although he had…just for a moment. Actually, maybe she'd grabbed his hand while the plane was taking off. She couldn't remember. She hated takeoffs and landings. She hated flying, period.

Now it was really underway…another long, tedious tour. She loved and hated touring. She loved the idea of it, but hated the actual execution, which is why Denise had hired Kyle Winchell. She'd probably hand-picked him because he was so handsome and charming, as if that might bring her more easily to heel. But Caressa heeled for no one.

She would be rid of him soon enough. She didn't need the distraction of him on the tour. She was already thinking of him more than she liked. His mouth was full and expressive—his smiles wide and his frowns intimidating. When she annoyed him his lips went all tight and straight in a pursed line. She noticed the movements of his hands, which were never casual or careless. He was polish and cordiality on the surface, but she could sense darker currents underneath.

But he was not darkness now. He lifted her cello with almost tender movements. She watched, feeling some alien emotion. Fondness? Damn Denise. Caressa looked away, letting music crowd into her subconscious as she followed him off the plane. There was always music in her head and she never knew what kind it would be. Of late, it was Saint-Saëns most of the time, tormenting her and riddling her with doubts. She must have been crazy to take it on at this point in her career. Saint-Saëns' Concerto One was something cellists did at the height of their arc. After this, there would be nowhere to go but down.

Caressa sometimes suspected that she wanted to go down.

"Caressa?" Denise said her name sharply, and she yanked her gaze from Mr. Winchell's broad back. *You can call me Kyle*, he'd said on the plane, right after she asked him to call her Caressa. *Mr. Winchell* fit him better, with his perfectly tailored dark suit and serious expression. He couldn't be much older than her, but he seemed older.

Caressa trailed after him and Denise fell in behind her. Saint-Saëns went silent in her head, replaced by thoughts of what Mr. Winchell might look like with his suit off. The idea of it made music start again. Wild, unruly arpeggios. The more she thought of it, the more her nipples tightened against the scratchy mesh of her sheer bra. She pulled her cardigan shut in front of her, lest he turn around and see. When they climbed into the limo, she placed her cello between them like some kind of shield.

God, the music was making her crazy. She just wanted some silence, just for a moment, a minute. She was going out of her mind, and Kyle Winchell wasn't going to do anything but make her crazier. Somehow, she was sure of that.

* * * * *

Kyle looked around the well-appointed hotel suite. There was something about a classy hotel that got his sap flowing. Pleasure, comfort, wealth...sex. Why couldn't he get off the sexy thoughts? Caressa was not exactly a seductress, with her prickly distant attitude, but she obviously made some jack because they were staying in a Presidential three-bedroom suite on the top floor of one of San Francisco's ritziest hotels.

Caressa disappeared into her room immediately, saying something about taking a nap. They had an eight o'clock dinner engagement with the conductor of the San Francisco Orchestra, and they were all still on New York time. Denise decided to nap too, but Kyle was too wound up to sleep. Instead, he unpacked for their five-night stay, a trick he'd learned in his travels. Unpack, and any place felt like home. When all his clothes were in drawers and closets, he went to the window. The cityscape was gorgeous, although he thought he heard the rumble of distant thunder. He wandered back out into the main room and finally decided to do a short workout in the gym before he had to corral The Prodigy to her eight o'clock dinner meeting.

By the time he returned and showered, the distant thunder had turned into a storm. Rain beat against the windows, obscuring any view of the city. Denise was in the kitchen fiddling with the coffee machine.

"Caressa go to the gym with you?" she asked.

"No. I thought she was resting."

"I knocked a few minutes ago and there was no answer."

Kyle went and knocked too, then looked back over his shoulder at Denise.

The older woman sighed. "Don't be afraid to go charging into rooms after her. She doesn't open doors if she doesn't feel like it. It's almost seven-thirty, and we'll be late if she doesn't get herself in gear."

Kyle cracked the door, then pushed it open. The room was dark—and empty.

He turned to Denise. "She's not here."

The look she returned pretty much told Kyle everything. *Not my problem anymore.*

Kyle pulled out his phone and dialed Caressa's cell number, which he'd been organized enough to program into his phone before they even got on the plane. Unfortunately, her phone rang out in the silence of her empty room. *Damn it.*

"Try downstairs," Denise suggested. "Maybe she was too hungry to wait for dinner."

"She doesn't leave messages?"

"Not often," said Denise with a sigh.

Well, she will after this, thought Kyle with annoyance. He looked in the restaurant and then the gym, and then started asking hotel employees if they'd seen a woman fitting her description. Finally, one of the room service waiters said he'd just seen a young woman fitting her description heading up the service stairs.

"And the service stairs go where?" Kyle asked with a sinking feeling.

"Up to the roof."

Kyle could hear the rain pelting against the windows of the lobby. "I guess I'll check it out."

The hotel manager looked mildly alarmed. "Shall I send someone to come with you?"

"No," Kyle said. "She was probably just getting some exercise. If you would show me to the stairs…"

"Why don't you take the elevator up and go from there?"

"Fine."

The manager followed Kyle to the elevator to key in the button for the rooftop floor. "Don't hesitate to call me at once if there's a problem."

Oh, there's a problem all right. There's a wandering prodigy on the loose and when I find her I'm going to wring her talented little neck. She knew she had a dinner to go to. She knew they'd all be looking for her. Passive-aggressive little brat. He rode the elevator up thirty-five stories to the door that opened onto the roof.

Damn, it was pouring. No way was she out there. He shoved open the door and a wall of rain hit him. He looked around. Lightning lit up the dark sky, followed by a deafening boom of thunder that made him jump.

Jesus Christ, she *was* there. Stupid fucking prodigy lacked a brain. She was standing less than twenty yards away, leaning against a metal light pole and looking at him with a smirk on her rain-soaked face.

* * * * *

She really hadn't come up here to get a rise out of him, although the expression on his face was priceless. Super pissed, super scared. Super everything. He was super in so many ways. She only came up here because there were so few really powerful storms, and so few places to really experience them. But man, he looked angry. He ventured closer, a few feet away, so she could see the striking eyes, the white teeth set in a grim line. She stared at his light shirt, quickly soaking through as the rain attacked him. She was already soaked to the bone.

"Are you insane?" he yelled. "What's wrong with you?"

"I love storms," she yelled back. "I really love them!"

How to make him understand? It was the only time a force greater than music could overtake her. She looked up at the sky, at the spitting clouds. The rumble of thunder resonated in her shoulder blades and down her spine.

"Do you also love thirty-thousand volts of fucking electricity stopping your heart and frying your brain? Step away from the fucking lightning rod at least."

She smiled at him, doing a twirl around the metal pole in a playful approximation of a stripper. "You curse like a sailor, Mr. Winchell."

"This isn't funny, Caressa. Come inside before you get struck by lightning or manage to kill yourself falling off the roof. You're on top of a thirty-five story building."

"Oh, really?" She ran for the edge just to hear him gasp, and he did. He didn't just gasp, he made some noise between a grunt and a yelp and lunged for her, but when she kept backing away, he stopped.

"Okay," he said, holding up his hands. "You made your point. You're a psychopath. I get it."

"I'm not a psychopath. I told you, I just like storms."

She was drowning. *Drowning.* Her hair was drenched, a sodden tangle heavy on her back. Her clothes were stuck to her skin with cold, driving rain. She blinked raindrops from her lashes. She wouldn't fall. She was a survivor. *Didn't die. Didn't die. Didn't die.*

"Don't worry. I won't die," she yelled through the clamor of the storm.

"You may not die, but I'll beat your ass black and blue for this, you little idiot."

She laughed. "Will you?"

He advanced and she took another step backward. He froze, his entire body a rigid, quivering monument to just how messed up she was.

"Damn it! Enough. You're too close to the edge now. Really too close."

She didn't even need to look back. She could tell how close she was from the look on his face. His features were crumbling from the stress of what she was doing to him. He felt helpless and she could tell he hated it. She didn't much like him this way either. She liked him when he was all bravado and snarky attitude, not this serious face.

"Come and get me," she said so quietly she wasn't sure he could hear her over the storm.

"No," he said after a moment. "You come to me. Right now."

She gazed at him—soaked, angry male. His button-down shirt, that miracle of tailoring, was plastered to his broad chest and muscular arms. His dark hair was even darker now, glossy black in the driving rain. His blue eyes looked black too. Furious. But not defeated. He stood straight and alert, and his shoulders looked strong enough to catch the zigzagging lightning like a spear and fling it back from whence it came. Strong enough to catch her if she did manage to fall off. *Don't fall. He won't catch you, you idiot. You're in this alone.*

If he were music, he would have been a *crescendo*. He would have been *allegro* and *fortissimo*. She was *morendo*...fading away. She jumped as thunder boomed like a gunshot and lightning lit the air around them into a blinding white out. When he spoke, it was with slow, emphatic conviction.

"Caressa, you have a dinner meeting at eight o'clock. It's time to get ready. Right now." His voice was all control, even though his temper seemed poised to shatter. She couldn't stop looking at his fists, his restless fingers.

"Dinner? I was looking forward to that ass-beating you promised me."

"For fuck's sake, I'm not playing games with you. We could both be struck by lightning up here and guess what? It won't end well. Come away from the edge right now or I swear to God I will fucking push you off."

She was fading, feeling sick all of a sudden from the way he looked at her. Everyone looked at her that way, like she was trouble. She was always bad. She was never good enough. She thought he was handsome and strong, and yes, even funny. She wanted to flirt. She wanted to kiss him—and he wanted to push her off. She wanted to stand in the pouring rain forever, until she turned to water herself, flowing away down the gutters to the street and down to some river or ocean. She loved him and she hated him. *Kyle Winchell, I hate that you make me feel this way.*

"I have a fucking dinner to get ready for," she muttered. She moved forward, away from the edge of the roof, and tried to walk around him, but he intercepted her. He took her wrist and yanked it. She yanked it back but only ended up hurting herself when he didn't give an inch.

"Let go of me," she snarled, suddenly as furious as he was.

"When we get inside."

They wrestled one another until they reached the rooftop door. He pushed her through and released her as soon as the door slammed behind them. She ran ahead down the stairs, dripping water behind her. She hoped he slipped on it. She still wanted him to kiss her. Her wrist ached where he'd grabbed it.

She hated his guts.

* * * * *

"Miss Gallo, on behalf of the San Francisco Orchestra I just want to say how delighted we are to participate in this collaboration. I have personally been following your career for many years. Your talent is…amazing."

Caressa looked at the portly conductor from under her lashes, ignoring her aunt's nudge under the table.

"Eh, Caressa is very excited too," Aunt Denise finally responded. "Her career has been a…a wondrous arc, and to be playing as a guest with such fine orchestras as the SFO, well…it's obviously a dream come true. Isn't it, Caressa?"

She looked up at the conductor again. They were all so pompous. So critical. They were all the same. They didn't love music, they loved authority and order. They loved to exploit her talent to fulfill their own visions. She pasted a wide, fake smile on her face. "Of course it's a dream come true. Yes."

She could feel *him* glowering on the other side of her. Kyle. Mr. Winchell. The thundercloud. Thanks to her rooftop shenanigans, they were fifteen minutes late to dinner. All her fault, as usual, although her aunt blamed it on traffic. Her aunt had also strong-armed Mr. Winchell into accompanying them, and so they had shared a cab shoulder-to-shoulder, with him a rock of indignation beside her.

Her long, thick hair was still wet even now, but his hair was dry, glossy brown and shining again. His eyes were still dark, though. She turned and gave him the same big, fake smile she'd given the SFO conductor, whatever his name was. Kyle didn't smile back, only looked at her with that troubling gaze.

Aunt Denise and the conductor were talking about the musical program now, and Caressa drifted, half-listening. Sometimes she felt like participating in these forced meet-and-greets and sometimes she didn't. Tonight she most definitely wasn't in the mood. Fortunately, no one ever asked for ID at these posh restaurants, and Aunt Denise hadn't said anything when the waiter poured her wine, although Kyle had given her a dire look. Whatever. She drained her second glass and made a few lackadaisical replies to the conductor's obsequious questions. After several unsuccessful attempts to draw her into conversation, the conductor turned to Kyle.

"It must be exciting to you, I suppose. These tours. Getting to watch her performances."

Kyle was silent a moment. "I don't know. This is the first tour I've been on."

"Oh. But you must be very proud of her."

It dawned on Caressa that the conductor mistakenly took Kyle for her partner. She took another big swallow of wine and put her hand squarely in Kyle's lap. "Oh yes, he is very, very proud of me."

Kyle's hand closed on hers like a vise, lifting it and enclosing it in an iron clasp. "Caressa, perhaps you should slow down on the wine. Or eat something," he said, nodding at her untouched plate of steak and pasta.

She snickered and looked up at the earnest conductor. "He's just my assistant, actually."

"Oh." The conductor looked embarrassed, and Aunt Denise shifted and rubbed her forehead.

"That's why he never smiles," Caressa went on airily. "He's only here to make sure I don't...I don't know...choke on my steak or something. Make sure I chew fifty times. He's really a stickler about the chewing thing."

"And the over-imbibing too," Kyle said under his breath.

She tittered and put her hand in his lap again, only to find herself once again intercepted. "Yes, an assistant," she said. "All the most important cellists need one. I might, you know, trip and impale myself on my bow or something without his assistance. He has a really important job."

The conductor nodded at Kyle. "All joking aside, it is an important job. The music world would lose a luminary if anything befell our Caressa. It's good that you're here to help her."

"I try," Kyle replied tightly.

Caressa giggled again. "He spanks me when I'm bad though. At least he threatens to." No one laughed, but Kyle turned a few more shades of furious at her side. "I'm totally kidding," she said in the tense silence. "It was a joke."

Yeah, maybe she shouldn't have had the wine after all. The conductor and Aunt Denise gave a token chuckle, but Kyle's scowl deepened and he wouldn't meet her eyes. Caressa drew in a deep breath and drank some water to try to clear her head.

"So, Miss Gallo, have you found Saint-Saëns' Concerto a challenge?" asked the conductor, who she now remembered was named Andreas.

She twirled some linguini on her plate, framing responses, then picked up her wine again. *I certainly have found it a challenge, you fuckhead.* Probably too rude. *Every time I hear it now, I want to gouge out my eardrums with an ice pick.* No, a little negative. *Saint-Saëns is the devil and you are his errand boy.* That made her giggle and choke on the wine she'd just sipped. It backed up into her sinus cavity and she put her napkin to her nose, staring down at the red spots she snorted onto the linen. She started laughing harder. Damn, she was a mess. Kyle made an impatient sound and reached for her wine glass, putting it down on the other side of the table.

"I am not drunk!" she protested, still unable to stop giggling.

Aunt Denise smiled at the conductor. "She so rarely imbibes. She's very focused on her music all the time. Then she cuts loose…"

"Of course. Who can blame her?" The conductor smiled too.

Caressa wanted to applaud. *Well played, Aunt Denise!* Her aunt had become so adept at glossing over her meltdowns. Of course, she'd given her enough practice over the years. Years and years and *years…*

God, so many years. And now Saint-Saëns and his fucking concerto like an albatross around her neck. With it, she was something. Without it, she was a failure. If she could have, if she had any balls at all, she would look at Aunt Denise and the conductor and say very calmly and clearly, "I am actually not capable of playing it well enough. I don't really want to try. Can we just call this all off?" God, she was fucking dizzy. She wasn't much of a drinker. She put her fork down with a clank against her plate and put her head in her hands. A silence fell over the table.

"You look tired, Caressa," her aunt said.

"I am tired. I'm sorry. I think maybe I'm a little drunk."

Aunt Denise reached across the table to pat her arm, although Caressa knew she'd rather slap her. "We've got the first concert tomorrow night. Perhaps you should go home and rest. Mr. Winchell, do you mind?"

"Not at all."

Kyle sounded relieved. Caressa pushed back her chair and tried to look up at him, but the room tilted, then tipped completely to one side.

She staggered and groped for him. "You know, I always forget that I don't do well with red wine…something about…I don't know…"

His arm came around her back and steadied her. "Maybe the fact that you're not legally old enough to drink yet."

She snorted. "I'm sure that's part of it."

He caught her under the arm as she stumbled against him. "It's been a long day. Let's just get you back to the hotel."

She didn't say anything more, just concentrated on walking as he led her from the restaurant. Why did people have to stare? So rude. And her hair was still wet. She should never have gone out in the rain.

He got her right into a cab and she slumped against him even though she meant to keep her distance. She didn't need him. She just needed some rest, some peace. She fell into his arms when he opened them and ended up completely horizontal across his lap. *Shit.* She was so tired, so tired. Next thing she knew, he was carrying her into the hotel.

"Thirty-five," he said to someone in the elevator with them. "Thanks."

"Got your hands full, I see," said the other person with a hint of laughter.

Kyle didn't answer, or if he did, she didn't hear.

* * * * *

Kyle stayed up late, partly to be sure she didn't traipse up to the roof again in her inebriated condition, and partly because he was too wrought up to sleep. He knew he had to leave. He could think of easier ways to earn money than hauling insane cellists down from rooftops in the middle of electrical storms, and he didn't need the drama of her obviously far-reaching problems.

Still, a part of him regretted giving up on her so quickly. He'd weathered some real storms in life with the help of friends, but Caressa seemed to have no friends to help her, aside from a business-minded aunt and a tour manager who couldn't even be bothered to come on the actual tour. And an "assistant"—him—hired to wrangle her like some temperamental animal. No wonder The Prodigy rattled her cage.

But he couldn't endure another rooftop incident. He would never forget the sight of her rushing to the edge of the roof, for no other reason than to yank his chain. Her needs were beyond his capabilities. Which was saying something, since Jeremy Gray had been one hell of a messed-up motherfucker.

Still, Jeremy Gray had basic control of himself when it came down to it. Caressa Gallo did not. Part of him considered phoning his old boss for his always-straightforward advice. *She's even more fucked up than you, Jeremy. Yes, I'm serious. But there's something about her… Should I stay or should I go?* Damn, there *was* something about her. Probably the most important reason of all to leave.

So he knocked on Denise Gallo's door the next morning to tender his resignation. She was understandably angry.

"You signed a contract!" the woman blustered. She was keeping her voice down, but surely Caressa knew what he and her aunt were discussing. "I told you we preferred not to shuttle people in and out. Caressa needs consistency. Predictability. I told you she was high-strung—"

"High-strung? She's a maniac, and I would have guessed an alcoholic too, except that alcoholics don't get drunk on two glasses of wine."

"Last night was unfortunate. Caressa has never done well with wine."

"Then why do you let her drink it?"

"She's a grown woman, Mr. Winchell."

"Grown woman is pushing it. I've seen three-year-olds who were more in control of themselves."

"It's not my job to control her. That's what I hired you for."

"She needs psychiatric help, which I'm not licensed to provide!"

Denise shook her head, rubbing her neck in frustration. "She does not need psychiatric help. She needs limits and structure… She's just… She gets frustrated sometimes. Isn't that understandable?" She glanced at

Kyle, then away, frowning. "I mean, maybe if you were to...turn on the charm, so to speak?"

"I'm sorry. What exactly do you mean by 'turn on the charm'?"

She flushed a little around the ears, and cleared her throat. "I don't mean to be indelicate, but..."

"Yes, let's be indelicate. What exactly are you talking about? Are you suggesting that I romance her as a system of control? Is that seriously what you're suggesting?"

Now Ms. Gallo went on the defensive, blustering and reddening. "No! I mean... Well, she's a lovely girl, Mr. Winchell. She can be quite charming when..."

Kyle crossed his arms over his chest, floored by the sudden clarity of the situation he found himself in. "When she's getting some masculine attention? Is that what you mean to say? And I don't really see this 'charming' side of her you keep alluding to. Maybe if I wore less clothes."

"You're making this sound much more sordid than it actually is."

"I'm sure that's not possible. Why didn't you just advertise for a gigolo if that's what you wanted?"

"Mr. Winchell, you're overreacting."

"Just answer one thing for me. Did you hire me with this intent all along?"

"No—I mean, I considered—I looked for a good fit. For someone I thought she might get along with. Caressa is... Mr. Winchell, you must understand, she is not like other women. I just want to help her. I'll do anything for my niece."

"Yes, but I won't. I've been there, done that. 'I'll do anything' always ends badly. I learned that the hard way."

"Don't get angry. You have to understand that my main goal is to keep Caressa happy."

"Your main goal is to keep Caressa playing her cello so you can bask in her spotlight and keep the money rolling in."

"How dare you suggest such a thing? Caressa plays the cello because she loves it. I wouldn't expect a non-musician like you to understand. If you saw her play—"

"I'm not going to see her play. I think it's best if I leave this morning."

Ms. Gallo moved to block him at the door, her bluster and anger transforming into desperation. She put a hand on Kyle's arm.

"Mr. Winchell, please. Caressa needs companionship. She needs structure. I've tried hiring women, girls her age. I've tried finding her friends. I've tried psychologists and psychiatrists. I've tried medication, but it interferes with her playing and that hurt her most of all. I've tried everything."

"Have you tried letting her make her own friends and live her own life?"

Ms. Gallo was silent a moment, then let out a long, defeated sigh. "I really thought you might understand."

"I'm sorry to disappoint you, but I'm afraid this assignment is not going to work out for me." Kyle opened the door and left, resisting the urge to slam it behind him. He was barely a few steps away when Ms. Gallo opened it again.

"Kyle. Please. If you leave, who else will help her?"

"I don't know and I don't care," he said over his shoulder. "I just know it won't be me."

Chapter Three:
Connection

Kyle threw his suitcases on the bed, trying to master his temper. It was happening all over again. The obnoxious bulldozing of personal lines. *Do this, do that.* There must be something about him that screamed for exploitation. He remembered the first time Jeremy Gray had called him into his bedroom. Three girls on the bed, fake boobs thrusting and red lips panting. He'd been twenty-one at the time and he didn't think twice. He didn't think twice for many years, through countless threesomes and foursomes and moresomes as Jeremy's "assistant". He'd enjoyed them all immensely, until he looked in the mirror the next morning.

No more. Those days were over for him.

Kyle focused on packing, emptying his drawers with methodical precision. He had a particular way he liked to pack. He liked control and organization. Yes, he was good at creating structure. Denise certainly had him pegged. And damn, it's not like he hadn't imagined whipping Caressa into shape, gorgeous mess that she was. Denise wanted him to "charm" her into submission. Kyle would have employed other methods. Her uptight aunt would have been up in arms.

But whatever. The sooner he put the Caressa chapter behind him, the better. His days of self-sacrifice were over. He was looking out for Kyle now, who was almost a year sober and tired of other people's insanity. He lined up his shirts beside his boxers in the smaller suitcase, then turned to the closet to get his suits. He sensed her there before he turned at her soft knock. She was just out of bed, looking tired and rumpled in a tee shirt and sleep pants. She took in the suitcases, then looked back at him, pushing her hair from her eyes.

"I'm leaving," he said.

She was silent a moment, just standing there in the door. "I'm sorry, Kyle. I didn't think I made you that angry."

"Really? Hm. Interesting perspective."

"I'm sorry," she said again.

"You don't want me here anyway, right?" he snapped. "The 'policeman'? When I'm gone you can do what you want."

Kyle was folding his shirts carefully into his suitcase, even more agitated now that she was near him. She came over and sat on the edge of the bed, well away from him, as if she read his dangerous mood.

"If you go, she'll just hire another one."

Kyle paused in his packing and fixed her with a look. "Yeah, well. Poor guy. Whoever he is."

Caressa looked down at her hands. "Am I that terrible?"

"You tell me. You're clinging to a pole in the middle of a lightning storm one moment, and embarrassing me at dinner the next. Now you turn on the innocent, apologetic act as if that makes everything better. You're rude and you—you don't even brush your fucking hair."

She ran a hand through the wild curls springing like a halo around her head. "It's too curly to brush."

"Maybe try some conditioner. I dunno. Whatever. I wish you the best, but I'm leaving."

"And I never even got that spanking," she said in a voice laced with sarcasm. So much for the angelic act.

Kyle snorted and returned to packing. "Get out."

"Look, I just drank too much! And that thing on the roof— It's not— I didn't—"

"Get out, Caressa. Please."

She pursed her lips and got up off the bed, heading to the door, but then she stopped and looked back at him. "I wish you wouldn't go. I'm really sorry. I really wish—"

He spun on her. "You know what I wish? I hear a lot of talking from you, from your slick Aunt Denise, but I don't feel like I'm getting a lot of honesty. Or reality. So what I really wish is that you would just stop talking, or else say something that sounded like truth to me."

"I wish you would kiss me."

She said it so quickly, it couldn't have been premeditated. She flushed, stammering. "I—I mean...last night I did. I was just...thinking about that."

Kyle stared, considering his options. He could turn and continue packing, ignoring her comment. He could give her a fucking piece of his mind. Or he could kiss the damn brat and get it over with.

No. Trouble. *Big* trouble. He schooled his face to nonchalance and tried to sound pedantic.

"Caressa, that would be such a bad idea."

"You wanted honesty." She dug her toe into the carpet as he returned to packing. "It would help me."

He sighed, turning from the luggage again. "Help you how?"

"I don't know. It would make me feel better maybe."

"Feel better? You're like, this super talented musician. You're playing, what, thirty venues this summer? Most of them already sold out? I don't understand what the fuck is going on here."

"What don't you understand? I'm not happy!"

"So quit! Do something else that makes you happy."

"I can't."

"Jesus Christ, this is ridiculous." He turned to packing again, jamming tees next to neatly rolled-up jeans. "Seriously, grow up and get a life already. You can't let your aunt pimp you out if you're this unhappy. Be an adult, put your foot down. Say, 'I'm done, Aunt Denise. Sayonara'. You're acting like this petulant child, over this false prison you've completely fabricated in your mind. Just quit if you're unhappy."

"I can't quit!" Her voice quavered, almost broke. "I don't want to quit, but it's hard to keep going. I'm stuck and I can't... I can't..." Her hands made helpless grasping motions. "I want to do it, I want to play, but I can't ever be good enough. I'm chasing this ideal that I can't meet, and I just need... I need to—"

"Go up on the roof and make me think you're going to fling yourself off?"

"No! Jesus. Can't you just stay? Please."

Kyle scowled and shut his suitcase, heading back to the closet for his shoes.

"I'm sorry, but no. I value my sanity too much."

He returned to the bed, glancing over, but she was gone. Good. What a nutcase. Her and Aunt Denise and Paul the tour manager could all fuck themselves. He started arranging the shoes in the larger suitcase, trying not to think about her words, or the way her voice sounded when she said them. *I'm stuck... I can't ever be good enough... I just need...*

He would need to call Walter. How the hell was he going to explain this situation? He would have to make up some kind of excuse for why he was leaving, or else tell him the bald truth. That Caressa was too much to take on, for all she was talented and beautiful. Someone would be happy to deal with her drama, it just wasn't him. It wasn't his problem.

He had finally convinced himself of that when he heard the first quiet strains of music from her room. He wasn't a musician, but he recognized warm ups. He tried not to listen, sitting down to compose an email to Walter.

Walter,

This new assignment has not gone as planned. Having spent time with Denise Gallo and her niece, I've realized that I am actually not a very good fit for the requirements.

Kyle stopped typing as the methodical scales halted in the other room. He listened for footsteps, hoping she wouldn't make another appearance. He looked over to the door which was still standing ajar, but heard no movement.

No, he heard something else entirely. Caressa Gallo began to play a song, and Kyle listened, his fingers poised over his laptop keyboard. The song went on, an aching, furious melody. He had been told about her virtuosity, read her file, seen the wealth of accolades and press about her online, but none of it had prepared him for what he heard.

Against his better judgment, he went closer to the door just to listen. He didn't know the piece she played, only knew it was emotional. Long strains of reverberating sound clashed with sudden changes of tone and tempo, the notes slow at times, and then so fast that he couldn't believe any human could play them.

He pushed the door open. She faced the window so her back was to him, and her hair obscured her fingers on the cello strings. Her legs cradled the instrument and she leaned over it like a lover. He had a sudden wish to see her face, but he couldn't have gone closer at that moment, not while she was playing. She seemed unapproachable, majestic. Untouchable.

She stopped abruptly and turned to him.

"What?" The genius transformed again into the rude, conflicted girl. "Get out. Isn't that what you said to me? I'm saying it to you now." She stabbed her bow in the air, gesturing. "Get out."

Get out. Listen to her. It would be for the best. "Were you telling me the truth?" *That's not getting out, idiot.*

She turned her back on him and sliced the bow across the strings, eliciting a strange, discordant squeal.

"Were you telling the truth?" he asked again. "About feeling like you're not good enough? About wanting…wanting me to kiss you?"

She was silent. Something in her hunched, defeated posture kept him standing where he was against all his inner instincts.

"I don't want to talk anymore," she said quietly, and started to play again, the same haunting piece.

"What's that song you're playing?" he asked over the music.

"Moeran's Cello Concerto."

"I've never heard it before."

She flexed her knee and stopped playing again with a sigh. "Not many have. Moeran never got popular. He was an alcoholic. A failure. In the end he was most famous for his ability to memorize train schedules."

"Oh, well, see? You're already worlds ahead of him."

She turned with such a virulent look that he backed up a step. "It has nothing to do with being ahead of him. It has to do with the fact that I understand exactly why he memorized train schedules. *Exactly* why."

"If you hate it so much, why do you do it?"

"Get out."

"Answer me. Explain it to me. If you can tell me anything that makes sense, I'll kiss you."

"Get out!"

He knew he was making her angry. He couldn't stop. "What kind of help do you need? Is Aunt Denise drugging you and holding you here against your will? If you want to memorize train schedules, why the hell don't you put down your fucking cello and do it?"

She stood up, gripping her bow in her hand, and he braced, expecting her to throw it at him. Her gaze seared him. "Get out!" she screamed. "Get out! Get out of here!"

He watched her just a moment before he decided. He'd wanted truth, and he'd gotten it in all its raw glory. She was desperate. She was enslaved to a talent she couldn't control. She was drowning and she didn't have a life vest. He crossed to her and took her bow away, because he was afraid otherwise she would eviscerate him with it. He slid one hand in her ridiculously messy hair to hold her still for his kiss. The last coherent thought he had before he pulled her close and pressed his lips to hers was that, for being such a tangled wreck, her hair was amazingly lovely and soft.

* * * * *

There was no choosing, no thought. Nothing but the feel of his stubble against her chin, and the strength of his arm as he grasped her. He was pulling her hair with his other hand, the hand that had taken her bow away. She still held her cello, a fact she completely forgot until he released her to guide it to its side on the floor. He did it so carefully, while she tasted him on her lips and stood feeling shocked. Then he was back, kissing her again.

She knew it was only because he'd heard her play. People always changed when they heard her play, which was why she couldn't "put down her fucking cello" as he'd exhorted her to do. Her music was the most wonderful thing about her. The *only* wonderful thing about her, she thought sometimes—but if it had won her this kiss, she didn't care.

He kneaded her neck as his mouth slanted over hers. His lips were warm and strong. She tasted his anger and his longing, and answered it with her own furious lust. His hands were on her hips, sliding down to cup her ass. The kiss deepened and she felt his hard cock against her front. *It's not you he wants. Just the music.*

She didn't care. She wanted this, just this one thing from him. If he left her afterward, so be it. Her fingers fumbled at the front of his jeans, wanting to free him and touch him, curious to feel the manly shape and heat of him.

For a moment his hand closed on hers hard, and she thought he would tell her no, but he only dragged her over to the door and fell against it, slamming it. There was no need to lock it because he pulled her to the floor in front of it, effectively blocking anyone from coming in. He came over her and she drew in a deep breath. It was really happening. She could feel him so hard and strong against her, so powerful and dangerous.

She started to panic, but her desire for him won out over her fear. She'd finish what she'd started. She ripped open his button fly as he plunged his hand down the front of her sleep pants. She moaned against his mouth as he kissed her again, harder, deeper. His fingers played over her clit, skillful touches that weren't too hard or too soft, but just right. Her hips jerked and sought for more of the building pleasure. Then he slid those amazing fingers down to her pussy, stroking and tempting, fanning the fire he'd lit the moment she laid eyes on him.

She wanted him. She was terrified, but desperate to feel him deep inside. She wanted him to soothe the longing that had her arching wildly against his hand. She reached for his cock as he freed it, gripping it with trembling fingers. It was so large, so firm. How would he feel sliding into her?

"Please! Kyle!" She would beg if she had to. His hand left her pussy abruptly and he pulled away. She moaned in complaint but he was back a moment later. He placed a finger against her lips.

"Complete silence, or we're stopping." His expression was serious, intent. She nodded, going silent as a mouse. With his other hand, he was rolling on a condom he'd magically produced, from his wallet perhaps. *Thank God.* She shimmied out of her pants as he yanked them downward. He reached under the front of her wrinkled tee shirt and squeezed her breast as he surged forward into her. She clenched her teeth at the sudden pain, trying not to cry out, but a strained mewl of shock escaped.

He stopped still. "Now? Really, Caressa?" he hissed in her ear. "*This* is your first time?"

She looked up at him, reeling from the sensation of fullness, the fact that he was inside her, joined to her. She grasped his shoulders, terrified he would leave her at this ground shaking moment. "There weren't a lot of opportunities before now!"

"Jesus." He looked mildly traumatized.

She moaned, moving her hips up against him. "Just…please!"

He fell on her, all his weight, and muffled her helpless moan of relief with his hand. She felt his hard stomach muscles against hers, as he slid and arched and slid again. His cock filled her completely, powerful, amazing possession, leaving her empty each time he withdrew.

She clutched him, needing him closer. Her insistent cries seemed to rile him up and he rode her harder, rougher, his knees braced on the floor. She reached up and pulled his hair, squirming under him as each stroke drove her closer to losing her mind. Her breath rushed against his palm as he silenced her whimpers. His other hand roved and squeezed— her breasts, her nipples, her tensing ass cheeks. His own quiet grunts and gasps against her cheek thrilled her, one more novel sensation to build and bloom into frenzy.

She felt close, *so* close to completion. Her legs grasped him and her hips bumped against his. "Yes, good girl," he urged her. "Come on. Good girl."

Good girl. The way he said it, the novelty of a man saying such words to her—it tipped her over the edge, and she contracted around his hard length with a hiss of breath and a shudder. Every wave of the orgasm was excruciating, melting bliss, a hundred times more intense than any of the orgasms she'd ever given herself. He held her tight, pressing his cheek against hers as he tensed above her. His hand fell away from her mouth. She lay still beneath him, feeling battered and sore, and yet joyfully replete.

He pulled away and she looked up into intent blue eyes. They were still joined together, but the passion had burned out, leaving behind a confused realization that they'd just fucked each other's brains out half-dressed on the floor. He brushed gentle fingers across her cheek, up to her temple.

"Crazy girl. You should have told me it was your first time."

"You didn't give me a chance," she said. "Anyway, I only asked for a kiss."

His lips twitched, and then widened into the most beautiful smile she'd ever seen. "Caressa Gallo, I think maybe your crazy is rubbing off on me."

She watched the smile fade, but his eyes were still warm. She tightened her fingers on his arm. "Does that mean you won't leave? At least not yet?"

He rolled his eyes, a faint smirk on his face. "It would be kind of rude for me to leave a half hour after I deflowered you."

"*Deflowered* me? What kind of word is *deflower*?" she asked with a giggle.

"It's a Texas word. We don't have twenty-year-old virgins in Texas, by the way. At least I've never heard of one. This is a new thing for me." He drew his fingertips down the line of her jaw, suddenly very somber. "Are you okay? I can't help thinking I could have done that better."

She shrugged. "Don't worry about it. It's just sex."

"It fits anyway, doesn't it?" he said. "For you. Suitably intense. I'm glad." He looked at the condom as he took it off and dropped it in the nearby wastebasket. "At least it wasn't a bloodbath. I might have fainted."

He touched her then, stroking his fingers over the reddish blur smeared inside her thighs. It felt like an incredibly intimate thing to do, and it struck her, finally, full force, that she'd given her virginity to this man. Thrown it at him, practically.

"I'm glad it was you," she said, as if daring him to disagree. "I mean, I'm not going to get all sentimental about you or anything."

"Of course not," he said. Was he laughing at her?

"I mean, I'm just not like that," she said. "But I was…curious. And I'm glad it was with you."

God, that smile. The fond way he was looking at her almost stole her breath. His fingers still stroked her, slid through blood and her own slick, undeniable response to him. He leaned back, propped on one arm.

"Can I ask you something, Caressa? And please tell me the truth. Were you really on the roof because you like storms, or was there some other reason?"

"No. I really do like storms."

His gaze unnerved her. She began to turn her head but he caught her chin and made her face him again. "Are you okay? Really okay?"

She thought for a long moment. *Was* she okay? "Honestly, I'm not sure I'm one hundred percent okay. But I didn't go up there to fling myself off, if that's what you're asking."

"You didn't go up there to get me to kiss you either."

She gazed back at him. His lips were set in a firm line, and his face was dark and stern. She shook her head. "I was just trying to feel alive. Can you understand that?"

The fingertips left her chin to brush back a lock of her hair. "I'll help you feel alive now and again, if you'll just stay off the rooftops."

She looked up at him from under her lashes. "Will you spank me if I don't?"

He shook his head at her. "You don't know what you're playing with, young lady. You really have no idea."

"I have some idea. I'm not totally sheltered. But are you...are you really into that stuff?"

"I'm beginning to think *you're* really into it," he said with a laugh.

"I'm just interested, that's all."

"It can be pretty interesting. But these are private things you're asking me about. At the end of the day, Caressa..." His gaze wandered down to her breasts and back up to her face, with a slightly guilty frown. "At the end of the day, I work for you. You're my boss. This was special to me, and that's the truth. But let's not make things too...complicated."

He drew away from her, leaving her feeling empty, vulnerable again. She watched as he straightened his shirt and did up his jeans. With a sinking feeling she put her own clothing back to rights. Her cello was still lying on its side where Kyle had so carefully placed it.

She didn't want to look at it. She didn't want the music...she wanted the sound of his sighs and her own groans of pleasure. He extended his hand and she let him pull her up. She was suddenly overcome with squirming, sickening fear. He would pretend it hadn't happened. He would say something to keep her at arm's length, something awful and impersonal. He would look at her again like she was beyond hope.

But no. He hugged her close and pressed a kiss against her ear. "Caressa, let's keep a secret, shall we?"

She nodded. She wouldn't tell anyone what they'd done.

"Not about this," he said softly. "Let's keep it a secret that there's more to you than cello strings and ticket sales. What do you say?"

Her smile turned into a quavery laugh, and then a cloudburst of tears. *There's more to you than cello strings and ticket sales.* She couldn't have explained how much those words meant to her at that moment, but he probably already knew.

* * * * *

He lay on her bed and watched while she practiced for almost two hours. Every so often he thought she might be crying again, although it was hard to tell since she was facing away from him. Little sniffles, a shake of the shoulders. When he asked if she was all right, she completely ignored him. She played the same passage again and again and Kyle watched, feeling like a stranger, even though he'd buried himself in her just an hour before. He could still smell her on his skin, his lips. Her hair was so beautiful. Her body had been so responsive, so wild. Wild like her. He had even taken her virginity, a startling privilege.

But now she seemed unknowable, extra-terrestrial. She was from another planet, because no human created music this way. At least, she wasn't from his little planet of order and organization. Even so, he wanted her again.

He had to decide what to do, where to go from here. He ran the possibilities through his head. Become her boyfriend? Chance-y. Become her fuckbuddy? Enjoyable, but empty sex had made a mess of him before. Refuse to sleep with her? Restore their relationship to something wholly professional? Not now. Not a chance in hell.

If he was honest with himself, there hadn't been a chance in hell from the start. As much as he fought it, he was a sucker for the wild ones. As soon as he'd climbed in the limo that first day, as soon as his eyes fell on her, he'd felt an attraction he hadn't wanted to admit. Not just a physical attraction, either. He wanted to help her. He wanted to protect her. Okay, and fuck her.

Now he'd have to face Denise Gallo in all his hypocritical glory. Less than ten minutes after he'd berated the woman for suggesting he romance Caressa, Kyle had taken her to the floor, popped her cherry, and filled her to the hilt with his cock.

He stretched on the bed, sitting up. Time to change that line of thinking, or he'd do it again, cello practice or no. At least Denise couldn't object if Kyle insisted on a condom allowance to cover the endless rogering of her niece that Kyle planned. Ironically, Caressa did seem to have become more cooperative since he'd fucked her.

But the kink-curious comments…

She really did have no idea what she'd be jumping into if she beckoned him that way. He would have to consider long and hard before they got into power exchange games, because once they did, they would form an attachment. Mindless fucking was easy. Dominance and submission, not so much.

He was drawn from his thoughts by the sudden silence in the room. Caressa put down her bow and rested against her cello. She looked exhausted.

Kyle watched her, trying to read her. "Good practice, Caressa?"

She shrugged. "So-so."

"You should take a nap. You have a performance tonight and you already look tired. You haven't even had lunch. What would you like?"

"I'm not hungry."

He turned and picked up the phone, then dialed room service. Without consulting her, he ordered a turkey club sandwich and a salad.

"I don't like tomatoes. And I hate turkey," she said as soon as he hung up.

"Then next time, when I ask you what you'd like, I suggest you make a choice. Otherwise I'll order what I choose and you'll eat it whether you like it or not."

The look she gave him was priceless.

"Come here, Caressa." He made his voice brisk and businesslike, but when she came closer, he pulled her down with him on the bed and nuzzled her ear. "Are you nervous about tonight?" he whispered.

"I'm terrified."

He didn't know why her quiet admission startled him. Perhaps it was because he assumed this was all easy for her. Perhaps it was the word she used. Not *scared* or *worried. Terrified.* Perhaps it was because it was the most frank and candid sentence she'd said to him in their short acquaintance.

He hugged her closer. "Listen. If you eat your sandwich and take a nice, peaceful nap, I'll give you a little reward when you wake up."

"What kind of reward?" she murmured against the curve of his neck.

"A really, really nice reward."

She sighed and stretched against him. "Will you stay here and sleep next to me?"

His fingers spread open on her back. She was no longer the awe-inspiring cellist, just a young woman obviously starved for closeness and connection. Kyle supposed, for all his outrage, that was really his most important job here. He was past the point of walking away. But he'd do the unpacking later. He kissed her again and said, "You bet I will."

Chapter Four:
Nerves

Caressa dreamed of him—the look in his eyes, the way he'd fucked her. When he shook her awake, she came to awareness already breathless and wet. He was taking her pants off again, tossing them to the floor. He kissed her, warm soft lips overtaking hers as he ran his fingers over her skin, her hair. She was already arching against him, craving him before she was even fully awake.

He stopped her with a firm hand on her hip. "Wait. Don't move."

She watched him cross to the door, his jeans perfectly sculpted to his waist and the muscles of his ass. He pulled at his sleep-rumpled shirt and ran his fingers through his hair. Then it hit her. Aunt Denise.

Her aunt wasn't stupid. Surely she would realize that Kyle had spent the greater part of the day alone in the room with her, and what they'd been up to, despite Kyle's game efforts to put himself in order. He looked back at her once more and mouthed the word "Stay."

Caressa watched him go and listened for any sign of conversation. Aunt Denise must have gone somewhere because she heard only silence.

Kyle returned with a handful of condoms and a broad smile. Caressa smiled back, hoping her wanton impatience wasn't written all over her face. She wanted him. He locked the door and came to stand beside the bed. He obviously understood exactly what she was feeling, judging from the smug expression on his face.

"Take off your shirt," he said. It wasn't a request, it was an order. She thought about refusing, about playing the brat, but found she didn't want to. Her fingers were already seeking the hem of her tee. Her bra was awful, some padded cotton thing in white, not the least bit sexy. Why didn't she have any alluring bras or panties? God, he was staring at her so intently, and he was still fully dressed, which made her even more embarrassed. She stopped, losing her nerve. He cocked his head to the side.

"What's wrong?"

"You're staring at me."

"Because you're lovely and I can't wait to see your tits."

She frowned. "My bra is totally unsexy."

"Take it off then. Give it to me." Caressa hesitated. "Now. Come on, hand it over."

Slowly she took off her shirt and reached back to unhook the matronly white bra. At the same time, he moved closer and reached down to cup one exposed breast, then pinch the nipple. She drew in a sharp breath of shock, but before she could pull away, he took the bra and walked away from her to throw it in the trash.

"Kyle!"

"You don't like it."

"Yes, but—"

"No buts. You make a lot of money. You shouldn't wear a bra you don't like."

She opened her mouth to protest again but he silenced her with an index finger placed against her lips.

"Hush. And sit up straight," he said. "Show yourself to me."

Caressa was reeling, feeling a thousand things at once. She didn't know whether to be angry or embarrassed. Or devastated. Or turned on. He said it again, more softly, encouragingly.

"Show yourself to me, beautiful girl."

Beautiful girl. She didn't know if they were having sex or something else altogether. She'd never thought of herself as particularly beautiful or desirable, but he was looking at her as if she were. She put her arms back on the bed and sat up straight so the whole front of her was exposed. She thought her breasts were okay, but her body was pretty average. Not fat but not skinny. Nothing impressive like his amazing physique. She knew, she *knew* he'd probably been with a thousand women, just because he was so sexy and good in bed. He apparently even kept a stash of condoms in his luggage. As for her, she'd been with one guy—him.

"Caressa."

His voice drew her back into the moment, and he reached for her again as he had before, taking her breasts in his hands and manipulating them, not roughly, but not gently either. She hovered somewhere between pleasure and panic. Each time his fingertips squeezed or tugged at her nipples, a hot piercing sensation flared between her legs. She found she couldn't stop the tiny sighs and lust noises that came unbidden from her throat.

"Undo my pants," he said, his hands never stopping their caresses. She undid his fly with shaking fingers. His cock was thick and fully hard, straining against his boxer briefs. "Take them down," he said in a husky voice. He leaned to kiss her mouth as she yanked at his jeans. Finally she slid her hands between the boxers and his skin, working the designer jeans down over his ass.

He groaned softly against her lips, kicking off the jeans and pulling his shirt over his head. He was so golden, so perfectly formed. She could hardly believe he was hers to take, this man that women must die for. She reached out for him and he came over her, his warm, flat stomach pressing her to the bed. *Put on the condom. Fuck me, fuck me!*

He reached down to part her thighs, and the feel of that alone sent her pussy throbbing into overdrive. She grabbed at him, clutched him, but he pulled away again, this time tormenting her breasts and sensitive nipples with tingling strokes of teeth and tongue. She tried to pull her thighs together to soothe the ache in her clit, but he made a sound and wrapped his strong, elegant fingers around her legs so she couldn't draw them closed.

"Kyle," she gasped. But he was kissing lower now, down her stomach to the apex of her mons. *Oh, Jesus.* She tried in earnest now to pull away, to protect herself from his unbearable sensory assault, but he held her down, spreading her pussy lips and flicking his tongue against her clit.

She trembled, her head thrown back as powerlessness and ratcheting arousal froze her. She was a sexual being at his mercy, and each lick, each nibble, each kiss felt more powerful than the last. "Oh, please." She arched her hips against his mouth. "Oh, please…just…please…"

"Please what?"

She looked down at him. He was looking up at her with a smirk and those eyes…those deep blue eyes… He knew exactly what she wanted.

"Kyle, please!"

"You want me to keep going until you come?" She groaned, not certain what she wanted at all, except for fulfillment. He blew against her pussy, then nibbled it softly. "Mm. You want my cock, maybe? You want me to fuck you?" Her fingers tightened in his hair as he looked up at her, watching her as he slid his tongue from the wetness of her pussy all the way to the tip of her clit. "Say it."

"Please make me come. Please." The words came out instantly, without thought.

"With my mouth or my cock?"

"Your cock. Please! When you're inside me it feels…it feels…" *It feels like something I've always needed but never knew before. It feels like I'll die without you there.*

He had the condom on in an instant, surging up between her legs and positioning the head of his cock at the hot, wet place he'd tormented with his tongue. She held onto him as he pressed inside, a long, slow invasion that brought the hum inside her to full, astounding vibration.

"Kyle. Kyle!" Just like that, she was up and over the cliff. He kissed her to muffle her frantic cries as her orgasm shook her. She contracted on his length and shuddered with delicious relief. She felt him chuckle against her lips.

"Again, Caressa."

"Nooo…" she moaned, but he only smiled and flipped over with her, so she was straddling his powerful hips. She braced her hands against the broad expanse of his chest, certain she couldn't bear another round. But then she felt the simmering ache start to build again in her clit as he pulled her against his pelvic bone.

He put both hands on her ass cheeks and squeezed them, parting them and fingering her ass. *No, no, no…* It was so dirty, and yet so pleasurable that she couldn't voice the words to make him stop. She couldn't pull away—he had her impaled and captured. He started to grind his hips against her and then reached to take both her nipples between his fingers. He pinched them hard, until the pain blossomed into something else. Shocking pleasure. Her pelvis throbbed with need, and her thighs tensed against him.

"Yes… That's a good girl."

His low, whispered encouragements helped her sink even deeper into the intimacy of the moment, and then he was forcing her down hard on his cock, roughly squeezing her ass. He pinched her breasts and groped at her thighs. He slapped her tensing ass cheeks, a shocking pain that tipped her over the edge into the same wildness he'd driven her to before.

She came so hard she lost control of what she was doing. She thought she hit him on the face or the chest, but she wasn't sure. She collapsed on him and he caught her, clasping her close as he found his own release. She lay still as he bucked through aftershocks with sharp, rough thrusts and breathless gasps against her ear.

For a long moment he continued to squeeze her, and then his arms relaxed in slow degrees. She pressed her lips to his neck and opened her teeth against his skin. She wanted to bite him but she didn't.

"Caressa," he sighed. "Caressa..."

She licked him instead, tasting salt and aftershave, and feeling dark prickly stubble like a trilling cadence against her tongue.

* * * * *

She was surprisingly easy to bundle up and get to the concert. Kyle hid his bemusement at her spacey subordination to his curt instructions and commands. *Shower. Pack up your cello. Eat a little bit, you're nervous.*

She did only eat a little bit. They were running behind schedule, so he took a hairdryer to her hair, carefully, with a diffuser. She watched him in the mirror as she did her makeup, occasionally complaining about the heat. It was all novel to Kyle. Jeremy had never done his own primping. If he'd needed makeup, the set or studio makeup artists handled it. He had his hair trimmed every few days, styled perfectly by his own personal hairstylist.

Caressa, on the other hand, did everything on her own. He supposed it was probably for the best, since she grew more nervous with each passing moment, and the mindless tasks seemed to occupy her. Makeup done, she pulled out a black outfit that looked like mourning. A silk top with a soft-shaped neckline that framed her face, and black slim trousers. No jewelry, no rings, not even a watch.

After all the care he'd taken with her hair, drying each curl into spiral perfection, she wrenched the mass into a low ponytail and secured it with a plain black elastic. With her dark lipstick and muted makeup, she looked severe. Where was the questing, reckless siren he'd just de-virginized?

"How do I look?" she asked as he stared at the final effect.

"Stunning." And he was stunned. The transformation from sex-drunk girl to master musician was complete and irrefutable. For his part,

Kyle dressed in a tux at Denise's request. He didn't ask if the tux would be an every-night thing, or just an opening-night thing. Either way, he knew he would always feel underdressed next to Caressa.

The three of them rode in the limo as before, Caressa hunched behind her cello with her hands clasped firmly in her lap. He thought he saw her fingers moving in nearly immeasurable movements. In the tension of the silent compartment, Denise leaned toward him. "You'll have to stay backstage."

"Oh, I'd planned to. I didn't expect to watch from the seats."

"She's nervous now…but she gets more nervous," she said cryptically. "Just stay close."

In the dressing room Kyle understood. The terror Caressa had claimed earlier hadn't been an exaggeration, or humor. She paced. She wrung her hands. She breathed so fast that Kyle's lungs hurt. She checked her cello three, four, five times, and then they took it to the stage and she really had nothing to do. Kyle came to stand by her, stilling her jittery pacing.

"Take some deep breaths, sweet pea."

She gave him a strained look as he took her hands. He'd imagined sweaty palms, but they were icy. "God, are you that cold?" He pulled her close. She felt so small, so shaky.

"I'm nervous. I'll be nervous until I'm out there. I just want to get out there and begin."

"And then what happens?" he asked.

She was silent a moment as Kyle stroked the soft, captured hair so sleek against her scalp. That such wildness could be tamed. It gave him hope. "Then what happens?" he asked again.

"The music takes me. I slip down into it like a warm bath. Like a trance or something. Like waves…"

Kyle considered that a moment. It was the same thing alcohol and drugs did for him not so many months ago. He was still pondering that when the stage manager stuck his head in and asked for Caressa. She broke away from him and Kyle stepped back, catching a speculative look from Denise. God, he'd been handling Caressa just like a lover. Of course, they *were* lovers, but Kyle wasn't sure yet how Denise felt about that. Charming her into submission was one thing. Fucking her repeatedly was another. Maybe Denise would fire him, send him back to New York on the first available flight after the concert was over. But no, she wouldn't do that, not when he had Caressa doing what Denise needed her to do.

Caressa was already striding onto the stage by the time Kyle reached the wings. Applause swelled, the dignified, rich sound of a concert audience. At some unseen signal from the conductor, the members of the orchestra raised their instruments. Caressa sat in the middle of the stage alone, settling her cello between her knees and taking her bow between sure fingers. She looked utterly calm, utterly composed. Kyle supposed she was slipping...slipping down... He remembered that feeling, the soothing comfort it brought.

She drew the bow across the strings and the first note of the concerto sounded, soft and yet magnified by the fact that a hundred musicians waited to pick up the strain. From the wings, Kyle listened and watched as the song developed, his eyes glued on Caressa in the spotlight. He'd heard her play, but this was something new, with the orchestra accompanying her and her fingers flying across the strings. She, alone, held the entire audience in the palm of her hand.

She looked so vulnerable.

Her body twitched and swayed as she played. Her face screwed into a mask of concentration only to brighten at the onset of a few light notes. It was hypnotic just to watch her. She was inside the music, just as she'd said. He felt a strange sense of pride, even though he'd had no part in her training or grueling practice sessions to arrive at this place she was today. As the piece drew to a climactic close, Kyle thought to himself, such talent. *Amazing.* For the first time since the concert began, he remembered to look over at Denise listening beside him.

Denise was watching Caressa just as intently, only her lips were drawn down in a small frown.

After the concert, all the way back to the hotel, Caressa sobbed and wouldn't allow either Kyle or her aunt to soothe her. Denise just looked out the window, her jaw tense. Caressa leaned her forehead against her cello, a pile of tissues beside her. Kyle sat and felt like the kid who showed up at school only to find he'd studied for the wrong test.

* * * * *

Caressa fled to her room and locked the door as soon as they got to the hotel suite. She didn't want anyone to see her. Especially *him*. That dumb, concerned look on his face. Jesus. Did he really not understand how badly she'd played?

It had to be his fault. All that kissing and fucking and...kissing... She should have been practicing, not kissing him. And the way he'd bossed her around, making her eat a turkey sandwich when she hated turkey, blow drying her hair so it got all frizzy and poofy. She always pulled it back anyway. He just didn't get it, he didn't get *anything*. He was upsetting her routines—

She froze at the knock on the door. It wasn't her aunt's knock. "Go away," she yelled.

"Open the door," he said in a calm voice.

"I said go away!" God, his stupid voice. She hated how it sounded like caramel, all smooth and melty around the edges. Where had he said he was raised? Louisiana? Texas? Again he knocked, two sharp raps in succession.

"I'm trying to sleep!"

It was a lie. She was huddled beside the bed where she'd dropped and pulled her knees up to her chest, trying to forget about the mistakes, the patronizing applause... She heard the knob rattle and knew he was picking the lock. The door swung open and she turned her back on him.

"Caressa—"

"Get out!" She screamed it, the same way she'd screamed at him that morning. "Get out, get out!" It felt good to scream at him, or rather at the wall, because she couldn't look at him and scream the way she was screaming. "Get ou—" The final 't' was muffled by a large hand and his hiss against her ear.

"Stop it, you diva."

She hit out at him, turning and attacking with everything she was worth. He parried, pushing her back and pinning her down with embarrassing quickness.

"You're an angry little girl, aren't you?" he asked, his hands flexing on her wrists.

"I'm not a little girl, you jerk. I'm not a diva."

"No? You act like one."

She fought with renewed energy. He slid his hands from her wrists to cover her palms, still pinning her with his body.

"Let go of my hands!" No one touched her hands. Ever. But he ignored her shrieked command, his fingers closing around hers. His chest was pressed to hers, a cage. An anchor. He waited for her to look at him, but she wouldn't do it.

"Go away!"

"No."

She finally chanced a sideways glance at him, and what she saw really devastated her. He admired her. Still. "You don't understand, Kyle. It was terrible."

"I liked it," he said without pause.

"Because you don't understand."

"No, I don't," he agreed a moment later, with an ironic lilt to his voice. "How can you say it was terrible? The applause went on and on. They were shouting 'Bravo!'"

"Yeah, they're idiots. They do that every time. Dress up and go listen to the pretty music from the fancy orchestra in their flashy tuxedos. They're like you, they don't know. The reviews will tell the story tomorrow. You fucking idiot."

His face changed then, and his fingers tightened around hers until she squirmed to pull them away. "Apologize."

"Let go of my hands."

"Apologize. *I'm sorry I called you a fucking idiot, Kyle.*"

She shook her head.

"Say it. *I'm sorry I called you a fucking idiot. I'm sorry for trivializing your experience and ranting at you like a shrill bitch.* Say it."

"Fuck you!"

"Say it. I can hold you here all night. Do you need me to repeat it?"

"I want to go to bed."

"As soon as you apologize."

She pouted. Damn, she had an itch on her arm. He wouldn't let go of her hands no matter how hard she pulled, and she had to scratch it. She squirmed against him and...oh my God.

He smiled down at her. Smug asshole. "Say it, Caressa."

He was hard, and he was pressing against her in a way that had her body rebelling against what her mind was telling her to do.

"No. Go away," she insisted, a little less forcefully this time.

"*I'm sorry...*"

"Jesus. Fine. I'm sorry I called you an idiot!"

"*And ranted at you like a shrill bitch.*"

Caressa heard a snort and a laugh and realized it had come from her. And then more laughter bubbling up before she could stop it. She wanted to be angry. She hated him. She *despised* him. No. She adored him.

"Say it." He was laughing against her lips, kissing her. "Say it, you crazy little wingnut."

"I'm sorry...I'm sorry I ranted at you like...like...a shrill...hahaha...bitch..." She could barely get the words out, she was laughing so hard. Tears were streaming from her eyes and then she wasn't really sure where her laughter ended and her tears began. Kyle kissed her again and again, licking the moisture from her cheeks and nibbling at her lips. Their bodies bumped together in laughter and a deeper, more intent purpose. He was groping at her pants, pulling at the waistband.

"Don't rip them," she said.

"Take them off."

She scrambled up, still not sure if she wanted to hate him or worship him. The conflict of her feelings lodged somewhere in her middle, near her heart, but between her legs there was warmth and wetness. She undressed and he undressed too with a complete lack of self-consciousness. She stared because she still couldn't quite get over the sight of him—the sculpted perfection of his torso, his muscular legs and his hard, upstanding cock.

She made a sound and backed away as he advanced on her, condom already in his hand and quickly rolled onto his thick length. His eyes never left her. In fact, his eyes were so intent they frightened her. She started to fight him as he backed her to the wall, for no other reason than the shit storm he stirred in her. He ignored her half-hearted slaps and shoves and pressed against her, slipping his hands beneath her knees to draw her thighs up and around his hips. She braced herself and bumped her head back against the wall, holding on for dear life.

"Say you want me, Caressa."

She gazed at him with bared teeth. "You're always telling me what to say."

"Then say what you feel. Say *yes*, or *no*—"

"Oh…" She moaned. "I don't want to talk." She couldn't summon words. She heard music, banging clashing chords, and felt his cock parting her, easing up into her. Why did he need her to talk? Couldn't he hear it? She gave a sing-songy whine and shifted her hips to take him deeper. His knees, or her elbows perhaps, thumped against the wall in the silence of the hotel suite as he began to move in her, each thrust lifting her higher. She banged her head again but she didn't care. His teeth closed on her neck and she wanted him to bite instead of nibble. "Kyle…"

She arched her hips into his thrusts, wanting to urge him on, but not knowing how. She ground against him and his fingers tightened on her hip where he held her. His cock pinned her and possessed her, and then found a spot that had her falling faster, rising higher. Her moans intensified as she sought satisfaction.

"Shhh…"

She heard his shushing as if from a distance. She grasped his shoulders and dug her nails into his golden skin. "Help me. I can't—Closer, please!"

With a groan, he slid an arm under her and turned, carrying her to the bed and collapsing over her. The force and rhythm of his thrusts increased as he plundered her, his hips pounding against hers. His pubic bone contacted her clit, rubbing over it in an unbearable tease. She pulled her knees up to draw him closer, to urge him on, and then he delivered a stinging slap to the outside of her thigh. Another, and another again. The sound was loud and she jerked, at the same time the chaos inside her transformed into a single strain of completion.

"God, Kyle!" The orgasm came on her like a gunshot, an explosion. Every nerve seized and her thighs clenched around him as he stiffened above her. He gripped her thighs where they still stung from his blows and pressed her down, down, down. She wanted him to hold her down forever, to fill her and not let her go. Her pussy clamped down on his hard thickness, a jolting release made even sweeter by the way he shook and shuddered above her.

When he fell against her she lay still, not wanting to stir and cause him to move. A moment later she heard a chuckle and a soft gasp of breath against her cheek.

"I suppose we could have been quieter."

Caressa didn't answer. Quiet was the last thing on her mind. God, the way he fucked her, like an animal rutting, like a wild man. He had slapped her thigh, hard. She still felt the warmth of his handprint.

And she had liked it. Very much.

He finally drew back to lie beside her, turning questioning eyes on her. "So…you got your spanking. Did you enjoy it as much as you hoped?"

She looked past him, over his shoulder. "What do you think?"

He tweaked her chin and tsked at her. "Don't be a smart ass. Tell me if you liked it or not."

She forced her gaze back to his, stared into those blue eyes that pinned her as effectively as his cock. "I still feel it." She didn't know what she meant by that…if she meant the burn on her thigh or his cock still firm and stirring in her. "You've got quite a libido working there."

"I do all right," he sighed, pulling away from her. He kissed her, not gently, and rolled off the bed. He stood over her and she felt suddenly naked, vulnerable. She pulled the sheets over herself and looked past him again.

"Can I sleep in here with you?" he asked.

"No."

He studied her a moment longer, then shrugged. "It's late, and if I sleep in here I'll probably just keep you up later than I should."

"You've already done that."

He stretched his gorgeous limbs, refusing to rise to the bait. She watched and pretended he didn't make her heart beat faster and her mouth go dry. He started to dress and she turned on her side, remembering everything that his ruthless seduction had driven away for precious moments. The concert, the horrible flubs. The undeserved applause. The piece had slipped ahead just out of her fingers. She'd thought she had it once or twice, but overall the performance was average at best—

Ohhh... He was leaning over her, licking up the side of her neck. She shivered and almost reached for him, reached to pull him back down beside her, with his spicy, manly smell and his voice like caramel.

"You still taste like tears," he whispered. His tongue slipped behind her ear, teasing and tempting. Then he kissed her gently on the forehead and was gone.

Chapter Five:
Involved

Kyle stayed in bed late the next morning. He'd adjusted to West Coast time easily, as if he'd never been away, but he didn't want to get up and face Caressa and her Aunt Denise. Not yet.

Yesterday's carnal shenanigans had surprised him only briefly. He hadn't been with a girl in ages, so of course passion would quickly flare to life with a new, exciting partner. Flare. Froth. Combust. Conflagrate. She set him on fire, possibly because she was such a flaming maniac herself.

Of course, he'd worked with erratic types before, very successfully. For five years, he'd managed to keep Jeremy Gray's crazy on low boil. But was he "working" with Caressa, really? Or was he doing something else altogether? His phone buzzed and Kyle smiled to see Jeremy's number on the display screen. He'd always had impeccable timing.

"Hey, Jeremy. What's up?"

"I heard you were over on the West Coast."

"Are you here?"

Jeremy laughed. "I'm in Denmark."

"What time is it there?"

"I don't know and I don't particularly care."

Kyle almost asked, "Is Nell there?" but instead bit his tongue. Then he realized he hadn't even thought of Nell in several days. Jeremy was barreling on, bombarding him with questions. "What?" Kyle asked.

"The new job. How's it working out for you? With the violinist?"

"Cellist."

"Oh, excuse me. Whatever. What's she like?"

Kyle laughed. "Intense. Honestly, she's giving you a run for your money in the tortured *artiste* department."

"I wonder what you ever did in life to deserve it. Really, she's as bad as me?"

"Probably worse. But...I don't know. I'm actually enjoying myself. In a way, I think she needs me. I think I can help this woman if she'll let me."

"You always did have that hero thing going on. Hopefully no bullets involved in this case."

"Trust me, I'm not getting anywhere near this girl and firearms."

They both laughed, and then Jeremy abruptly changed direction. "Still sober, I guess?"

"Yeah, of course. Nine months, three weeks, four days. I need all my wits about me right now."

Jeremy was quiet a moment on the other end. "You're already fucking her, huh?"

"Damn. How could you possibly know that?"

"Well, I'm right, aren't I? I can tell by the tone in your voice when you talk about her. Just be careful. You have enough demons of your own. Don't take on anyone else's."

"My demons are...subsiding." They both knew what—or who—he was talking about.

"That's good. I'm really glad to hear that. All right, I've gotta go. Just hoping everything was working out. Maybe we can catch one of her concerts when she's swinging through Europe. We'll be here for a while."

"Sure. I'll send you some dates."

We. Him and Nell. Kyle still felt the prick, but the sting was not so deadly. Maybe Caressa was helping him as much as he hoped to help her. He hung up with Jeremy and showered and dressed, anxious to see what mood she was in today.

But when he went out into the main room, only Denise was up, sitting quietly over coffee and bagels. His first impulse was to retreat and shut the door again, but he wasn't generally a pussy and he didn't intend to start acting like one now. Instead he crossed the room and joined her, sitting across the table. Her glance was not a friendly one. Kyle cleared his throat.

"So…about your suggestion to charm her."

"Mr. Winchell, I really don't want to know."

"Denise—"

She held up a hand. "I really don't."

"You don't have to keep paying me if you don't want to."

"Of course we'll keep paying you." Denise's lip curled down at one corner. "I only hope for her sake that you're practicing safe sex."

"I'm pretty responsible that way," he said with a touch of pique.

"Responsible? Really?" She sounded peeved, and looked down at her hands. "I want to say that I'm disappointed in her. That I'm angry with you, Mr. Winchell. But I feel it's not my place."

Kyle let those words sink in, reaching for a sesame bagel and smearing it with strawberry preserves. "Why disappointed? And please call me Kyle, for God's sake."

"She did not perform at her best last night."

"And you blame me?"

"I don't know who to blame. But she wasn't herself."

"It was the first night of the tour, right? Was she supposed to already be at her peak? She's not allowed to have opening night jitters?"

"Well, of course she can. But it was the premiere night. A lot of reviewers attended." With a flustered gesture, Denise indicated three newspapers beside her. "There were a couple more online."

"What did they say?"

"Uninspired. Uneven. 'Not her usual luster'. Read them yourself."

Kyle chewed slowly, feeling inexplicable fury. "I thought she was spectacular."

"Well, you know nothing—"

"Nothing about music. Yes. Why don't we reiterate it one more time? Look, her performance really moved me."

"I'm not surprised, judging by the noises that came out of her room last night," she said with a sniff. "You think everything she does is spectacular. The music world doesn't work that way."

Kyle bit back words he knew he was better off not saying in the heat of the moment, choosing instead to pour a glass of orange juice from the iced carafe on the table. "She can't see those," he finally said, nodding at the papers.

"She'll ask to see them as soon as she gets up."

"Don't show them to her. Tell her she had a rough night and she needs to move on. Reading bad reviews is only going to agitate her further."

"Further than you already have?"

Kyle drew in a deep breath and fixed the middle-aged woman with a look. "Listen, *Aunt* Denise. If you want to fire me, feel free. I'm still not leaving. Not unless she asks me to. She needs—"

"Handling. Just like I told you. But this isn't the type of handling I had in mind."

Denise lifted her eyes and Kyle turned to see his rumpled lover standing in the door to her bedroom.

"Come and get some breakfast, Caressa," Denise said.

"I want to see the reviews."

"No," Kyle said, at the same time Denise said, "Later."

"Are they that bad?" Caressa sat at the table beside Kyle and eyed the stack of papers beside her aunt.

"They're not bad at all. It was the first night of the tour. Let's not overreact. Have some breakfast," he said, pouring her some juice.

Caressa sat and looked at her aunt, ignoring the tray of bagels and muffins Kyle slid across to her. "Thanks for hiring him, Aunt Denise. We've already fucked three times."

Kyle choked on the bagel he was chewing and Denise sat up straighter, turning narrowed eyes on Caressa.

"You think you're shocking me?" her aunt asked. "I heard you—all three times. So thanks for the scoop, but I already knew. And my, don't you look proud of yourself?"

"Ladies." Kyle rubbed his eyes and then put his hand on Caressa's arm. "Listen. I need you to not even look at those reviews. Okay? Tonight is another concert. Have some breakfast, practice for a bit, and then we're going out."

"Going out where?"

"Shopping. But we'll only go on one condition. You do not so much as touch those newspapers. No looking online. In fact, all I want you to do is eat and practice."

"No sex?" Caressa chirped, smirking at her aunt. Denise glared at her and pushed back from the table, stalking off to her room and slamming the door.

Kyle frowned at Caressa. "Nicely done."

"I hate when she looks at me that way."

"Your aunt and I had already discussed…things. She would rather just not know, and you can't keep poking her with it."

"Or what?"

"Or it ends. I know you live to find weapons to use against her. I refuse to be one of them. Now eat something."

"I'm not hungry."

"Eat. Or I'll spank you again," he added with a gleam in his eye.

"You would like that, wouldn't you?" Caressa said, but she reached for the tray and helped herself to a blueberry muffin.

"*You* would like it, I know that much," he muttered under his breath. She chuckled and stared out the window, but he detected a slight blush in her pale cheeks. She would like it all right. She'd love it, the little perv. So many decisions. He'd already made the first one when he'd tackled her yesterday and taken her on the floor. Now he had to decide whether or not to cater to her obvious curiosity about BDSM.

What a joke. Of course he was going to cater to it. He was already imagining various scenarios, all of which included bondage, perverse hardware, and gags. She would definitely need to be gagged, with his cock preferably, but anything in a pinch. The girl had a sass of a mouth, and a bedroom persona to match. Nell had been so submissive and pliable when he'd watched her with Jeremy, and Kyle had always considered her the pinnacle of sensuality. But Caressa was just sex in a rocket, primed 24/7 and about to go off. Different, but equally compelling. Perhaps *more* compelling, because Kyle never knew if he was going to survive her next heat blast.

* * * * *

Kyle took her to a shopping mall, a ritzy outdoor promenade not far from the hotel, and Caressa walked beside him feeling conspicuously out of place. The mall was full of people her age, twenty-somethings in stylish clothes and trendy accessories. She was wearing jeans and a gray tee shirt, and a pair of old tennis shoes. Kyle walked beside her with that stealthy lope of his, looking like someone who'd just stepped out of an issue of GQ. He was wearing jeans and a tee too, but it looked different on him, sexier. He fit right into this crowd of hipster young professionals. The other shoppers jabbered on cell phones and clustered in laughing social groups. Many of them were couples, walking, talking, holding hands. Flirting. Kissing.

She wanted to take Kyle's hand but she didn't. Her obvious dork cachet would sully his golden-California-boy aura. Lots of women looked at him, and then looked at her. She could read the look on their faces. *How did she snag hotness like that?* She started to lag behind but then he took her hand and pulled her up to walk beside him.

Near the end of the promenade, he pulled her into a shop. She looked around and heat rushed to her face. It was a lingerie place, and the employees all looked like damn supermodels. A girl straightening rows of panties looked up and smiled at Kyle, impossibly vixenish and gorgeous. Caressa narrowed her eyes at her and turned away in the direction of the door.

"I'm not into this," she muttered.

He pulled her back. "You said, and I quote, 'My bra is totally unsexy'."

"Yeah, I want to be unsexy."

"No you don't. Come on, let's just look around."

Caressa snorted, shooting another unpleasant glare at the girl behind the counter who appeared to be mentally undressing Kyle with her heavily-made-up eyes. "This is so stupid and tacky. 'Oh, I just fucked you. Allow me to buy you some sexy panties and bras'."

"I'm not buying you anything. You're picking some things out for yourself. What do you like? What do you want to have on next time I pull your shirt up over your head and start fondling your breasts?" He said the last part quietly, next to her ear, and she shivered a little. Then she stepped away from him again.

"I'm not the sex kitten type."

"I don't doubt it. But you're not a grandma either. Your bras and panties have to go." He leaned back against a faux-finished gold leaf column and gestured around the boutique. "Look around. Take your time. Buy what you like. You've made plenty of money in the last few years, Caressa."

She would have refused, but something in the last comment struck her. She *had* made a lot of money, and she'd worked hard for all of it. Why was she wearing boring department store underwear that embarrassed her? *Because you have no social life and no one to wear something nice for anyway.* Well…until now.

She flicked a glance at Kyle and moved away from him, running her fingers over the panties and bras displayed on shelves and racks. Some of it was quite nice…soft shimmery satin, with tiny details like lace and bows. She stopped at a simple ivory bra with a row of impossibly tiny buttons down the front. It was plain but it was…fine. Delicate. One of the salesgirls spoke beside her, making her jump with her loud, abrasive voice. "Would you like me to start a fitting room for you?"

Caressa stared at her. She'd never shopped in a boutique like this. Kyle answered when she didn't. "Yes."

"What size are you?" the girl continued, staring openly at Caressa's breasts. "34B? 32C?"

"Um…"

"Let's go measure you."

The girl had Caressa by the arm, steering her to the back of the shop so quickly that all Caressa could do was throw a panicked look back at Kyle. He smiled and nodded. God, did he just wink at her? The girl pulled her into the changing area, into a cramped, curtained room. She waited expectantly for Caressa to…what? Undress? She was shorter than Caressa, petite with blonde hair and wide blue eyes perfectly lined with eyeliner.

"It's easier to measure if you undress first. Then we'll know what size to grab," she suggested perkily.

"Oh, okay."

Caressa took off her shirt and again felt a deep pang of embarrassment at her pedestrian cotton bra. She did look like a grandma. She took it off with as much bravado as she could muster and waited while the salesgirl whipped a narrow tape measure around her chest. "My name's Bridget, by the way."

"Hi, Bridget," Caressa said. Her voice cracked on the last syllable as Bridget matter-of-factly laid the tape right over her nipples.

"Looks like a 32C to me. So…is that guy your boyfriend? He's yummy."

"Oh, um. No. Just a friend. He actually works for me," Caressa said dryly. She was an accomplished musician after all, and she'd probably made more as a twelve-year-old than this girl was making slinging bras and panties as an adult.

But Bridget just said, "Oh," in that perky, cheery voice of hers and left Caressa to dress again. When she was decent, she went back out into the store and picked out a few more bras she liked. Nothing too frilly, but nice classic colors with subtle details. A sky blue bra with a black velvet bow that enthralled her. A beige one in a sort of retro style with black and white lace. As she chose them, Bridget pulled out matching panties. Kyle was still across the store, chatting with the other shop girls who were throwing themselves at him in a disgustingly desperate way. Fine. Let him flirt with them. Better than having him watch her with that dissecting gaze.

Finally she ducked back into the changing room and tried the fit on the undergarments. Most of the sets she'd chosen suited her perfectly. They were so much more well-designed and flattering than her cheap, plain cotton crap. She ended up not being able to part with any of it. God, so much money. She ran a fingertip over a tiny edging of ivory lace. She didn't care.

Kyle stood beside her as she checked out. The shop girls had finally fallen silent, deciding at last, she supposed, that he really wasn't available. She wondered what he thought of the things she'd picked out. She wanted to look over and ask, but then again, she wasn't buying it for him. He was right, she made a lot of money. She should have underwear she liked, and if he didn't like what she chose, he could go fuck himself. She'd told him she wasn't going to get all sentimental over him and she meant it.

She paid for the sets with the debit card Denise had given her a couple years ago, that she only used now and again for online purchases and quick trips out for food. God, she had plenty of money saved up from concerts and royalties. She was paying *his* salary, wasn't she?

"I like the things you got," he said as he fell into step beside her back out on the sidewalk.

"I didn't think you even noticed what I got, you were so busy chatting up those girls."

"They were chatting *me* up."

"I'm sure you're constantly wrestling with that problem."

"Why so grouchy, darling?"

Caressa rolled her eyes. He was headed for another store, an upscale women's clothing boutique.

"Kyle!"

"Come on. I just want to help you. Dress you up a little. Do you really like those clothes you wear? You're so spirited, so talented. Why are your clothes so...bland and lifeless?"

"That's how concert musicians dress."

"Says who?" He was pulling her past counters full of artisan jewelry and pottery to racks of variously textured sweaters and jackets, tops and blouses. "Who made the rule that that's how concert musicians have to dress? I guess you could wear whatever the hell you wanted as long as your fingers are the ones playing the notes."

"It doesn't work that way. There are conventions of dress—"

"I'm not talking about what you wear onstage. I'm talking about you getting a sense of style and being happy with the way you look."

"I am happy with the way I look."

"Then why do you hide yourself under layers of gray and black?"

"Because, unlike you, I don't want to be stared at."

He made an impatient sound and started browsing through lush cardigans and embellished tank tops. "This store reminds me of you. Very impressive and great quality, but completely crazy underneath." He held up a shirt with asymmetrical gathers and an unfinished, beaded neckline.

"No. Well..." She sidled over to a nearby table of filmy blouses. God, she loved ruching. Little bows, nothing garish... Buttons. She loved buttons that were unusual. She really loved itty bitty buttons. And textures...

By the time she left, Kyle had a fistful of bags in both hands, and Caressa was feeling buoyant and beautiful. Why not have fun dressing in her own style when she wasn't performing? The black was getting old. She'd bought tops in rust red and rum pink, jackets in green paisley and aqua blue. She'd bought sweaters with short sleeves and pedal pusher shorts in plaid. She'd bought a white tank top with silver and yellow bows all over it. Denise would hate it, but Caressa loved it.

"We should get back," said Kyle. "We'll save shoes for another day."

Caressa laughed and felt an almost insane urge to skip along beside him. For a few hours she'd forgotten all about Saint-Saëns and concert reviews. She'd felt like a normal person, out and about living life for once. She'd bought a bunch of clothes she liked and enjoyed the fresh air and sunshine. She hadn't heard any music but the sound of Kyle's laughter and whispered encouragements in her ear.

* * * * *

He left her at the suite to rest before the concert and headed off to the hotel gym with the newspapers from the table stuffed in the bottom of his bag. After he worked out, he sat in the sauna and flipped to the Arts sections to read over the reviews. Denise was right. They weren't exactly condemning her work, but not congratulating her either. All three reviewers brought her age into things. *While Caressa Gallo has grown up before our eyes, her performances still smack of immaturity.* Kyle felt a strong urge to smack the reviewer. She was twenty fucking years old, not exactly a seasoned adult yet.

He folded the papers and set them aside in disgust. When he'd taken this job, he hadn't bargained on any of this. He didn't know how to help her. When Jeremy had gotten bad reviews, it had always been reviews of the movie as a whole, not him personally. In this case, Kyle couldn't see how Caressa wouldn't feel personally attacked.

Damn it. He wanted to protect her, shelter her somehow, but he couldn't. He wanted to stand behind her on stage and glower at the audience, daring them to think any less of her for missed notes or botched phrasing. He didn't even know what the fuck phrasing was, but he was sure Caressa did it more beautifully than ninety-nine percent of the master cellists in the world. He showered and returned to the room in a snit, to find Caressa in a similarly touchy mood.

"You read them anyway," he accused.

"Denise always buys me my own copies."

"Damn it. I told you not to read them." He could see her searching her brain for some childish retort. He held up his hand. "Don't. Just don't say anything."

"I don't want to. Get out of my room."

"They were wrong, you know. It's just their opinion."

"They weren't wrong!"

"Stop with the yelling thing, Caressa. It doesn't intimidate me and it just makes you sound like a crazy woman."

"Maybe I am a crazy woman," she snapped. "All I know is that I screwed up yesterday and it was all your fault."

"Somehow I doubt that."

"You and your fucking seduction and—"

"Wait. Seduction? Sex goes both ways, sugar. I don't remember you resisting or saying no."

"How am I supposed to play with you…doing this stuff to me? I need to concentrate on music, not fucking and shopping and whatever the hell else you want to do at any given moment. You're too…disruptive!"

"Fine, I'll leave you alone then."

"I would appreciate that."

"You probably wouldn't have enjoyed all the things I had planned for you tonight anyway," he added casually, studying one of his nails.

"What are you talking about?"

"Nothing. If you want to be left alone, I'll leave you alone. I thought you liked our time together so far. But whatever. You need to be ready to leave for the theater at six-thirty."

He turned his back on her and left. A risk. He prayed she wouldn't run back up to the rooftop, or stage some other similarly dramatic scene. But she did nothing, and at six-thirty she came out of her room in her armor of black silk and smoothed-back hair. At the theater she marched out on stage as if to do battle, and from the look on Denise's face, this time Caressa prevailed. Kyle tried to feel happy for her, but disgruntlement reigned.

The next three days passed in a tense standoff. Kyle did everything he'd agreed to do as her assistant, but that was the extent of their interactions—in reality anyway. In his mind, Kyle interacted with her until Caressa could barely walk. He fucked her, tied her up, gagged her, teased and tormented her. He made her moan, and when she fought him he held her down and fucked her harder.

If she was having similar thoughts, she hid them well. They got on a plane to Portland and Caressa sat alone with her cello case in the two-across seat. Denise glanced over at her and then back at Kyle.

"It's probably better this way."

"Mm." Kyle thought for the hundredth time that he should resign and let the constant temptation that dogged him fall into someone else's hands. But he wasn't capable of walking away from her, not now. "Whatever makes her happy, I guess," he said, only because Denise seemed to be waiting for some answer from him.

"Everything I do is for Caressa's happiness," she replied in an unctuous tone.

"Do you really think she's happy?"

"In her own way she is. This is what she lives for. It's not always easy for her, but she wouldn't have it any other way."

"Are you sure of that?"

"She put the music ahead of *you*, didn't she?" She didn't say it cruelly, but Kyle got the message loud and clear. Denise shifted and clasped her hands in her lap. "Please, whatever you do, don't try to make her choose. You'll end up with more of a mess than you can manage."

"I would never ask her to choose."

"Not in so many words, I'm sure. But she's already conflicted."

"Why does it have to be either-or? Why can't she have a relationship with me and still do her music too? This unhealthy obsession—"

"You don't understand."

"I understand that she's living half a life, and the half is all music. I took her to the mall and she was walking around like Alice in Wonderland. She's twenty years old. What does your life look like when you're twenty and you've never even hung out at a mall? What has she ever done that normal kids do?"

"She's not a kid."

"Not now. But five years ago she was. What was she doing five years ago?"

Denise bit her lip and didn't answer.

"Let me guess. Practicing her cello, appearing at concerts, and poring over reviews."

"Yes. And that's exactly what she wanted to be doing."

"How do you know? What else has she ever been allowed to do?"

"It's not a matter of 'allowing'! She does all of this by choice."

Kyle stopped, glancing over at Caressa. She could see they were arguing, and quickly looked away. "By *choice*. Yes, that's what I hear," Kyle said in a lower voice. "But it seems like only one choice is allowed. What if she chooses to be with me? What if she chooses a real life instead of this musical bubble she's living in?"

Denise looked over at him, her deep brown eyes sincere and resolute. "If she chooses, she chooses. You are not listening to my words. *You* do not make her choose. It must be her choice. You understand?"

"I would never force her to choose," he grumbled, sitting back in his seat. But part of him knew that's what he was already doing. Poking, peeling away the protective layer that kept her focused and productive. He wanted to show her the wide world she'd forsaken to become a musical virtuosa. But was he doing it for her—or for him?

It was just a short flight and soon they were preparing the cabin for landing. He looked over at Caressa and saw her fingers curled around the handle of her cello case. He wanted to be holding that hand. He wanted to make her happy, make her laugh in that same giddy way she'd laughed at the mall that day. There was no malice in it, no desire to ruin her, just a desire to help her discover things, and yes, perhaps woo her a little bit.

But more and more he realized that Caressa was already involved in a primary relationship—a dysfunctional one. Caressa was inextricably entangled with a horsehair bow, a glossy wooden body and four quivering strings.

Chapter Six:
Instrument

Caressa lay awake in the dark tossing and turning, unable to find peace. Tonight's concert had actually been the best so far. They'd traveled to a three-night appearance in Portland and on to Seattle for another three days. Caressa had always loved Seattle for some reason. Perhaps because it always rained in Seattle. Kyle had made a joke about Caressa not going up on the roof on the way home from the last night's show, when rain had lashed the windows of the car and lightning had lit up the gorgeous planes of his face. She hadn't found the joke particularly funny. That night hadn't been a joke to her, when she'd first stared at his chest, at his fingers. When she'd first had to admit that something moved her besides music.

The shows were going fine, but she felt like shit. She'd thrown up a wall between them and he aggravated her by stubbornly staying on his side. He still managed everything, kept her on schedule, made sure she had room service and dry cleaning. He got her to interviews and appointments. He hauled her cello on and off planes and through hotel lobbies, up and down elevators. He never once bumped it or banged it into the wall.

He never touched her either.

She tried to tell herself it didn't matter. The music mattered. She kept her mind on music all day without a problem. The better she played, the better she felt. She practiced and felt the concerto that was once her enemy becoming more like a friend. New aspects of the work opened up and she embraced them, sometimes in the hot chaos of a performance and sometimes as she sat quietly eating or resting. She was actually fine until she turned out the lights at night and remembered the feel of him holding her down, pressing into her. Her body betrayed her will, and wouldn't let her forget.

She finally gave up on sleep and threw off the sheets, sitting up and hugging her knees to her chest. She'd moved the bed against the wall because she knew he was on the other side of it, and now she leaned against it as if he might feel her in the next room and know she needed him. Needed him? God, did she really need him? She had a handle on the concerto finally, and she was getting into the rhythm of life on tour.

He *certainly* didn't need her. Everywhere they went, women gawked at him. A lot of them openly made passes. Ugh. He might have a woman with him right now, in the hotel room next to hers. She pressed her ear against the coolness of the wall but she heard nothing.

Well, she couldn't just sit in the room and stew. Tomorrow was a traveling day, so she could stay up late if she wanted to. She got dressed and put on a little lipstick and grabbed her key to go downstairs. She'd go hang in the bar, do some people-watching. Maybe try to buy a drink without ID. She looked a little older with her hair pulled back.

As she left, she caught the door so it wouldn't slam. If Kyle was in there fucking some lucky woman, God forbid she would disturb him. Maybe he was sleeping. She thought just a moment of knocking on the door. After the rooftop incident he'd told her to always keep him advised of her whereabouts, but it wasn't like she was leaving the hotel. She shrugged and continued down the hall.

The bar was like every other hotel bar she'd ever been in. Slick and yet depressingly sterile. Dark and a little smoky. Not very crowded, which screwed the people-watching idea. She sat at a table near the door, glancing around and gathering up her courage to try to finagle a drink from the bartender. She was almost twenty-one anyway. Maybe she should just show the guy her ID and hope he'd spot her a few weeks. Just as she decided to try it her problem was solved, because a businessman appeared at her elbow with two beers in his hand.

"Hello. Lonely?"

Caressa looked at him, not sure what to respond. *Yes, I'm lonely. No, not for you.* Not that he wasn't attractive in a rich businessman kind of way. He was pretty short and not classically handsome, but he exuded success and power. He was probably some corporate higher-up on a business trip. When she didn't answer, he held out one of the beers, a question in his eyes.

After a moment, she took it. "Thanks."

"Can I sit down?"

"Sure."

He sat beside her, not crowding her. He didn't seem to be too drunk or sloppy. "So, are *you* lonely?" she asked, turning his question back on him.

He laughed. "Not really. Just bored. I've been in a hundred of these hotel bars. Hundreds of hotel rooms. They get old."

Caressa looked down at the beer bottle. It was some brand she'd never heard of, probably some expensive import. She took a tentative sip. "Yeah, I know."

He looked surprised, or perhaps amused. "Aren't you a little young to be jaded by travel?"

She shrugged, made nervous by the way he scrutinized her. She hated the taste of the beer, but she didn't want to be rude and not drink it. She took another miniscule sip and let the bitter liquid sit on her tongue. "I travel for a living," she finally said.

"Doing what?"

Caressa hesitated. How much should she tell him about herself? He was a complete stranger. Her eyes darted around the room. It's not like she wasn't safe here. It's not like he could make her do anything she didn't want to do, no matter how rich and assertive he seemed. She inched away from him a little and smiled, toying with the neck of her beer bottle. "I'm a musician," she said. "I play with various orchestras. I'm touring right now."

"Ah." He looked duly impressed. "What instrument do you play?"

"Cello."

"I used to play a little sax back in the day." He smiled ruefully. "I didn't keep up with it. Doubt I could play a note now."

"Really? Music is like bike-riding. You never forget."

"Maybe. My name's Michael, by the way."

"Hi, Michael. I'm Caressa."

He shook her hand with a warm, firm grip. She thought he shook it a little too long. "Caressa. That's different. So I take it you're not a Seattleite."

"No. I'm a New Yorker."

"I'm from Toronto." She watched him take a deep drink of his beer and tipped her bottle back too. He was old enough to be her father. She got the feeling he liked that. She turned a little from his intent gaze, and then noticed a tall, dark-haired man sitting at the far end of the bar. His face lifted and all-too-familiar eyes latched on to hers. She quickly lowered the beer bottle from her lips, but he was already up.

"Um..." was all she managed to get out before he arrived at the table.

"Making new friends?" Kyle bit out.

"Excuse me?" Michael's voice bristled.

Kyle pushed her beer back to his side of the table. "Yeah, she's not old enough to be drinking that. And really not old enough for a business-trip hookup either. If you'll excuse us," he drawled, pulling Caressa from her chair and leading her toward the door.

"Let go of me." She pulled her arm away, too embarrassed to look back and see what Michael was making of this.

"What are you doing down here?" he asked.

"What are *you* doing down here?" she shot back.

"I was trying not to have a drink, Caressa. Although I'm legally of age to do so. Unlike you."

"I'm almost twenty-one. And what do you mean, 'trying not to have a drink'? Why were you in the bar, then?"

"That's a story for another day. So were you seriously planning to hook up with that toad?"

"He was very nice."

"Said the hopelessly naive victim. He's a married businessman on a trip wanting to screw you after he got a few beers in you."

"How do you know that?"

"How do you *not* know that? Seriously, you scare me sometimes."

He was leading her to the elevators. She pulled away, turning on him. "Don't talk to me like that. Like I'm a stupid, naive idiot!"

He looked around the mostly deserted lobby and steered her into the elevator as the doors opened. She stood as far away from him as the small compartment would allow, her arms crossed over her chest. "Maybe I wanted to sleep with him. Did you ever think of that?"

He gave her a look that silenced her. When they reached their floor, he walked her to her room. "I asked you to tell me whenever you're going somewhere. Especially alone."

She didn't reply, just looked at the floor. She hated this, being lectured like a child. He hadn't been interested in lecturing when he was busy fucking her. She wanted to say that, how much he hurt her, how cruel he was to desert her, but he hadn't deserted her. She'd forced him away. She looked up at him, torn by emotion and confusion. Big mistake. He looked down at her and she knew he saw everything she felt but couldn't say. The irritated lines of his face softened.

"I didn't really want to sleep with him," she said.

Still his gaze held hers. She reached out for him with one hand, hating herself for doing it, but unable to do anything else. Her fingers met the hard planes of his stomach and moved lower to play over the crest of his hip. The words—*I wanted to sleep with you*—were unspoken but understood. The softness in his face transformed again into something intent and dangerous. "There is..." She stopped, remembering how she'd leaned against the wall to listen for him. "There is this wall between us."

"You put that wall there."

"I know, but..."

He waited. She didn't know what came after that *but...* After a moment he put his hand over her hand where it was toying with the waistband of his jeans.

"Would you like to spend tonight with me, Caressa?"

Time seemed to stand still. She wanted to answer in a thousand different ways, but finally she just whispered, "Yes."

"No walls though," he warned her. "Just you and me, and all the things I want to do to you."

"No walls," she agreed. *Whatever. Whatever you want. Do all those things to me.*

* * * * *

Once the door closed, she lost her nerve a little. He stood as if ready to...what? Do something to her. He intended *something*, and that both excited and scared her. She had come to think of Kyle in two ways...as a cool, responsible assistant and a rough, impassioned lover. Now he seemed a strange combination of both—coolly calculating and sexually threatening. She skirted the outside of the room, coming to stop beside the TV.

"So...I'm kind of scared to hear about these 'things' you just alluded to."

"You should be scared." He was still staring.

"You're a massive pervert, aren't you?"

"You have no idea. But you are, of course, free to tap out at any time." He finally moved, taking off his shirt and laying it over the chair to his right. His hands went to his jeans, unbuckling the belt and popping open the buttons with that same dexterity that made him seem so dangerous from the start. "I doubt you'll leave though. What's that they say? 'Curiosity killed the cat'."

"Are you going to kill me?" She gawked as he kicked off his jeans, revealing a very distinctive bulge in his boxer briefs.

He chuckled. "You've survived thus far." The boxers came off and he stood before her in all his breathtaking, masculine glory. She had the sudden impulse to drop to her knees. But before she could do anything, he crossed to her and put his hands on her, on her neck, on her shoulders, down the sides of her hips, and then to the curve of her buttocks. He kissed her, impulsively, sloppily, as if he hadn't meant to but couldn't quite resist. He pulled away and unbuttoned the printed blouse he'd helped choose for her, to reveal the delicate ivory bra she'd chosen for herself. He paused, running his fingers over the tiny row of buttons.

"I like this," he said quietly. "Understated and yet ornate, like you."

"I'm not ornate," she said. "What does that even mean?"

"You'll see." He unbuttoned her jeans and slid them down over her hips with flat, warm palms caressing every inch of skin on the way. God, she was already so wet for him. She wanted what she'd had before. She wanted him to throw her down and fuck her so her skin was scraped against the rough hotel carpet.

He knelt, not yet removing her panties. "Very nice…" He slid his fingers down the tiny row of buttons at the front, matched to the ones on her bra, and then his tongue traced the path his fingers took. She could feel the wet, warm trail through the sheer silk as she looked down in wonder at his broad shoulders, his dark hair. She moaned as he pressed his lips to the apex of her cleft.

At the same time, his fingers slipped up her panties and parted her, and one delved into her soaked pussy. She whimpered and grasped his shoulders. The pleasure was crippling, immediate. The teasing of his tongue through the silk was magnified by the slow in-and-out invasion of his finger. Soon, another finger pushed up inside, filling her, stroking her. She wanted to rip off the panties and feel his tongue against her clit, not this horrible, half-fulfilled state of craving and wanting. Her fingers twisted in his hair and she moaned out a wordless plea.

He pulled his fingers away and yanked her to the floor with two strong hands on her hips. He crawled over her, one solid knee pressed to the juncture of her legs. She ground against it, unthinking, a hapless creature of pure, wanton desire.

"No," he said. "Not yet."

She stilled, confused. *Not yet?* He was killing her. He left his knee where it was and pulled down the cups of her bra, exposing hard, pink nipples. He gave her a look, of challenge or perhaps warning, and then he put his lips on her and suckled her. Warm wet arousal became frantic alarm as his lips and teeth tightened on the sensitive bud. God, it *hurt*! But it felt...so...amazing...

He was watching her, smiling softly. "You like that."

She shook her head but he only laughed. He lowered his lips to the other thrusting peak and gave it the same rough but sensual treatment. Her hands sought something to hold onto...the carpet, his neck, his hair. She cried out, the pressure to come almost unbearable, building and swirling in her pelvis so she thought she would explode from it. Again she pressed against his knee, spreading her legs, thrusting against him—

The reaction was immediate. "I said not yet." His clipped reprimand was accompanied by a sharp slap to her thigh. She gazed back at him, the sting barely registering over the surging wave of horniness. She felt wild and completely wanton in a way she'd never felt before. He pushed himself off her, sitting on his knees between her legs. She could see his cock was thick and full, jutting up out of a thatch of dark hair. God, she wanted it—but he was making her wait.

"Please..." she begged, hardly knowing what she was begging for. Anything. A touch. A taste.

"Yes, you'll get it," he said. "When I say. Not yet."

She moaned again and he ignored her, pulling down her panties and tossing them aside. "Part your legs. I don't want you to come yet. I know you're hot and horny, but we can't have you getting yourself off whenever you feel like it."

Can't we? His hands pushed her thighs apart and she complied, driven more by the demanding tone of his voice than the insistence of his fingers. He forced her legs wide open, past the point of comfort to the point of embarrassment, at which time he finally seemed satisfied. "That's better. You can come when I say. I know it's hard to wait, but you do what I want right now. I think you like it that way. I can see how wet you are from here. I can smell you." He touched her carelessly, drew rough fingers across her pussy in a tease that brought unassuaged longing to a brutal peak. He brought his fingers to her nose. "See? Taste yourself. See what you taste like."

She couldn't believe he ordered it, and worse, couldn't believe she obeyed. She licked his fingers, desperate for something—anything—to be inside her. She sucked her scent and taste so avidly she embarrassed herself, but the look on his face told her she was doing the right thing. *Things…things I want to do to you.*

She hated this and loved it. She wanted him to fuck her, to fulfill her needs—but she liked it just as much that he was refusing to. She had the feeling that if she didn't do exactly as he told her, this magical game would end and she would be far less satisfied than if she continued to obey. So she waited, trembling like a leaf, as he stood and went to get something from his luggage. He returned with a black permanent marker. She watched with a kind of wonder as he removed the lid and knelt between her legs again.

He spread his knees so her thighs were pushed open wide, then reached beneath her to remove her bra. Once it was off, he placed the point of the marker between her breasts. He drew a long, straight line all the way down from her breasts to the top of her pubic hair. She watched, barely breathing. He drew a second line beside the first, and this time she shivered a little at the feel of the felt tip against her stomach. He put his other hand on her hip.

"Be still."

"It tickles!"

"Be still," he said again, his gaze pinning her. "Let me."

Let me. Her body wasn't giving her a choice. It was honed in on the slightest stimulus he gave her. The narrow tip of the marker nearly undid her as he began up at her breasts again to draw a third line all the way down, and then a fourth. At some point during the fourth line she understood what he was doing. He moved the pen to the side of her stomach, drawing a narrow outline of a curve, and then a mirror-imaged one on the other side. She could see they were exact replicas of the ones on her cello's body.

"What are those called?" he asked, tracing the figures with each hand.

"F-holes," Caressa replied, feeling strangely close to hysteria.

He nodded, a faint smile. "Apropos."

A few more lines down over her breasts and around her hips to outline, and then he sat back and capped the pen. He studied her, running long, tender fingertips up the strings of her body.

"Caressa. I can play you, if you let me. Let's make music, you and me." She swallowed, never doubting for a moment he could do it. In this type of music, he was a maestro. "But I like to be the conductor," he continued. "Can you understand that? I like to be the one setting the tempo. I want to be the musician, doing the phrasing."

She gazed up at him, transfixed. "Where did you learn about tempo and phrasing?"

"From you, of course. Everything I know about fine music, I've learned from you," he murmured, drawing his fingers down from her quivering f-holes to the base of her instrument, aching and yearning for his touch.

* * * * *

The drawing had been complete improvisation. He'd wanted to find a way to explain his desires to her without coming off like a tyrant or an asshole. He quite simply liked to be in charge. It's what made him good as a personal assistant, and it's what drove him to become a dominant once Jeremy had introduced him to that world. Kyle understood her desire to submit, her reckless need to challenge and be brought to heel.

But he was after more than just control here, just as she was after more than chastisement. He wanted connection, and he felt like connecting with her would be like weaving himself into a tapestry. An incredibly involved and lengthy process, but one which might produce a masterpiece.

He gazed down at her now, his beautiful instrument. He leaned over her on one arm, the other stroking her, making her jerk and shudder beneath him. She was so wet, so responsive.

"What a good girl you are," he said. "Keeping your legs wide open as I told you. It's hard, isn't it?"

"Yes."

"*Yes, Sir.*"

She hesitated, but only for a moment. "Yes, Sir. It's hard."

He noted the charming blush. "Is it embarrassing?"

"A little."

"Turn over." He helped her turn onto hands and knees, obstructing her when she tried to draw her legs together. "No. I want you open to me. I don't care if you're embarrassed."

She made a small sound of protest and buried her face in her hands as he spread her wider still. "Now, stay."

He got up and went to dig a condom out of his luggage, and then took up his jeans, drawing his belt out. She stiffened a little but stayed still. She looked gorgeous—ass up, back arched so perfectly. At least for the moment.

"Don't move, Caressa."

"What are you going to do?" Her muffled voice sounded quavery.

"Spank you. A real spanking. I hope you like it as much as you thought." He smiled to himself, imagining she drew herself up a little straighter. "If you say 'enough' I'll stop. Okay?"

"Okay."

"*Yes, Sir.*"

"Yes, Sir," she said. She seemed to brace herself. He doubled the belt over and landed the first stroke, not hard enough to scare her, but hard enough to count. The only reaction was a curling of her fingers into tight fists. He hit her again, this time concentrated on one cheek. She gave a little whiny moan and he cracked the other cheek. She was already nice and pink. No need to drive her to her limits the first time around. He wouldn't make it that far. His cock was close to exploding.

"Okay?" he asked quietly.

"Yes, Sir."

Another blow, harder. She yelped and drew her knees in just a bit. He used his foot to push them back open, none too gently.

"Be a good girl, Caressa."

"How—How many—?" she asked.

"As many as I think you need. You're beautiful like this, by the way."

She made another lovely, frustrated sound. The belt was perfect for this task, weathered and supple, certainly very sting-y for her, but not likely to bruise her much. He gave her another middle-strength stroke, and another. "It would be kinder of me to tie you down, wouldn't it?" he asked, watching the telltale trembling, the tension in her spine. "I can see you're trying very hard to be still. Or is the trembling from something else...?"

She shook her head, but her whole body arched as if begging for him. He was suffering as badly as she was. His control broke and he fell on her, the belt flung, forgotten, to the floor. He grabbed her hair and pulled her back to him, his cock nestled between the hot apex of her thighs. He pressed his cheek to hers, his lips against her ear. "My God, you're a spectacular little slut, aren't you? You make music I've never heard before."

She shook her head, and he felt moisture on her cheeks. Tears? Had he miscalculated?

"What is it? What's wrong?"

"I've never heard this music before either. I don't know what to do."

"Do you want me?"

"Oh, yes. More than anything."

He grabbed the condom he'd set aside, rolled it on in record time. His hands wrapped around her hips, grasping, no doubt, just over the drawings he'd made on her, the "f-holes" as she called them. He squeezed her breasts and pinched her nipples as he drove into her, feeling her convulse around him as the pain registered. He pounded against the red cheeks he'd punished, fucking her deep.

God, she made him crazy. He pulled her hair and bit her nape, breathing in her sugary, salty scent. She was like a wild, liquid thing in his arms, shuddering and shivering until she cried out and arched back against him. He came too in a pounding wave of sensation, his fingers pressed against the strings he'd drawn down the center of her chest.

He turned her over when he was able, collapsing down beside her. There were still tears, and he tried not to be troubled by them. Not only troubled, but affected too much. *I love you.* The words rolled through his brain, a shocking revelation. But he couldn't really feel that, not so soon. It was only her vulnerability, the way she gave herself up to him when her life was so much about defiance and control.

She ran her fingers down the strings to where they met her dark pubic hair.

"How do I get this off now?"

"You don't." Kyle traced after her fingers and took her hand in his. "It's permanent. At least for now."

They showered together then, and yes, the marker didn't come off, not the least bit. He didn't want it to. Nor did she leave when he gave her the opportunity, even though it was nearly two in the morning.

"I want to stay," she said. He nodded and gestured to his bed. She hesitated. "Should I go get my pajamas?"

"Not a chance in hell."

He slid in beside her and looked at her a long time. He wished he knew what was going on behind her steady gaze. The tears were gone now and she seemed calm, more peaceful than he'd ever remembered seeing her.

"You liked it?" he asked finally.

"Yes." She answered as if it was painfully obvious, and he supposed it was. She had enjoyed his dominance. She had slid down into submission like a fish into an ocean.

"Why?"

94

She thought about it a moment. "Because I...I liked doing something right. When you said...when you said *good girl...*" She paused, her voice suddenly tight with emotion. "It's been a long time since I've really felt like I've done something well."

Kyle frowned as he brushed an errant curl from her forehead. "Caressa. You've made countless people happy with your music. You've made CDs, you've performed at hundreds of concerts. You're a familiar name in the music world. A music celebrity. Why do you think that is?"

She shrugged. "Because I'm young. People think it's interesting that I can play so well at my age."

"So it's just your age? You don't think it's because of the music? Because you play in a way that moves them, that astounds them? There are thousands of cello players in the world, really good cello players. And you're probably in the top five."

"That's debatable."

"Right now, at this moment in time, I believe you are. Okay, let's say top ten. Still. Do you really believe you haven't done anything well? That you don't do something well every time you walk out on that stage?"

He traced her drawn-on strings, toying with her, trying to make her see what was so blatantly obvious to everybody else. She looked away. "I don't know. I don't ever feel like I really play well."

"The music world disagrees with you."

"What about those reviews?"

"That was the first night. Jesus, Caressa, they've been raves since then." He sighed and rolled away from her onto his back, shoving his fingers through his hair. "You really scare me sometimes. You really worry me."

"I should just sleep in my own room," she grumbled, turning to climb out of his bed.

"Stop." He put his hand on her shoulder. "Please. I'm just trying to understand you. Why you feel this way."

She turned to frown at him. "I don't want you to understand me. I just want you to tell me what to do, and tell me I'm a good girl when I do it."

The silence in the room was stifling. Still he stared at her, measuring, deciding where to go next. She looked away, and then dragged her gaze back to his and held it. After another moment, he made a small, negative sound.

"I don't know, Caressa. This seems unhealthy to me. You should be living life. Dating, forming real relationships, not fucking around with a guy like me. Music shouldn't be making you feel bad, to the point that you need a lover to keep it together. A dominant. Isn't that what you want?"

"Isn't that what you are?"

"I suppose. But I usually choose my partners based on sexual attraction, not psychological neediness."

She looked crushed. "You're not attracted to me?"

"If you really believe that, you're more fucked up than I thought."

"You just basically called me a needy psycho."

"I didn't mean it that way. Look, it's clear to me that you need help. I'm willing to give it—although I promise right now, you won't always be thrilled with what goes down. I'll give you a wall to bang your head against, but if you get hurt, you're not going to get cuddles and sympathy from me. It won't be a game, Caressa."

"I don't want a game. I just want—I want more of what we did tonight. I...I really like the way it feels when you take control of me like that. I didn't know how to tell you..."

"I think you tried a few times, in a ridiculously roundabout way. Come here." He pulled her close, whispering kisses across her forehead, down to her cheeks. "Caressa. I want to help you. That's what you hired me for."

"My aunt hired you."

"Because you needed me. You knew it the minute I got into that limo with you the first day, didn't you? And it scared you and you've been trying to push me away. Well, no more roundabout with us. No more dishonesty, no more tantrums."

She swallowed, pressing her cheek against his. "It's scary to need someone," she whispered.

"I know it. But I won't fail you. You don't fail me."

He thought she might cry. She almost cried. He enveloped her in a hug and she clung to him. He didn't tell her about his trip down to the bar, about how he came so close to buying a drink. Just one drink. He didn't tell her he actually needed her as much as she needed him.

•

Chapter Seven:
Infatuation

He held her hand most of the flight to New York. Not romantically, but possessively, because he wanted to, even though she kept pulling away. At one point, he closed his fingers around her wrist and smirked at her. *I have some equipment to pick up at my place*, he'd told her on the way to the airport. He'd refused to elaborate, preferring that Caressa spend the flight speculating on what type of equipment he was talking about. It was better than her worrying about the plane crashing, which was how she normally spent her time in the air.

For his part, he speculated on other things. How they would spend their time in New York, or more precisely, how much time she would want to spend with him. Last night's re-connection had been arousing, but the next morning her signals confused him. She was distant, cool. Insular.

If she wanted distance, she could easily find it during their time in New York. He had his own place in Hudson Square and she had hers with her Aunt Denise in Soho. But he was her employee, so he would have to stick around at least some of the time. She had seven performances at Lincoln Center, and a couple press events and interviews, to include a ritzy gala meet-and-greet to raise funds for the New York Philharmonic. Her New York appearances were a big deal. Perhaps that explained her prickly mood.

They arrived late in the day, merely because the time changed going eastward. As soon as they landed, Caressa called a man named Dominic Fiorenzo to see if she could come by his shop with her cello. The man was ostensibly a repairman of fine instruments, but Caressa spoke of him as nothing less than a god. A couple hours later, after dropping his bags at his apartment, Kyle came for Caressa in a rented car large enough to carry her cello. They drove out of the city to the Jersey suburbs, arriving at Signore Fiorenzo's shop just at dusk.

"*Caressa mia!*" The old man hobbled from behind the counter as soon as they entered, pulling Caressa into a fatherly embrace. Kyle looked around the old shop while he took her cello out of its case. It was on a nice enough street but it was a real hole inside, cluttered and dusty. Kyle tried to subdue any overt expressions of horror, but the OCD side of him was affronted beyond repair. Caressa didn't even seem to notice the mess, pushing aside a stack of mildewing books to sit down on a chair behind the counter. She played a few notes to show Dominic the problem, some tone or string problem, and sighed in relief when the repairman recognized it at once. She looked up at him anxiously.

"Fixable?"

"*Sì*, I fix. Play for me again, let me hear."

She played a few notes. "I know it's just a little off, but…"

"No, I hear it."

"Will it take long to fix? I have a performance tomorrow."

"*Sì, sì*, I fix. You play once more, Cara."

She played and he listened carefully, making a subtle adjustment to the strings. Caressa played again and he nodded.

"Peg slipping. It is summer, *sì*? They slip and slide. No damage. I repair peg here for string A, this is all."

"New pegs?"

"Perhaps. No, not yet. You let me play with it? You wait, or you come back in two hours?"

"Okay, we'll come back," said Caressa. Dominic had already hopped up and started rooting through some bins behind the counter. Then he ducked into the back room, a glimpse of which made Kyle feel physically sick. Kyle followed Caressa out of the shop onto the quiet suburban New Jersey street.

"Hey Caressa, have you ever seen that TV show about hoarders?"

She tsked. "He's messy but he's good at what he does. So do you mind waiting around a couple hours? There's a diner down the street."

"Yeah, let's eat." Kyle could think of other things he'd like to do with her for two hours, but they'd require, at the very least, the use of a hotel room. They ordered coffee and sandwiches at a greasy spoon instead and sat to eat across a wobbly table from each other.

Caressa sighed. "You know, I'm so tired of hotel food. This actually looks good to me."

Kyle eyed her sloppy reuben. "Yeah, traveling gets old fast. It's nice to be home for a little." He put ketchup and mayo on his burger, trying to think how long it had been since he'd dined in a small town dive like this. Not since Spur. Strange to find this sleepy suburb just a few miles out of the city.

"So who is this guy, Caressa? You must really trust him, to leave your cello with him."

"He's the one who found it for me in the first place."

"Really?" He tried to reconcile the scruffy, disorganized man with the "priceless" value of Caressa's beloved instrument.

"Dominic is a direct link to Sergio Peresson," she explained. "Before Peresson died, he and Dominic were friends. They worked on instruments together. Dominic used to do work on du Pré's cello."

"What's a du Pré?"

Caressa snorted. "Not what. Who. Jacqueline du Pré. She was a famous cellist." She paused, stirring her coffee thoughtfully. "People sometimes compare me to her."

"She was crazy too?"

Ah, nice eye roll. Caressa stared down into her cup and shrugged, her sandwich barely touched. "She was a lot like me, I guess. She started young. She was truly a genius, and yes, a little crazy. She was really...I don't know. If you watch the old films of her playing, it's so obvious that she...that she had a gift. That she was something completely singular. One of a kind."

Kyle took Caressa's hand. "Then you are a lot like her."

"No, I'm not," she said, pulling away. "Anyway, Jacqueline du Pré got multiple sclerosis. She had to stop playing. Can you imagine?" Her voice faltered a little, and she took a deep breath. "She played her last concert when she was only twenty-eight."

Kyle thought she might cry. "That's tragic," he said quietly. "Are you afraid that will happen to you?"

Caressa didn't answer, just flipped her sandwich over and ate some of the corned beef. "I do like having a link to her. I like that she played a Peresson too. I wish I had her cello, but after she died, they loaned it to some friend of her husband's. I would have loved to play it, just once."

Kyle frowned, finishing off his burger. "Someday, some cellist is going to wish to play Caressa Gallo's cello." He immediately wished to take the words back, thinking them too morbid, but she surprised him and slid him a flirtatious look.

"Like you played it?"

He hid a smile, remembering "f-holes" and black lines on skin. "Well..."

Later, after they picked up Caressa's cello, he took her back to Denise's Soho townhouse. It seemed a home-y enough place—a lot warmer in character than his minimally-furnished walk-up. He didn't see much of it, though, since Caressa dragged him past her aunt and right upstairs to her room.

Again he felt a strange flashback to his youth in Texas. He'd had to sneak upstairs with girls back then, to avoid the kind of looks Denise shot at him as he followed Caressa to the second floor. And the girls he'd snuck upstairs with in Spur had been a lot less...complicated than Caressa. He sprawled beside her on her twin size bed, still unsure of her mood. She had a way of flirting and then withdrawing, as if she scared herself. Maybe she did. He had to remind himself that she'd actually been a virgin a few short weeks ago. Her bedroom was a virgin's bedroom, girly and frilly in a way that didn't jibe with her serious persona.

"Hey, you didn't practice today," he said, remembering.

"I know. It feels strange to not play for a whole day."

"Why don't you play me something?"

"I will, if you go get my cello from downstairs."

It was late, but they were still on West Coast time, and wide awake. He hoped the neighbors wouldn't get too upset about a late night concert. "Okay," he said, standing and stretching. "I'll go get your cello on one condition. You need to be stark naked by the time I get back." He pointed a finger at her. "Stark. Naked."

She gave him a coy look, neither agreeing nor refusing. He went downstairs and got the cello case, and considered taking the cello out. But then he imagined tripping on the way up the stairs and landing at the bottom in a pile of splintered wood and metal, and decided to haul the whole hard-sided case upstairs. "Damn it, Caressa," he gasped as he pushed her door open. "You better be naked after this—"

He looked up to find her standing beside her desk. The lines he'd drawn on her were still there, faded after a couple of showers. She was beautiful, like a Grecian statue. His palms itched to cup her breasts, to run over her hips. His whole body wanted to grind against her. He made himself stand still, made himself look at her. He never enjoyed her this way. He always just fell on her, unable to control his urges. God, her breasts, her flat belly, her flawless skin. She gave him an assessing look, as if she knew what he was thinking. *Yes, I'm having trouble controlling myself. You made me this way.*

"Sit down," he said firmly. "Open your legs."

After a short pause she did as he asked, silently and deliberately, and hot liquid lust jolted his cock to life and resonated down to his balls. He busied himself opening the case and extricating her cello, trying to leash the desire that threatened to overwhelm him. God, jumping right in and barking orders at her, was he? The most exciting thing was that she'd obeyed. He carried her cello over, stopping in front of her to take in the delicious sight of her spread thighs, her pussy. She reached for her cello but he stopped her. "Wider."

She swallowed, gazing ahead at the steadily increasing bulge in the front of his pants. "Wider," he repeated. "Obey me." *Do it, do it. Play along. I want this so badly.*

With a faint, self-conscious smile, she complied, spreading her thighs so he could see the glistening center of her pussy. My God. *My God.* He ran his fingertips over the top of one knee. "Good girl," he said, wishing he could yank both her knees up, rip down his zipper, and impale her. *No, no, play with her first. She wants it. Look at the expression on her face.*

He reached with one hand to fondle her breasts, unable to help himself. She whimpered when his fingers closed on the sensitive tip of one nipple and pinched. She shivered and drew her legs closed again. He stepped closer, spreading them with his legs so the choice to obey was taken from her. He could just unzip, unzip and take her... *No.*

He thrust the cello at her. "Play for me. Something sexy, Caressa."

"Yes, Sir."

She knew exactly what the honorific did to him. She started playing, beautifully, with consummate skill, but he could barely hear her above the blood beating in his ears. Her parted knees were a revelation, a masterpiece, tapering down shapely calves to flexed feet on the floor, all of her sinuous body cradling her instrument and drawing such sounds from it...

He started to strip, knowing he had to be as naked as her and that he had to be inside her. She slowed a little, a faltery note—

"Keep playing," he said. "Don't stop."

She obeyed, playing, but still watching him. When he was nude he crossed his arms over his chest only to keep them from reaching out for her. She looked up into his eyes and then down at his cock, and her lips parted. It was as much as he could take.

He stilled her bow, then took the cello and laid it on its side with the very last of his control. "Come. On your knees." *Those lovely knees, kneel on them for me. Obey me, beautiful girl.*

She looked up at him, hesitating. Of course, she didn't know how to do what he was asking for. He would show her. He would show her everything, give her everything. He would adore her forever for the way she looked up at him from her knees.

* * * * *

Caressa wanted to be his good girl. She would do anything for him when he looked at her that way. She felt loose and pliable as he took her face in rough hands, then leaned down to kiss her, deeply, passionately. She leaned back and moaned into his mouth as he explored her with his tongue, delving inside and insisting on more, more, more. Then he drew away and parted her lips with gentle fingers. "Open for me, Cara."

He said *Cara* like the Italian, like Signore Fiorenzo said it sometimes. She knew it meant "dear" or "beloved." The way he touched her and kissed her made her feel beloved, and she opened even though she was scared and uncertain if she could serve him the way he wanted. He guided his cock to her lips, and she clutched for his thighs, trying to balance, trying to sit up off her heels and accommodate him.

"Okay," he whispered. "I know. Do your best."

She knelt all the way up and he held her shoulders, letting her taste and explore him at her own pace. She swirled her tongue around the bulbous crown of his rod, thinking of kissing it, but not wanting to draw away. She took him deeper instead as he moved his hips forward, a sliding, smothering intrusion. She felt a frightening loss of control, a threat, but then he drew back, his fingers tightening and stroking across her back.

"Jesus, Caressa, you have no idea how great that feels. Don't stop. Suck me. Lick me." His words drove her like direct stimulation to her clit. She was so hot for him, for his godlike body and his quiet, explicit orders. He made her want to touch herself. She wanted to rub herself off, but somehow she sensed this act wasn't about her.

He grabbed one of her hands and pulled it between his legs, showing her without words how to fondle and caress his balls. She still sucked him while he manipulated her hand, trying to do everything he asked of her. He took her other hand from where she'd braced it against his leg and placed it at the base of his cock where her mouth couldn't reach. She felt awkward and clumsy in her movements but he was clearly enjoying himself, which gave her the courage to keep on. His groans and whispered encouragements mounted in intensity and his hands grasped in her hair. She panicked a little. Was he going to come in her mouth? No. He pulled away with a soft hiss.

"Bend over the bed." He yanked her up and gave her a little shove in the right direction. Before she could bend over all the way he was behind her, sheathed and ready, once again nudging her legs apart. "Wide. Open to me, always, you little slut." He said slut like an endearment, like *Cara*. Beloved slut. She was burning for him.

As soon as he parted her, as soon as he touched the head of his cock to her, she was trembling, close to orgasm. Everything he did…the way he looked at her, the way he touched her…it was a whole new world of wonders. She reached back, not knowing how to center herself in the midst of the storm he created inside her. She was scared he would hurt her, and scared he wouldn't hurt her enough.

"Kyle…" she pleaded.

He took her hands and held them hard as he slid inside her to the hilt. He wrestled both arms behind her back and trapped them there, pressing down on her, restraining her. She ground her clit against the edge of the bed as he withdrew and fell forward again. "Please, please, Kyle…"

"Ask me nicely."

She searched for words, coherent thoughts. "Please, Sir. Please make me come. I want to come."

He reached under her with one dexterous hand, the other still clasping her tightly by the wrists. She felt like crying with relief as he touched the exact part of her that ached for contact, that triggered fireworks one touch at a time.

"Here?" he asked. "It feels good, doesn't it?"

"Oh, God," she wailed. She struggled against his fingers, arching up to press her back against his chest.

He held her hands even harder, fucking her faster while he touched her. "Let go, Cara. Let me make you come."

She collapsed on the bed again, impaled. He took her roughly, his fingers sliding over her clit in rhythm to his thrusts. She felt the taut circle of his fingers around her wrist like a brand. She stopped struggling and let the crippling release wash over her, thankful for the mattress beneath her as her legs gave way.

Sensation burst wide, flooding her pelvis, her breasts and nipples. She rode the waves as he continued to pound into her, urging her to complete fulfillment before finding his own. Only then did he release her hands, which felt lifeless and floppy. All of her felt loose and floppy, except for the part of her he still cupped, lazily sliding one of his fingers in and out. He tangled his other hand in her curls, pulling her hair just enough to make her moan and come back to awareness.

"I like fucking you, Caressa Gallo," he said. "I can't seem to help myself."

She peered back to find him wearing that casually sexy grin he was so good at. He was irresistible when he flirted. Really, it was ridiculous. "Get off me, you perv."

"I see how it is." He laughed, withdrawing from her limp form and tossing his condom in the trash. "You only summon up the 'pleases' and 'Yes, Sirs' when you need something. Like a big fat cock where it counts the most."

She turned on the bed, laughing with him. "Is that wrong?"

"I don't know. You tell me." He effortlessly pulled her over one arm while his other hand started battering her ass cheeks with wicked, shocking spanks.

She yelped and reached back to shield herself from his assault, but he only grabbed her hand and smacked her harder. She was laughing too hard to cry out, but it hurt. She yanked at her hand again and soon they tumbled to the bed in a tangle. She tried to get away but he held her down and landed a few more fiery cracks.

"Stop. Stop!" she howled. He finally released her.

"You're making me hard again anyway."

She glared at him, then down at his cock, which was indeed hardening again. "Jesus. You're like a machine."

"Lucky for you. Now, just lie still. Stop trying to turn me on."

"Trying to—what?" Caressa protested. "You're the one who's always attacking me!"

"Shh…lie still." Kyle pinned her down again with a firm hand on her stomach, and with the other hand, began to toy with her curls. "Crazy girl," he murmured. "Your hair…"

"Don't touch it if you don't like it."

"I like it. It's just a mess." He began to twirl some of the curls beside her face, letting them drop against her cheek. She watched his eyes, so deep blue. His full, sensual lips, his aristocratic nose. She tried to fight the feelings flooding her chest. Love and need. Infatuation. That's all it was. She couldn't love him, she couldn't need him. She didn't have room in her life for a force as big as him. She turned her face away, but he turned it back again. "What? What's wrong?"

"Nothing." She sifted her brain for something to say under his scrutiny. "Why didn't you come in my mouth?" *Oh, great one, Caressa.*

Kyle gazed down at her in mild amusement. "Did you *want* me to come in your mouth? You little cum-hungry—"

Caressa dissolved into laughter.

"I wanted to, but I didn't know if it would freak you out. You should ask me to get tested before we start swapping bodily fluids anyway. If you want to go without condoms. And you would have to go on the pill."

"I'm already on the pill. One of the things we tried for my mood swings. It kept my periods regular so I stayed on it."

"Didn't do much for the moods though, did it?"

She pushed at him. "I hate you sometimes."

Kyle chuckled and pulled her closer. "I'll get tested if you want. Then we can go bareback. And I can splooge in the back of your throat as much as you want."

"Kyle!"

"Cause you seem to want it. You seem to crave it, you little— *oomph.*"

They were wrestling again, her shoves and elbows no match for his brute force. He just rolled on top of her and grinned down at her.

"Just admit you're thirsty for my cum and we can stop arguing about it."

She shoved at him, still laughing. "Cut it out. Hey, I have something else to ask you, seriously. As my assistant."

He composed himself and rolled off her to his side. "I'm at your command."

"So, you know that thing tomorrow?"

"That thing? You mean the big meet-and-greet and Lincoln Center fundraiser at which you are the spotlight guest? That thing?"

"Yeah, that. I was thinking about…maybe. I don't know. Dressing up a little."

"Of course you have to dress up. You're the guest of honor. So what were you thinking about wearing?"

Caressa was silent a moment. "I don't know. I usually just wear my concert clothes—"

"Oh, no, no, no, no, no." Kyle shook his head. "I pictured you in more of a Galliano-type number. You know, those dresses where it looks like you're being slowly ingested by a mountain of silk and lace."

"Stop," she said, laughing and poking him in the side. "I mean, I used to wear these really… I don't know. Dumb, babyish dresses. Aunt Denise picked them out. I thought maybe you could help me find something more…"

"Mature?"

"Yes."

"Sure, I'd be happy to. It's going to be close finding something by tomorrow though. You should have asked me sooner."

"You're my assistant. You should have known this was coming up and already picked out what I was going to wear."

He thumped her on the head and chuckled. "You wouldn't listen to me anyway. But what kind of style are you interested in? Any particular designers?"

"Designers?" Caressa wrinkled her nose. She sometimes forgot that Kyle used to work for some big movie star. "I was thinking about something classic. Sort of like…" She got up and walked over to her bookshelf, getting an old folder she'd filled with photos and clippings. She flipped through until she found the one she was searching for. She looked down at the young, blonde-haired woman, playing the cello in a champagne-colored off-the-shoulder gown.

"Here." She took it to Kyle. "I don't know the designer, but I like this."

He studied the yellowed magazine clipping. "Let me guess. Miss du Pré."

"Yes, it's Jacqueline. I mean, I don't want to be exactly like her. I want to have my own style, but I think…I think it's pretty."

Oh man, his smile always killed her. He cupped her face and kissed her. "I like it too. You would be pretty in anything. But I see you in red. Or stark white. Something dramatic and textured."

She started to flush as he trailed kisses down her neck. "I don't know. I'm open to possibilities. But do you think we'll have time to find something nice by tomorrow?"

He looked back at her with a reassuring smile. "Don't worry. You know the last-minute instrument repairmen. I know the last-minute wardrobe folks. I'll make some calls."

Chapter Eight:
Heartless

Kyle could only stare.

They'd found a dress, and it was stunning on her. Ivory, not white. The bodice was sculptural silk, embroidered with very delicate, almost invisible pearls. He remembered tiny buttons on her bra, and this was that effect, only heightened. The dress was high-waisted, with a full skirt that rustled around her in elegant drapes and made her look even smaller and more delicate than she was. She wore no other adornment, only a small rhinestone comb he'd used in the back when he swept up her hair. She was spectacular. Denise looked as shocked as he felt, and told Caressa over and over how lovely she looked.

He felt quite suave and elegant too in his best tux. It was an important night, not least of all because she was going out there as someone new. A talented musician, yes, but a beautiful woman growing into her personality. She wasn't meant to be dark and tailored. She was blinding brightness. It thrilled him to see her that way.

But she paced. He knew Lincoln Center was a big deal venue, perhaps the biggest venue on the tour. They were still almost forty minutes out from her performance, too much time for her to get nervous.

"Caressa," he said. "Enough. Sit and take some deep breaths." He told her things like that every so often as they waited in these backstage dressing rooms, and she ignored them. He felt obliged to say them anyway. He could look at her and give her an order in his dom voice. *Sit, girl.* But that only worked in the bedroom. Here, he was the submissive one, as much as he wished he wasn't. She yanked at the carefully pressed folds of her gown.

"How can I sit in this anyway?" she fussed.

He suppressed a sigh, looking at Denise. "We already practiced sitting, remember? We practiced playing. It worked fine. You'll be fine. It's beautiful."

"It's not me. I feel stupid."

"It is you," said Denise in that cloying, patronizing way of hers. "You picked it out and you loved it."

It was true. She'd been like a starry-eyed child earlier, trying on thousand-dollar dresses and turning in front of the mirror. But he saw her starting to fray. He saw the unraveling before it even began. "Caressa—"

"This is—I can't wear this. I need my other clothes. Kyle—"

"Cara, no."

"I want them! Go get them. There's time."

"It'll take half an hour," Denise protested. "Forty-five minutes. Caressa, be reasonable."

"I can't wear this! Go downstairs and get some clothes then," she said to Kyle. "Black pants, black shirt. Go to Columbus Circle."

"You're kidding me, right?" He was exasperated, but she was frantic and ratcheting up.

"Why aren't you listening to me?" she wailed, in tears now. "Don't you understand? I can't perform this way." She spread her arms and gestured at her dress as if it were a time bomb about to go off. "Why won't you help me?"

"God damn it. You are fucking crazy, you know that?" He spun on his heel and did the only thing he could do, which was run to Columbus Circle and run back with a black Armani top and pants he prayed ran true to size. By the time he returned, Denise was gone. She always left the meltdowns to him.

He pulled at the zipper of Caressa's dress, tempted to rip it off her, wanting to tear it to a thousand pieces in his frustration. *Just do your job. This is your job. Whatever it takes to get her on that fucking stage.* She dressed in silence, putting on the new garments as he ripped the tags off. They fit, but nothing like the dress, which lay discarded now on the floor. "Do you want your hair down?" he ground out.

She didn't answer. By this point it was already nearly time for her to head out the door to the stage. Still in a temper, he reached for the comb and yanked it out. She spun on him. "I'll fucking do it." She ripped the pins out and brought the whole thing down. She had no elastic to pull it back with, and he didn't either. Bad assistant. Her hair stuck out from her head in all directions, a mass of unruly curls, gorgeous in its own disheveled way. He seethed and stared at her.

"You do not understand me," she screamed at him. The monster, his lover. "Stop looking at me that way! You don't understand!"

He bit his lip, wanting to hurt her. This wasn't kink though, this wasn't the cue for him to whip out the riding crop and give her an attitude adjustment. This was real life. This was someone he cared about out of control, a feeling sickeningly familiar to him.

She turned and left, heading to the stage. He followed at a distance, hating and loving her. She walked to her place front and center to vibrant applause, accepting her cello from the stagehand. She began to play, and even Kyle could see it was heightened, sharp. She put him in mind of a warrior, her hair like some wild headdress. He stalked back to the dressing room, leaving Denise to mind the prodigy. She was so frustrating. The most frustrating thing of all was how much he cared about her, and how little she cared back. He'd been there, done that. Read the novel all the way to the tragic end, blinked out on alcohol and cocaine.

She returned to the dressing room after the performance, looking exhausted but noticeably happy. At least there would be no post-concert meltdown today, no need to drag her to the cocktail party in the throes of artistic anguish. He'd already hung the dress away in the closet, tired of battle. He'd taken off his tuxedo jacket and thrown it over a chair. "I'm sure Denise is already there waiting for you."

She hesitated, scrutinizing him. "You're not coming?"

"I don't particularly feel like coming. No."

She looked down, then back up at him with a frown. "You only want me in that dress. You only want the elegant lady on your arm."

He paused, the temper like a living thing inside him. He couldn't let it out. He fell back on factual, impersonal phrases. "You wanted to go buy a dress. You asked me to help you. If you don't want to wear it now, don't. Whatever you like."

"I'd like you to come with me." She almost sounded apologetic. Almost.

"I'm not in the mood."

"Because you're angry about the dress."

"Fuck the dress, Caressa. Listen one more time. *I'm not in the mood.* Go on. Denise will be there."

"I don't want to go if you don't go."

"You *have* to go. I don't."

"Don't you work for me?"

He narrowed his eyes. *Don't say it. Don't say anything rash right now.* He let out a long, deep breath and picked up his jacket from the back of the chair. "After you," he managed to say in an almost normal voice.

* * * * *

Caressa lay in bed, wanting to cry but not quite able to. It was late, nearly two in the morning. Kyle had just dropped her off at home after staying with her at the party until the bitter end, long after Denise had surrendered to peace and sleep. He'd stood beside her through the endless blathering conversations, the praise and inane questions. *How did you come to love the cello? How much do you practice? What are your favorite songs?* She'd desperately wanted some of the champagne, anything to take the edge off, but he'd said no. He'd stood at her elbow the whole night and hadn't let her take a drink. Well, she supposed it was because of that red wine incident...

But there was more to it. What had he told her the night he found her in the bar? *Trying not to have a drink...* He hadn't taken one drink, while everyone around them grew progressively drunker. A cola. Some water. Nothing more. Why had he gotten so upset about the dress? *It wasn't the dress, Caressa. You screamed at him.*

She'd ordered him around. Again. She liked when he did it in the bedroom, but he didn't like when she did it back to him. But the bedroom was the bedroom, and outside the bedroom she had shit she had to do. It wasn't negotiable. He didn't understand that. The cool, reproachful look he'd given her at the door had taken away any of the pride she'd felt at her concert performance, as well as any pleasure she'd found as the center of attention at a Lincoln Center benefit. She tried to tell herself it didn't matter, but it *did*.

She rolled out of bed and picked up her phone. She scrolled to his number, then put it down again. It was late. He was mad at her. She picked it up a moment later and dialed his number anyway. When it went to voicemail she hung up. Then she dialed again.

"Hello, Caressa." Angry, gritty caramel this time. Not sweet.

"Kyle. Are you sleeping?"

"Not anymore."

"I'm sorry." She fell silent. That was the extent of what she'd planned to say. Silence on the other end. "Kyle, are you there?"

A big sigh. "What do you want?"

"I'm sorry," she repeated. "I'm sorry."

"Okay, you're sorry. That really doesn't comfort me because this thing you're saying sorry for—you're just going to do it again."

"I know. You don't understand, though—"

"Next time you tell me I don't understand something, I'm quitting. Do you understand *that*, you little nutcase?"

"I'm not a nutcase, I'm just…" She swallowed the impulse to once again say *you don't understand*. "I miss you," she said instead. "I wish you were here. Or that I was over there." Suddenly she ached to be with him. She wanted to touch him and apologize to him face-to-face, body-to-body. "Can I come over there?" She waited, afraid he would say no, but he said yes and had her write down his address. She took a cab, and was there a half hour later.

He answered the door in boxers and nothing else, leaning against the doorsill looking tired. He took her hand and led her through his darkened apartment to the bedroom, and she was kind of relieved he didn't say anything, or expect any words from her as he took her clothes off and dropped them on the floor. He pulled the covers up over them both and cradled her close to him in the dark.

"I'm sorry," she whispered against his neck. "I don't know why I act that way sometimes."

He was still, not offering any perspective beyond a light, soothing caress up and down her arm. Finally he said, "You're like something running through my fingers, that I keep grabbing at." He sought her wrist and his fingers tightened around it almost painfully. "I want to catch you. But I'm not sure that desire is coming from a healthy place."

They lay in silence for a moment. Caressa tried to gauge his mood. She remembered his rigid stance at the party, his clipped conversation.

"Why don't you drink, Kyle?"

"Do you *want* me to drink?"

"I'm just curious."

He laid back, away from her, stretching one strong, sculptured arm to rest behind his head. His lips drew down in a frown and his gaze was distant. She thought he would close his eyes and sleep, leaving her question unanswered, but eventually he spoke in a soft, ironic voice.

"I used to be as obsessive as you are. Over something. Some*one*," he corrected, looking over at her.

Caressa felt a pang of jealousy. She pretended nonchalance. "A girl?"

"A woman, yeah."

"She was your girlfriend?"

"I'd rather not talk about it."

"Your submissive?"

"Caressa."

"Was she beautiful?"

His hand slid over her hip and down between her legs. She tensed, wanting his skillful touch but assailed by a thousand different emotions. He pressed his face against her cheek. "She was beautiful, yes. She was *very* submissive. She was nothing like you."

Caressa felt an inexplicable rage, pounding chords in her head. He could so easily leave her. Any woman could make him happy. He was only with her out of circumstances. There were probably thousands more sexy and personable than her, women who were submissive just the way he liked, women happy for his control. He could have his pick of any of them.

"Why didn't she want you?" she asked, specifically to hurt him.

His hand stilled between her legs and he pulled away. "It wasn't meant to be. I used alcohol to numb myself, to try to get over her. It didn't work and I just ended up more miserable, so I don't drink anymore."

"Ever?"

"Ever. It's best if I don't, and probably best if you don't too. Promise me you'll never use alcohol that way, just to deal with life."

"I won't. I don't like the taste of it."

"Promise me. Not just alcohol. Drugs. Whatever."

"Did you use drugs too?"

She regarded him, seeing him in a whole new light. Stern, upstanding Kyle, who always lectured her. Perfect, capable Kyle. A user and a drunk.

"Promise me," he said again, dead serious.

A *former* user and drunk. "Okay, I promise," she sniffed, turning on her side. "I only have room for one obsession in my life anyway."

He flipped her over and pinned her down, his mood suddenly turning from remote to angry. "Why so many questions?" he asked. "If you only have room for one obsession in your life, why are you over here plaguing me?"

"Do you think you qualify as an obsession? Don't flatter yourself."

"You called me at two in the morning, Caressa. Seems pretty obsessive to me. But then you're not known for your reasonable behavior."

She lay still beneath him, trembling to control her reaction to his nearness and the irritation in his eyes. He was rock hard. She could feel the rigid outline of his cock pressed against her belly. Against her will, her hips moved, seeking more contact. She chanced a look at him, pained to find a mocking expression directed at her.

"Now you go soft and submissive, when you want the cock. Right? No screaming at me now. No giving orders. I see how it is." She searched his eyes for a teasing spark, but found only cool anger.

She pushed at him. "Get off me!"

"Oh, there are the orders. I suppose the screaming comes next." He kissed her with punishing force, one hand squeezing her breast roughly. She realized the flirting, the fucking was all an act. A ploy. He hated her, just like everyone else. The thought devastated her. She pushed him again, with all the force she could muster, and he let her up, let her barrel away from the bed to grab her clothes. *Not you too, Kyle.*

When he'd held her and pressed against her she'd wanted his warmth and forgiveness, not anger and hate. His hate destroyed her. She dressed on her way out to his door, not stopping when he called her from the bedroom. Fuck him.

She ran down the streets of Hudson Square until she hit Sixth Avenue and then kept going, not having the energy to flag down a cab. She needed air anyway. The few people on the streets walked around her, avoiding her, probably because of the look on her face.

She awakened late the next morning, still feeling wrung out and miserable. Battered. There was a reason her brain pinged out a warning every time he was near her, despite the reactions of her body and her heart.

If only he wasn't so…irresistible. She went downstairs to find her cello, needing the refuge of music. She sat and played some older songs, simple, elementary tunes she hadn't played since she was a student. It was so easy to play them well, to play them perfectly. Why must everything progress from simplicity to horrible, unmanageable complexity? She wondered what would happen if she changed her current concert repertoire to a recital of these childish melodies? She plucked at the strings, smiling to herself, and then she turned, hearing a deep, familiar voice chatting with Aunt Denise out in main room.

So he'd come. After his angry scorn last night, she'd expected him to quit or at least make himself scarce for a while. She strained to listen to their conversation through the cracked door at the same time she told herself she didn't care. But they weren't talking about him quitting. Denise was talking about Caressa's interview with some New York arts magazine, and Kyle was talking about seating preferences on the upcoming flight to Montreal.

She started to play again, feeling detached and wooden. Of course he wouldn't quit. He'd stick around so she could feel the maximum trauma necessary. She heard a sharp knock. She didn't look up, but she knew it was him. She could feel his presence like a weight on her. He came and sat on her bed, watching her, but still she ignored him. She chose something louder, with long sustained notes she played with aggression.

"Do you want to talk?" he asked over the reverberating noise.

"No."

"You seem upset."

"Because I hate you. I thought you were going to quit. I wish you would."

He got up and left and still she kept playing, mechanically, even though her heart was aching and racing in a panicked rhythm. Her tempo faltered and her bow slipped. She grimaced and played the passage again, then forged into a difficult part of Saint-Saëns' concerto, her showpiece. She wrestled with it, forcing her concentration, calling on all her skill.

But then he was back again, kneeling in front of her cello. She paused as soon as the marker touched her. She wanted to jerk away but he held her by the calf, drawing two eyes, a nose, a big cartoonish smiley face on one knee so it looked up at her. More mockery. He moved to the other side, drew an identical happy face. She would have laughed at the loopy artwork but the situation didn't seem remotely funny. He wasn't smiling at all. When he finished he drew away, capping the pen. He looked as if he might say something, but then he turned for the door. "I'll let you practice. Stage call is at six-thirty."

She knew it was. She put her bow to the strings, staring down at her knees. At the door he turned back and threw the pen next to her on the floor.

"You never smile, Caressa. Never. Anyway, I'll be here at six. Whatever you want to wear, have it ready to go to the theater."

She practiced for two more hours, but even music couldn't exorcise the demons tormenting her like the smiling faces on her knees. She stopped halfway through and went to the bathroom, scrubbing at the carelessly drawn pen marks, trying to obliterate them completely. Still, a shadowy outline of them remained.

* * * * *

They got through New York, Montreal, Los Angeles, Toronto, Philadelphia, Boston, Baltimore, Atlanta. The Fourth of July came and went. He and Caressa interacted with professional distance, maintained more by her withdrawn focus than any self control on his part. He let her be, and found his sanity slightly improved for it, although his desire for her chafed. It was Nell all over again, and he wondered, as Jeremy had asked, what he ever did to deserve it.

But she was stable, at least. She didn't scream at him or throw tantrums. She paced before shows but she got the job done onstage. Reviews were good, which seemed to sustain her in some equilibrium. He sent her dress ahead from venue to venue, hoping she might wear it one night, hoping she might ask to go shopping for more. But she was all black austerity again, with her hair tamed in a low, tight ponytail. She was stable…up until the Miami flight.

A series of inconveniences had them running late, and Atlanta traffic was gridlocked. Kyle looked at his watch, then at Denise.

"We're not going to make it. We better look at other flights."

Denise sent him a look he couldn't interpret. "We'll see."

Kyle chuckled. "Uh, we're still thirty minutes away, and the flight's in an hour."

"We can still make it. I don't want to take a later flight," said Caressa.

"There will be plenty of flights to Miami," Kyle reassured her. "It's just going to mean a longer wait."

"I don't want to take a later flight," she repeated, a little more intensely. Denise soothed her, telling her they would wait and see. Kyle watched with jaded half-attention. A meltdown was coming. Interesting. Over something so insignificant. They would probably only be delayed an hour and there was no concert tonight anyway.

But the meltdown started in earnest at the security checkpoint, in the form of violent, hysterical tears. She railed at the security workers to hurry up, and then screamed when they mishandled her cello in their haste. It was a miracle he got her through without an arrest, but her single-minded hysteria only mounted as she tore toward the gate.

He walked, wheeling her cello, since he couldn't very well run with it. They wouldn't make it anyway. The flight had been scheduled to depart ten minutes ago. Denise ran after Caressa, but Kyle headed for the ticket counter. He rescheduled their flight, and dawdled on the way back to the gate, hoping Denise had successfully soothed her niece.

But she wasn't soothed. He wasn't prepared for the shaking, disintegrating woman he was confronted with. He sat on the other side of her. "Don't worry. I got our tickets changed, hon." He ran his hand over her trembling back, the first time he'd touched her in a couple weeks. "It's okay. We can leave in half an hour."

"No!" He leaned back at the virulence of her denial, sitting up and looking around. Curious eyes were staring, wondering about the small woman beside the cello case screaming refusals and denials. Security headed their way. Denise looked at Kyle over Caressa's head as Caressa sobbed into her hands.

"Even you couldn't get her on that flight, Kyle." She shook her head. "I'm sorry."

Twelve hours. Twelve hours to get to Miami by car. Later, when they were an hour or so south of Atlanta in their rental, and Caressa had long since cried herself to sleep in the back seat beside her cello, Kyle looked over at Denise.

"Okay. Explain it to me."

She sighed. "Just drive, Kyle. Let's just get there, please."

"I'm not driving twelve fucking hours without some fucking explanation. Our flight would have already been there."

Denise looked down at her hands, rubbing some imaginary spot on her palm. "It's a long story."

"I have—let's see—about eleven hours."

Denise looked at Caressa in the backseat, and Kyle glanced at her too in the rearview mirror. She'd fallen into a deep sleep, perhaps lulled by the highway road noise, or perhaps just exhausted from losing her shit so completely. Denise still turned up the radio a notch before she started to speak.

"When Caressa was very young, just six or seven, she started traveling to appearances. Not tours, per se, but word of her got around. They lived in New York, and her mother and father were at the heart of the arts community. Her father—my brother—was a pianist, and her mother was an artist and designer. Caressa often performed for their friends at events around the city. Not because she was an accomplished artist at six or seven years old, only because she was a novelty. No, novelty is not the word for it."

She stopped and looked over at Kyle with a sheen of moisture in her eyes. "To have seen her play back then…I can't really describe it. It was like the angels talking through her cello. She was just a tiny little thing, playing these grand concertos. So little, so innocent, and the music she could draw from those strings…" She paused, collecting herself. "It really was kind of like watching a miracle. It was just that affecting."

"I believe it," Kyle said.

"Anyway, by the time she was eight, they were making trips to Washington, The Hamptons, even out to the West Coast. People talked about movie appearances, books, concert tours with the masters, big time stuff even back then. The thing was, she was still a child. An only child, and terribly spoiled. Doted on. She was the center of the universe for my brother and his wife. They let her get away with everything."

Kyle chuckled, imagining it clearly. It fit her to a tee. But Denise wasn't laughing.

"One weekend, they were scheduled to travel to a friend's home upstate, up in Saranac Lakes. Some artists' conference, and she was going to play there as a special guest. They were going to fly there. As you can imagine, she was a nightmare to drive with, even short distances, and she really loved airplanes. But she made them late, this day. Something about not wanting to wear the outfit her mother had chosen, or not wanting her hair brushed. Her hair has always been such a tangled mess…" Denise stopped, laughing almost wistfully. "As a child it was…"

"Forget about her hair. What happened?"

"Well, they missed the flight by minutes. She threw another tantrum about having to wait until the next morning to fly out, and her father just threw up his hands and hired a charter plane. A little four-seater deal. They had nearly arrived when the plane started to lose altitude. It crashed in the Adirondacks, in the middle of nowhere."

Kyle felt something turn and slide in his stomach. Horror. Dread. "They died."

"The pilot and her parents died. Caressa survived somehow with only superficial wounds. Perhaps the cello case in front of her kept her secured in her seat. Actually, her mother survived too. The crash anyway, although her wounds were mortal. She told... She said..." Kyle glanced over to see Denise choked up now in earnest. "She asked Caressa to play for her until help arrived. And she did...all through the night. It was a chilly autumn night, and she must have played for hours. At some point her mother died, but she kept playing on that banged-up cello. When they arrived, her fingers were mutilated from the metal strings in the cold. But it helped them find her...the sound of the music led them to her..." Denise stopped again, then continued on more softly. "If you look, you can still see the scars on her fingertips. So you see, whenever we miss a flight now..."

Kyle was silent, picturing Caressa's world at that moment. Eight years old, a little girl who'd thrown a tantrum that led to a charter flight and the end of her parents' life. Trapped alone on a mountain with her dying mother, who exhorted her to *play*...

Denise looked over at Kyle. "If you want to know why she's still playing, why she keeps playing even though it hurts her..."

"I've heard enough to connect the dots, I think. You might have told me about this before now."

"I thought she might tell you."

"She didn't."

Denise sighed and looked at her hands. "It's not a story she likes to tell."

Kyle felt frozen. He'd drawn silly faces on her knees, thinking that might cheer her up. "Does she blame herself still? Did she believe it was her fault?"

"Oh, she had months of counseling and therapy concerning that issue, but how can you know the mind of an eight year old? She was so obedient afterward, she would tell you whatever you wanted to hear. Whatever the right answer was. She was spectacular at being good, at least for a while. And she played as if that would exonerate her. She made such strides that her teacher had to pass her over to another, and then another. By the time she was ten, she was playing in front of big orchestras on regular tours."

Kyle grimaced, finally understanding the drive, the fury. The belligerence of her focused walk onto the stage each night. "She doesn't play because she loves it. She plays as a penance."

Denise sighed. "I don't know why she plays, Kyle. Who really knows?"

He looked over at her, angry, accusing. "You enable her."

She shushed him, looking back at Caressa. "Don't wake her. She's tired."

"Yes, she is tired. Tired of touring, tired of playing and putting herself out there to be judged. What a sick thing to do to a woman who already probably can't forgive herself."

"It's easy for you to play judge and jury," she spit back. "I'm the one who had to pick up the pieces. I'm the one in the family who stepped up, who took her on out of love for my brother. And if you think it was me forcing her to sit and practice in the weeks and months after their death—" She fell abruptly silent. "You can't understand what it was like. She was so haunted. I couldn't have stopped her."

Denise was crying now. Kyle knew he should let her off the hook. Apologize and smooth things over. *Of course, you did what you had to do.* But he knew a thing or two about enabling, about keeping quiet to achieve your own needs and rewards. "You need to tell her, somehow, that it's okay to stop if she wants to. You have to, Denise."

The woman shook her head, grieving now. "I can't make her stop. I don't know what to give her to replace it. Music is all she's ever known. I can't make it up to her. All that obsession and mourning. The way she cried... So many tears. I can't, Kyle. I don't know how to start that conversation."

"Wake her up. Let's have it now."

"No!" Denise gasped in horror. "No—"

"No. We can't have her stop now, can we? She has a tour to finish."

"Well, she does. You can paint me as the avaricious stage aunt, whatever. You can believe what you want. But I told you before, don't open this can of worms. Not yet. Soon. Someday she'll choose for herself to be done, and I'll respect that. But she's not ready yet."

"How do you know?"

"She chose Saint-Saëns herself. What else, but as a swan song? There's not much higher to go. She may not even realize it herself, but I believe she understands this has to end at some point. But she has to finish this tour. She's trying to prove something. She's seeking something."

"Expiation?" Kyle asked after a pause.

"Perhaps." Denise set her jaw, appealing to him. "If she is, will you be so heartless as to stop her?"

Kyle could be heartless. He had been heartless many times. He glanced in the mirror at Caressa in the backseat, clutching her cello as she slumbered in the reclined seat. No, he'd been heartless before, but in this case, his heart was too engaged.

Chapter Nine:
Inside You

Kyle and Denise decided to stop for the night just north of Orlando. Caressa heard Kyle call to make the arrangements while Denise took over the driving. It was just a few more miles now, and Caressa watched him from the backseat in the gathering dusk. His hand rested on one long muscular thigh, over dark designer jeans. His traveling clothes. He looked tired and she knew it was her fault. When they'd stopped a couple hours earlier for dinner, she'd apologized to him for wigging out about the flight change. He'd reached out for her, slid a hand behind her neck and pulled her close.

"It's okay," he'd said. That was how she knew Denise had told him the whole story. At least now she wouldn't have to tell it herself. She might have told him eventually, but probably not. It just made people pity her. Well, most of the time. Back after it happened, when she'd been at the hospital getting bandaged and rehydrated, when she'd been a bundle of shock wrapped in a warm blanket, she'd overheard one of the nurses. *She's lucky. It's a miracle she didn't die too.* She could still bring that voice to mind, the hushed wonder and the look in the nurse's eyes. No pity, just amazement.

But Kyle pitied her. He looked back at her now with that panther-dangerous face sedated into gentle sympathy. "We're almost there."

"I know." She wanted to snap at him to stop looking at her that way, but she bit her lip. She felt wrung out and fragile, not fit to do battle. To be honest, she didn't want to fight with him any more. She wanted him to hold her close again. She wanted him to fuck her hard and rough. He hadn't touched her that way—sexually, or even flirtatiously—for weeks. He'd been STD-tested and everything. If he wanted to... whenever...right now, he could pull her pants down, rip off her panties and take her.

She wondered how it would feel, skin-to-skin. No barrier between them. His hot, hard cock slipping deep inside. But if he even wished to do such a thing, he gave her no indication. In quiet times, when she least wanted it, she remembered every time he'd touched her, and how he'd touched her. *Where* he'd touched her. That commanding tone in his voice... He still used that tone with her, but only to tell her when to get dressed, when to practice. Things she had to do. Places she had to go.

Let me come to your hotel room.

The words were so loud in her brain as she stared at him, she was amazed he didn't hear them. He was watching the road, giving Denise directions. He had reserved them all separate rooms. Unfortunate. Well, she'd made her bed, so to speak. She'd have to lie in it—alone.

It was hot, mid July, so as soon as Caressa let herself into her dated, shabby hotel room, she cranked up the air conditioner. She stood over it now in a scanty sleep tee and panties, her hair still wet from a low pressure shower. Not the best hotel they'd ever stayed in, but again, it was her fault. He'd driven for nearly eight hours because she was an idiot, so she wasn't going to complain about the hotel he'd pretty much booked over the phone.

The air conditioning unit was so loud, or perhaps the room was just so quiet. She barely heard the knock on the door over the unit's rattling hum. She checked the peephole and swung the door open.

He walked in, seeming too big for the space they stood in, trailing that devastating Kyle-scent she knew by heart. He took in her state of near-undress and shut the door behind him. He was still in jeans and a tee. His belt was cinched over iliac furrows she wanted to lick. Was that the belt he'd used on her?

His expression was impossible to untangle, and she tried to keep her own emotions shuttered.

"I just wanted to be sure you were okay," he said quietly.

"I'm fine," she replied, trying for nonchalance. "You're the one who had to do all the driving."

"Don't be flip, Caressa. You know what I'm talking about."

She gave a wild laugh. "Am I okay? Do you really want to know? What do you think? I was doing well enough before you came along."

He slid a scathing look over her body again and turned to the door. "Okay. Good night."

"Wait!"

He turned and she reached for him. *God, please don't go away. Please, just touch me. Just hold me for a minute.* She was afraid he'd push her away and escape out the door, but he didn't. He clasped her close and pressed his face against her hair. She shuddered from the sheer relief of him holding her. "Kyle, I don't mean any of what I say to you. Ever. I'm just trying to drive you away."

A moment later his question came, muffled against her forehead. "Why?"

"I don't want to choose between you and..."

"Me and the music? Your aunt said that too. I'm not trying to make you choose anything." He pulled back, tracing a thumb along her jaw to her chin. "You're so afraid of being made to choose. It doesn't have to be me or the music. You have choices to make, but the way I feel about you isn't one of them. I've come to realize that I love you either way."

She sucked in a breath, trying to comprehend. Trying to believe. "You love me?"

"I'm afraid so. I've tried not to. Really hard." He gave her one of his charming smiles, his hands tracing down to her shoulders and then over her hips. His warm fingertips came to rest between the gap in her tee and the waistband of her panties. He sobered, gazing at her. "I've tried to convince myself it's just attraction. Passion. But it's not. It's deeper than that."

"I love you too."

"You don't have to say that just because I did. Not unless you mean it."

"No, I mean, you're right. I don't want to love you, but I do. I think I do. I'm pretty sure…"

His eyes softened, dark blue in the dim light. He leaned his head toward hers as if he might kiss her, but his mouth stopped just a fraction from hers, so close she could feel his breath against her lips. "I guess we shouldn't question it. Or think about it so hard."

Her soft agreement was cut off by a tender kiss, and then another. His hands trailed up her stomach again, up to caress her breasts. He was being too tentative, too gentle. She slid him a sideways look. "I don't want a pity fuck."

"If you expected a pity fuck I'm afraid you're going to be sorely disappointed. With that said, this is your last chance to send me away."

She didn't answer, only pulled at the hem of his shirt, pushing it up to press eager kisses against his chest. Her fingers worked at his belt buckle, and the buttons of his jeans. She peeled down his boxer briefs as he whisked off her shirt, flinging it to the side. He was already fully hard, and she explored his cock with her fingers as she fell to her knees. He stopped her, tipping her head back.

"I don't want an apology blow job."

She sank back on her knees and blinked up at him in frustration. "I changed my mind. I'm back to hating you."

He laughed, shoving his cock against her mouth. "I think what we have here is a power struggle. Let me take care of that. Open, girl." He was twisting her hair in a firm grip that melted her. She knelt up again and took him between her lips, thrilled by the aggressive way he thrust into her mouth.

He groped down her front, pinching her nipple so she whined against his thick rod. She wanted to beg for mercy but she also never wanted him to stop. With him, it never stayed gentle. She didn't want gentle from him.

When he pulled away she felt sharp disappointment, until he pushed her back onto the floor and pinned her down. She fought him a little, for no other reason than she liked to feel him restrain her. His soft chuckle spurred her on and she fought harder, knowing she would lose, but enjoying every second of his skin sliding against hers, his rough breaths and hisses.

He'd reached over to grab his shirt and he held it now, twisting it around her wrists over her head. He bound them tightly, knotting the shirt around them so she couldn't escape no matter how hard she tried— and she tried her very hardest to be certain she really couldn't.

"Shh, shh," he whispered, trying to settle her. "I want you bound."

"Why?" Her voice sounded rough from passion, or perhaps panic. He licked her, a slow, teasing slide up the side of her arm.

"Because I like you this way. Keep your hands over your head. Don't move them." She went still at the commanding tone in his voice, and her pussy throbbed, growing wetter and wetter. God, her panties had to be soaked. As if he could read her mind, he slid his hand down the front of her silk bikini, right down to the spot that ached with arousal, and then further.

His fingers curled inside her, and she felt the slippery wetness as he manipulated her firmly, possessively. Her hands flew down, hobbled together and unable to stop him. He pushed them back up with tsk. "Be good."

She stared into Kyle's eyes, spellbound by the intensity she saw there. He moved again, grabbing her shirt next and wrapping it over her eyes. The room had been dark before, but now she saw only blackness. She clumsily reached for the blindfold, but he stopped her and she struggled again, stilled by an impossibly strong thigh across her hips. Her breath sounded loud in her ear, and then came his whisper. "The other woman—she was so submissive. I thought I liked that, but I like that you fight back a little."

A *little*? She was insulted by that, but the fact was, he outweighed her by at least eighty pounds. She closed her eyes behind the blindfold, trying to calm down. He ran fingertips down her side and drew down her panties. He spread her legs wide, a position he seemed to enjoy putting her in. He prevented her from closing them with a leg splayed across her left thigh. "I know you can't see me, but I want you to trust me, Caressa. We're going to play a little game called 'I trust Kyle'. Okay? You can answer *Yes, Sir*."

Caressa turned her head, although she couldn't see him. She jerked as his lips brushed softly against hers. "Yes, Sir."

He kissed her again, then moved away. She wanted to reach out for him, but one of his hands steadied her arms before they could even move. She heard a whisper of movement and then felt fingers parting her and hot breath against her pussy lips. She shuddered as he deftly licked her clit.

"Oh God." She tried to clench her legs shut but he held her open, teasing her pussy lips with ardent skill. Behind her closed eyes she envisioned his mouth, his sensual lips, and ached to kiss them, even as she prayed he wouldn't stop. Each warm, slick stroke of his tongue was pure pleasure, and the way he held her down only made her burn hotter for him.

She felt herself losing control, twisting her hips for more and arching against him. But then he was gone, his talented tongue replaced by teasing fingers. She swallowed a groan, lost in her dark world of powerlessness and hunger. Her pussy ached for satisfaction, but he seemed determined to keep her at a steady low simmer.

"More?" he asked.

"Yes, Sir. Please!"

His fingers were working up inside her now, those long, manicured fingers stroking, building fire upon fire. God, she was soaking wet. He slid his fingers from her flooded pussy down to her asshole. She flinched as he pressed there, but he didn't withdraw.

"Trust me, Caressa."

I trust you, I trust you.

He toyed with her pussy and ass, filling her with his fingers and manipulating her, making her hips buck from the shock of his touches. She writhed on the floor in helpless blindness, not wanting to pull away, but still frightened by the intimacy between them. Without sight, every touch and sensation felt multiplied. From time to time, when it seemed too much, he made soothing noises that made her shiver. He was so experienced, so comfortable with this decadence, but the blunt eroticism was so new to her. Did people really play like this in bed? With no shame, no barriers of propriety between them? As he soothed her, he asked quiet questions. *How does that feel? Does that hurt? Does it feel good? Do you like it?*

She could barely concentrate, moaning answers and struggling against the thigh that held her pinned open to his probing assault. She felt like a top strung tight, about to go off but not quite able to. "Kyle...Sir...please!"

He laughed and, in a tumble of limbs, had her turn over on all fours, pressing her head down on her tethered wrists in the front. When she tried to drop her hips, he stopped her and positioned her with her back arched and her ass in the air. She felt exposed—and deliciously dirty—as he went to wash his hands and return. Then she could feel his cock against the back of her thighs. She shivered as his hands came under her chest, fondling her breasts. Then she felt his fingers at her mouth.

"Open."

She did, because his voice was so sharp and insistent. She felt soft silk against her lips, and realized with a start that he was shoving her own panties into her mouth. She tried to spit them out, pure instinct, but he persisted, pressing them in again until she capitulated. She was blind, bound, *and* speechless now. He took her faculties away so casually, and yet she knew there was a reason behind it all. *Trust me.*

He knelt behind her and she moaned softly, aching for penetration as he slid the head of his cock over her clit. She jerked and bit down on the silk wad in her mouth, wanting to beg for more, but unable to.

He leaned over her back so she felt his hard stomach against her, and then he took one of her hands in his. His hair tickled against the side of her face, and he smelled of sex and depravity. His other hand wrapped around her waist and she had the strange feeling of being adrift, tethered to the earth only by him. She couldn't see, she couldn't speak. She couldn't move or reach for him. When he started to press into her, she knew true submission. She surrendered to all of it.

He filled her and fulfilled her, driving deep with no latex barrier between them. Just like the submission, her arousal grew without conscious effort or intention. He felt so thick, so hot, pressing forward, riding her like he owned her. She began the thrilling climb to that peak, the shuddering clench and unbearable torture of coming closer and closer to the edge. She couldn't draw full breath, another blatant reminder of his dominance and her submission. Another reminder of all she was willing to give up for him.

She squeezed his hand, tighter and tighter. When he started to fuck her harder, in an uncontrolled, rough rhythm, she let go and he grasped her neck. Not choking her, no. He held his hand against her windpipe, and it felt protective, not dangerous. *I could hurt you. I could kill you now, but I won't. I love you.* He'd said he loved her, and she knew she loved him. She'd wanted his possession and she had it. She came, arching back against his cock. Her hands strained in their bonds, and he gave an animal growl that felt like a part of the ecstatic throbbing between her legs. It all converged like some avalanche, or a volcano erupting and burning her. *Brillante. Bravura. Crescendo magnifico.*

After, he took her panties out so she could speak if she wanted to. Perhaps he wanted her to, wanted to know her thoughts. But all she did was sigh and wait, his surrendered prisoner. A *fermata*, waiting at his discretion, trusting in the consummate skill of his touch.

* * * * *

Kyle shifted in his third-row seat, trying not to jar the portly woman beside him. She was bejeweled and clad in a dark silk gown. Her perfume was cloying. Kyle raised his fingers to his nose, discreetly. He could still smell traces of Caressa on his hands from the fervent finger-fucking he'd given her in the dressing room. He only let himself breathe in the faint scent for a moment, lest the growing bulge in his pants disturb the orchestra denizens around him.

He'd asked her to put on the dress again. Well, not asked. He'd ordered her to wear it, and when he'd left her backstage, she had it on still, minus panties. Whether or not she made it to the stage in that lovely state remained to be seen.

Either way, it suited him. If she panicked and changed, he could punish her for it. If she wore it, he could reward her. Either way she was his to love, to play with. They were in Cincinnati, on the leg of travels that Caressa jokingly referred to as the "Heartland Tour". New Orleans, Minneapolis, Denver, Albuquerque, Pittsburgh, Houston, Dallas—a series of quick trips and more intimate venues.

Since Atlanta, Kyle took great care to get them to the airport on time or even early. He also took great care to keep Caressa surrendered to him, because it seemed to make her happiest, and it sure as hell made things easier for him. When he told her to practice, she practiced. When he told her to drop to her knees, she dropped to her knees. He made her tell him how many mistakes she'd made after each concert, and punished her for them. She hadn't had a tantrum in weeks, and she'd never played with such concentration. Even Denise commented on it, but Kyle merely smiled and deferred to her talent. It was, after all, all for her.

Perhaps there would be a punishment tonight. The novelty of performing in her striking gown would surely result in a few mild flubs. The mistakes bothered her more than they bothered him and her audience, although his belt or crop seemed to give her some measure of relief. From her petty musical sins, anyway.

He never addressed the greater issue of whether she played from guilt, nor asked any specific questions about whether this tour was her swan song. He would eventually, but not yet. He was not willing to upset the delicate equilibrium they finally shared.

The house lights went down, not a moment too soon. Speculating about consequences and punishments had him going hard again, no doubt because those punishments were always followed by some pretty intense sex.

The Cincinnati orchestra played first, some charming concerto he could only think of as a warm-up. After it ended, there was a short, expectant pause, and there she was.

In all this time, he hadn't sat in the seats to watch her. She'd needed him backstage too much. Now when she walked on stage in her sweeping ivory gown, head held high, it took his breath away. She sat in a burgundy upholstered chair in the center of the stage, accepting her instrument from the spiffily-attired stagehand meeting her from stage left.

Kyle felt some insane pang of jealousy at the shy smile she gave him, but then he grew distracted watching her settle the cello between her knees. It was a series of movements that had fascinated him from the start—the parting of the legs, the placement of the arms and fingers. The way she leaned forward, watching the conductor, ready and intently waiting. He'd never seen it so clearly before, only from the obstruction of the wings.

With a start, he recognized the look as the same one she used when he was giving her his provocative directions and requirements. What had he said to her once? *I like to be the conductor. Can you understand that?* If she hadn't understood then, she seemed to understand now.

She began to play the unfolding, melodic harmonies so familiar to him. He could never catch the mistakes she claimed to make, but he knew the notes she played by heart now, down to every dip and rise of her bow. The dress heightened the graceful movements of her arms as the notes poured from her instrument. It had been a shock to him the first time he'd heard her play in a small hotel room, and even in this vast concert hall her cello sounded powerful. She'd explained the mechanics behind it once, that one of the qualities that made her cello so valuable was its powerful tone. Perhaps it was the tone that struck people, but it was the emotion behind the notes that held him spellbound.

When the concerto ended, Caressa bowed to a standing ovation. It was the first time he saw her look uncomfortable in the dress—and it *would* have been a problem if her lovely breasts were to tumble from the deconstructed bodice. Fortunately, they stayed put and Kyle exhausted himself with all the others, applauding until his hands hurt.

He shouted "Brava!" and her head turned, recognizing his voice over the others. *Yes, you good girl, in your lovely gown. You sexy little genius.* Her face lit up and she gazed at him for a long moment. As the curtains drew closed and the lights came up to signal intermission, the woman beside him turned with a smile.

"She's just…" The woman sighed. "Simply entrancing. It's as if she channels the music straight from heaven."

Kyle's lips twitched at her melodramatic assessment, but he had to agree. "She is certainly talented."

"My husband and I have been attending her concerts since she was a young thing." The woman introduced Kyle to her husband, a thin, distinguished-looking older gentleman. The couple's excitement and inspiration was palpable. They were fans. Kyle tried to describe it to Caressa later as he took down her hair back at the hotel room. She blushed and was typically self-deprecating. He brushed her hair up over her shoulders, pressing a kiss at the back of her neck.

"It was nice watching you from the seats."

"Nice?" She gave him a look.

"Breathtaking. Spectacular. Spellbinding." He reached around to cup her full breasts and pinch and squeeze them absently as he brushed out her hair as well as he could. She was nude, as he was. He required nudity whenever they were together in his hotel room, another form of control. If she wanted to play, she had to strip off all her defenses—and clothing—just inside the door. If she didn't want to play, she stayed in her own room. The system worked well, and she seemed to thrive on it. She knew once the door was locked, once her clothes were off, she was his to command, fuck, or punish at will. He tipped her chin up and scrutinized her lovely features.

"How many mistakes did you make today?"

His cock twitched at her woe-be-gone look. He wasn't a real sadist like his old boss had been, but he liked tormenting her. It was her reactions that aroused him, more than any desire to impart pain.

"Well…" She looked away over his shoulder and then back again. "The dress sort of distracted me—"

"I knew you were going to use that excuse."

"And you being in the audience! I was kind of nervous."

He stroked her cheeks with bemused affection. "Excuses. Tell me how many mistakes you made, followed by a *Sir*, girl."

"Only a couple, Sir. Plus one other time when my phrasing was a little off."

He waited. She bit her lip, thinking.

"And I guess I wasn't as strong as I could have been on the notes leading up to the last crescendo. I mean, I was close but…" She sighed. "Four mistakes, Sir."

"Hmm," he said, releasing her chin and guiding her to her knees. "That's going to hurt. Ten for each error makes forty. Sure there weren't any more?"

She swallowed hard. "No, Sir. I wouldn't lie."

He knew she wouldn't. She probably made less mistakes than she confessed to, but a hard session would be enjoyable for both of them. But first things first. At a silent, subtle gesture with his fingers, she dropped to her knees and started to fellate him. He'd trained her to respond to a variety of unspoken commands in the bedroom, although he still preferred to give her orders. But at times like these…

He grasped her hair with a sigh, leaning his head back and basking in her quickly developing oral talents. "Good girl," he murmured. "Now lick my balls…mm…" He tapped her head and she looked up at him with wide eyes eager to please. *Oh God, beautiful.* He yanked her back to his cock by the hair, plunging between her lips. He fucked her face, impassioned by the submission he'd seen in her eyes. He tried to press her boundaries, both physical and mental, as he reveled in the building sensation of possessing her mouth. Pressure built in his cock, radiating down to his balls and even to his thighs. He thought of her as she'd been on stage, regal and masterful, drawing music from her instrument. Now she was his—his to play.

He tried to prolong the delicious torment of her oral talents, tensing as she drew back to run her tongue across the front of his shaft, the crown and tip. She pressed her lips against his throbbing cock in a teasing kiss, then licked up a spurt of pre-cum with an avid glance up at him. The sensation alone nearly killed him, but then she made some small lust noise of pleasure or satisfaction and he was lost. He drove deep in her throat, holding the back of her neck as he emptied himself in waves of shattering release. She stayed still, receiving his cum, and then he pulled back a little so she could breathe better. She drew her lips across his cock as he withdrew, as if she couldn't bear to miss out on one drop. God…she was learning.

He gazed down at her in barely-veiled adoration. "You little slut."

"Yes, Sir," she answered without hesitation.

"You little cock-craving monkey." She gave an undignified snort that he suspected was her attempt at muffling a laugh. "You never get enough, do you?"

"No, Sir," she answered, again without hesitation.

"You'll get plenty of cock tonight, don't worry. After we take care of the matter of your punishment. Go lie face down on the bed."

She hurried to obey as Kyle went to rifle through his haphazardly assembled toy collection. He wasn't carrying a lot because of all their travels, but he'd picked up enough to make things interesting for her. He tossed cuffs on the bed beside her face, then some lube and a butt plug, trying not to laugh at the widening of her eyes.

He considered the clamps, but she was already going to endure a thorough ass-warming. On second thought, he threw the clamps on the bed too. The whole purpose of requiring her to service him first was to buy time to torment her for as long as possible before he fell on her again. He considered what was left. Ball gag. That would be necessary. He tossed it over along with a whippy little crop, then the ping-pong paddle she despised. She swallowed, gazing up at him speechlessly.

"Wish you'd stayed in your own room tonight?" he asked.

She moved her hips forward against the edge of the mattress. "No, Sir."

He chuckled inwardly as he cuffed her hands to the frame of the hotel bed and worked the ball of the gag between her lips. She didn't like being gagged, but submitted to it after a few crisp words on Kyle's part. The sound of repetitive strikes could be explained away as innocuous activities—cries and screams, not so much. At least Denise had not complained when Kyle started routinely booking her room on a separate floor.

He lubed the plug and slid one hand under Caressa's hips to hold her still. He pressed it to her tiny hole and worked it in. It wasn't a huge plug, but it wasn't as small as the ones he'd started her on either. She moaned behind the gag and arched her hips to accommodate it, grinding against the bed when it was fully seated. Little pervert.

Like everything else, she'd taken to anal play like a natural. He doubted there was any virgin in the history of the world who'd gone from lily white to so completely depraved in the space of a couple months, and he was pretty damn proud to be the one behind the transformation. At least partly behind it. A lot of it was her own insatiable curiosity and lack of inhibition. He watched her writhe just a moment for the pleasure of it, then gave her a sharp slap on the ass. "Control yourself. No coming until after the punishment or it's doubled. You know that, so behave."

She went still with another moan, pulling ineffectually at the bonds that held her tethered to the bed. He picked up the crop and started with a few warm up strokes. Her luscious bottom jerked and she tried to evade him by turning on her side. The only problem with hotel beds was that so few had good sturdy footboards for restraining naughty submissives. He knelt on the bed beside her, placing a knee at the small of her back and delivering three quick strikes to the tops of her thighs. She wailed behind the gag, shuddering under him.

"Enough, Caressa. If you're going to flail around when I'm just getting warmed up, I have no choice but to get stricter with you." Another slice across the back of the thighs brought another muffled cry and a burst of tears. "Are you ready to lie still and take your punishment?"

She nodded, moaning. She could take a pretty good whipping on her ass, but her thighs were another matter. He took his knee off her back. "That was ten so far. Ten more with the crop and then I'll let you have a little break." He still knelt beside her in case he had to subdue her, but she was reasonably still for the next ten blows. He'd gotten pretty good with the crop the year before in the BDSM clubs. He could hurt her pretty badly but leave just a few mild welts.

He knew to a pretty accurate degree how much he hurt her, because in the beginning he'd sounded her out after every punishment. She'd described the shocking "stripe-y" fire of the crop as compared to the deep sting of the paddle, and categorized his belt as some type of pain in between.

He studied her trembling ass cheeks as he placed the crop to the side. He was already half hard again. He ran his fingertips over the three welts he'd raised and the other criss-crossing lines, then pressed the butt plug deeper into her just to hear her moan. "I know you want me to fuck your ass, girl," he whispered next to her ear as he leaned to pick up the paddle. "You're just going to have a wait a bit longer."

But not too much longer. She gave him a pleading look, staring between him and the evil little ping-pong paddle she hated. That look had him rising to full mast. Maybe he was more of a sadist than he thought. He'd picked the paddle up on a whim in one of the hotel gyms and, after seeing the rousing effect it had on her, secreted the tool away in his luggage. He tapped her ass with it now.

"Up. Arch your hips up. Twenty more."

She made some lovely tortured sounds as she reluctantly proffered her ass cheeks for punishment. He paddled her hard and steadily, five alternating whacks on each cheek, letting the heat and sting pile up to an almost unbearable level for her. She keened behind the gag and ground against the bed, her legs clenched together. He paused and put a hand on the small of her back, tapping the edge of the paddle against the flange of the toy between her ass cheeks. "How did I tell you to position yourself?"

With a slow unwinding effort, she raised her sinuous hips, presenting her gorgeous bottom to him. It was lovely dark pink now. He'd make it red before he finished, and she knew the worst was still to come.

"Ten more," he reminded her. "And I want your legs spread wide for the last ten." She gazed back at him, pleading for mercy with her eyes, but knowing she would get none. She slowly spread her thighs, leaving herself vulnerable and open to his gaze. He put his hand on her back again and gave her a solid crack on the inside of her left thigh. She screamed behind the gag and cranked her legs shut.

"No way," he said, prying them apart again. "I said open. Spread wide. Every time you close them I start over with the last ten again. Do you understand?" She lay still, trembling, for a long moment, and then she nodded. He watched her eyes, for the safe signal of closing them tightly, but it didn't come. "Good girl," he said quietly. "You know you need this. Don't you?"

She nodded again, her eyes full of emotion. He was tempted to be softer, only because the moment felt so tender, but that wasn't how either of them liked to play the game. He gave her another crack on her inner thigh. This time, she actually spread her legs wider, as if desperate to obey. He walked around the bed and cracked the inside of her other thigh, and then returned to belaboring her ass cheeks with fairly hard spanks until they were deep crimson.

She kept her legs spread wide, a wanton creature determined to please him even though he was hurting her quite a bit. He caught the scent of her unmistakable arousal, and his own cock was heavy, his entire pelvis pulsing with need. He gave the last two strokes right over the toy's flange, at the sensitive underside of her buttocks. She gave a satisfying scream behind the gag, and Kyle knew he would die if he didn't slide into her tight anal channel.

He tossed the paddle aside and hurriedly uncuffed her, helping her ease down the bed and stand on unsteady legs. He unbuckled the gag, using his discarded shirt to swab away the inevitable drool, then bent her forward to take out the plug. She made a low moaning sound he silenced with a warning pinch to her inner thigh, and she leaned forward on her arms in resignation. Her full breasts hung down before her, swaying as he arranged her with her hips high and her legs spread. He remembered the clamps. Soon, but not yet.

He squeezed her hot ass cheeks, then parted them, pressing his cock to her tightening hole. He started to push in, then thought better of it and added a quick swipe of lube. Now even as she resisted, he eased forward, aided by the slippery lubricant that contained some nice warming agents too. He felt the familiar tensing, and then the relaxing as she accepted his intimate invasion. She arched her back and wiggled against him as he drove all the way in. He shuddered, finally experiencing that tight, hot friction he'd been craving.

"Oh, Jesus, Caressa," he burst out. She whimpered in reply as he paused, fully seated in her. He pulled her up off the bed with a tug of her hair and clasped her against his front, his balls still bumping against her ass. "Get me the clamps," he said through gritted teeth, indicating the two silver-chained clips on the bed in front of her.

He fucked her ass a little as she handed them over. He was trying to hold back, but the pleasure was so intense. He felt a building throb in his balls, and distracted himself pinching her nipples. They were already tight and erect, ready for the clamps. He reached over her shoulder to put on the first one and she made a yelping moaning sound. He clasped her closer and shushed her with a firm hand cupping her jaw.

"Quiet."

She fell silent, and he could feel her whole body tense as he opened the clamp over her other nipple. He let it shut and was rewarded with a satisfying clench of her sphincter around his dick. He started to move inside her again, in and out, fucking his little fuck toy. He gripped the chain between her clamps with one hand and clutched her hot, dripping pussy with the other, thrusting his fingers inside her cunt as he fucked her ass. Each time he tugged on the chain, she made a smothered crying sound and pressed back against him, all sinuous horniness. His wild creature.

"God, I fucking love you," he whispered against her ear. "I love you like this. Do you want this, Caressa? Do you like when I use you like this?"

"Yes! Yes, Sir!" She was breathing fast. He knew she was close to orgasm.

"Are you mine, girl? I'm inside you, deep inside you."

He tugged the clamps again, thrusting hard, and she gasped and clutched at his thighs. She went rigid and her ass pulsed on his cock in climax while her pussy soaked his fingers. He held her as she struggled, her animalistic movements making his own world turn in and spiral into orgasm. He fell forward onto the bed on top of her and wrapped both arms around her, squeezing her with all the desperate adoration he felt. She made a soft sound of satiety, going limp in his confining embrace.

"I'm inside you," he repeated again, more intently. "I won't let you get away."

Chapter Ten:
Gods

Caressa watched Kyle and Denise talking from her vantage point on the hotel sofa. They were out on the balcony, baking in the summer Dallas heat. Caressa stayed out of the sun. She always had, but now it was even more important. Kyle's designer friend had made her three more gowns to wear at performances and they were all strapless, off-the-shoulder numbers like the first one. Her typical lobster-style burn lines wouldn't exactly scream refined elegance. There was a black gown, and a flaming red one, and another ivory gown with lots of raw-edged fringe all over it. Caressa called it her "shag dress" and Kyle made a crack about shagging her every time she wore it.

She didn't know why she'd worried about leaving behind her old childish image, the staid clothes and the ponytail. It was too girlish for the way she felt now, something Kyle had known before she could admit it to herself. She wasn't a child anymore. Not *that* child. Her parents' prodigy. The miracle survivor, the one who didn't die. Maybe letting go of that girl was so frightening because in a way it was letting go of her last link to her parents.

She barely remembered them now. She looked at photos, remembered a few standout encounters, including the one she'd most like to forget—but never would. *Mama, I don't even remember what your voice sounded like anymore.* When she tried to remember it she heard only Denise, a nagging, nasal voice she hated. She didn't think her mother had sounded that way, but she didn't remember. She was forgetting, and she blamed herself.

It was because she was so self-centered. So obsessive, Kyle called her sometimes. "You need to live life—a *full* life." He said it all the time, an endless mantra. He dragged her out to museums and restaurants in whatever city they happened to be in. He made her watch the news and keep abreast of current events, something she'd never bothered with before. He quizzed her on world disasters and election results and disciplined her when she got it wrong.

She knew it was a good thing to broaden her horizons, but she also knew why he was doing it. He wanted her to stop playing. Well, not stop. He wanted her to stop playing *obsessively*. He couldn't seem to understand that was the only way she was able to play. She remembered not to say those words to him—*You don't understand!*—since he'd threatened once to leave if she did.

She didn't think he'd leave anymore, but he'd developed other effective ways to punish her when she rubbed him the wrong way. The worst punishment was always his disapproval or anger. When she really infuriated him he ignored her, a punishment she found unbearable in its cruelty. It straightened her out right away. It bothered her that he controlled her so easily. It bothered her more that she loved him so hard it hurt. He said he loved her too, but then he'd tap her cheek and say she was too young to know what love was. But she knew. She was much older than she looked.

Critics even noted her more mature appearance in their reviews, which continued to be supportive, for the most part. Denise started hinting at what Caressa might want to do for her birthday in August. She was turning twenty-one. Officially an adult, but she'd felt like an adult for so long already. Maybe they were doing party planning out on the balcony. But who would they invite? Kyle wouldn't want anything with a bunch of alcohol, so any big, fun party was out.

She didn't care about a party anyway. She just wanted him to be there. If he would just be there smiling at her and pulling her into one of those enveloping hugs of his, it would be a perfect twenty-first birthday celebration for her.

Denise was laughing now at something Kyle said. He was talking with his graceful hands, his long fingers, waving them around like a conductor. In a way he was her conductor, keeping her organized and on an even keel. And doing…other things.

She flushed and shifted on the couch, trying not to stare at him. Trying to discipline the thoughts in her head. He could keep everything on an even keel except for her wild, hectic feelings for him. That he couldn't control, because he felt the same too. Their encounters got hotter, and ever more emotional. He both energized her and drained her. He made her want to play more beautifully and skillfully than she ever had—and he made her want to throw it all away.

She frowned and forced herself up and off the sofa to her cello. It had been so long since she'd felt ambivalent about playing. Not about performing or everything that came with it, but the actual playing. She shook it off and ran her fingers up the ebony fingerboard of her instrument. She felt a sudden urge to cry, as if her thoughts might have hurt the thing's feelings, this piece of wood and metal that she toted around the country and played music on. That too she swallowed down. Focus. *Focus.* Kyle whispered that to her sometimes, or ordered it in a stern voice when he was giving her some perverse instructions. *Bend lower. Take me deeper. Suck faster. Focus.*

The sound of more laughter drifted from the balcony. Caressa turned her back on them, tuning her cello aimlessly just to have something to do. She supposed she should be happy Denise and Kyle were finally getting along better. She played some warm-ups and then settled into a meditative piece she liked. She was feeling unusually tired. Bored maybe? This was the last show before the tour moved on to

Europe, and then she would have just four more weeks of engagements. Going to Europe would liven her up again—at least she hoped it would.

She concentrated on the piece, losing herself in the notes, trying to find that space where she started to live inside the music, but she couldn't quite reach it. A few minutes later she heard the balcony door slide open and closed, and then felt Kyle brush a kiss against her cheek. She lifted her bow off the strings but he was already moving past her to his room in the suite.

"Don't stop," he said. "I'm going to the gym, and then I'll bring you some dinner before the concert tonight."

"Y-- Okay." She was supposed to keep the *Yes, Sir*'s in the bedroom, although it almost slipped out more and more these days.

"When you're done practicing, I want you to pack for a side trip we're going to take before we go to London."

A side trip? Another forced jaunt out into reality. She was sure there was a lot to do in Dallas, but God, it was so hot. "Where are we going?" she asked, not totally able to keep a hint of displeasure from creeping into her voice.

"My hometown," Kyle said. "Pack casual, for two days and nights, and pack comfortable. We're driving, and it's five hours to Spur."

* * * * *

They left in the morning. Caressa had been surprised that Denise agreed to let her go driving around Texas without her, but she seemed to think a rural getaway would do Caressa some good.

Her aunt was flying over to London alone and planned to see some friends. Originally Kyle and Caressa were supposed to accompany her, but Kyle switched their tickets. Caressa had a little meltdown about it, headed off by Kyle before it really got serious. "They're just tickets, Caressa," he'd said in a patient but firm voice. "Thousands of people switch flights every day, and nothing bad happens." After a few hours— and a thorough fucking in the name of distraction—Caressa sunk down into the idea that her flight had been changed, but that she would be okay. Well, probably.

Now here they were, en route to Spur. They had driven out of Dallas into lovely rolling hills and picturesque forests. The scenery was pretty, but Caressa had a feeling of leaving civilization. She didn't have the first idea how to drive. If something happened to Kyle, they would be stranded out here in the middle of nowhere. She slid a look at him beside her, navigating their black SUV along the narrow Texas highway. He was from *here*. This uninhabited, wild place.

She'd known he was from Texas. It had come up in some early get-acquainted conversation. She could actually hear a southern lilt in his voice sometimes, when he was really relaxed or tired. She liked it when she heard it, but he generally maintained a more neutral accent. She wondered if he was ashamed to be a country boy.

He'd worked for some movie star before he worked for her, in the glitz and glam of Hollywood. She admired his ability to fit in anywhere and do it flawlessly. He hung around backstage at her concerts in a tuxedo, looking better than anyone, even the conductors. In restaurants, airports, hotels, museums, television studios, he managed to look utterly cosmopolitan and unflappable no matter what was going on. It was something about his expression. Some control or steeliness. She loved when he looked that way...so capable. She also loved when that capable manner tumbled into smirks and glowing smiles that lit up his entire face.

"What are you thinking?" he asked over the hum of the road noise. It was his smile face, so relaxed and boyish. She couldn't help but smile back.

"You're happy to be going home."

"That's what *I'm* thinking. I asked what *you* were thinking," he teased.

She looked out the window, gesturing at the farmland and trees around them. "I just can't believe there are actually people and towns out here. It seems so...remote."

"We're just a couple hours outside Dallas, Caressa."

"I know! That's why it's so weird."

Kyle laughed. "It's called the country, sweet pea. A lot of people like it. I try to get back here a few times a year. Thanks for coming with me."

"I didn't realize I actually had a choice."

"You didn't. But still…thanks."

Caressa snorted and looked back out the window. She was going to live out in this country for three days. It was kind of fun. She was going to try to get into the spirit of things. Her cello was in the back seat, so it's not like he was trying to really shake her up. Maybe he was making her come so she could meet his family—or so they could meet her. Some sort of pang settled in her chest. Meeting family. What would he tell them about their relationship? That he worked for her?

"Kyle?"

"Yes, baby."

"Are you my boyfriend?"

She saw his brows draw together slightly before he schooled his face into that steely-handsome look. *Oh, great.* "I mean," she went on, "like…what are you going to tell your family about me? Are we even meeting your family?"

"Of course you're meeting my family. You'll probably meet my entire hometown. Spur's not that big. And we can tell them whatever you like."

She bit her lip, feeling peevish all of a sudden. Why should she care if he was her boyfriend or not? Stupid terminology for what was going on between them anyway. She shrugged. "Whatever. I don't care. I was just curious."

He was quiet, watching the road. Then he shrugged too. "I'm also curious, Caressa. Am I your boyfriend?"

"Oh God. Can we not talk about this?"

"Why are you getting upset?"

"Because I feel stupid now. Boyfriend and girlfriend is so…high school."

"You never went to high school."

She crossed her arms over her chest. He was constantly harping about the things she'd never done, the things she couldn't do because of her musical career. It pricked her every time and he knew it.

"Yes," he said a moment later, with great resolution. "Now that I think about it, I'm definitely your boyfriend."

"I don't want you to be my boyfriend," she grumbled.

"And you're definitely my girlfriend. Yes. I'm pretty sure that once we said 'I love you' to each other, we automatically became boyfriend and girlfriend."

"I'm pretty sure you make stuff up, you asswipe."

He chuckled, squeezing her knee. "I love you, Caressa. I want to introduce my family to my girlfriend. My talented, beautiful girlfriend. Oh, and 'asswipe' is one of those words we put on the list. You remember? Things you're not allowed to call me anymore? Now that we're in the country, I'll have to cut a switch. Plenty of trees to choose from."

She sank down in the seat and crossed her arms over her chest even tighter. She didn't know if she loved him or hated him. He was right though. There were plenty of trees.

* * * * *

Kyle decided to stop in the town of Loving for lunch to entertain her, and because of the strange conversation she'd initiated in the car. As a boy he'd always snickered at the *Welcome to Loving* sign along the highway, but now it suited where he was in life. *Welcome to loving. May cause headaches.* He sat across from her in a diner not unlike the one they'd visited in New Jersey so long ago. Actually, not so long ago.

All told, he'd only really known Caressa a matter of weeks. Did he *really* love her? After the Nell debacle he didn't trust himself to judge love, obsession, or lust anymore. With Caressa he felt all three, but he was as wary as he was head-over-heels for her. Anyway, *girlfriend* was too limited a word for what he thought of her, which was why he'd hesitated when she'd brought up semantics. Hell, he would be her boyfriend, her lover, her dominant, her cello valet, her take-out fetcher, her mood-management technician. Anything. He felt like everything to her, and she was like everything to him. *Okay, sure, boyfriend. If that's what you want. Whatever you want—I'm all in.*

But she was right. His family would want to know the semantics, the cut-and-dried circumstances of their relationship. He would tell his mom and dad and brothers and sisters that Caressa was his girlfriend. Then it would make sense to them when he kissed her, when he couldn't keep his hands from touching her. Lots of people met at workplaces and started romances, and that's more or less what they had done. His family would understand it, probably better than he did. His family were salt of the earth people. What they would make of Caressa was anybody's guess. If he was honest with himself, part of the reason he'd brought her with him was to see her as they saw her, however they saw her. He was still working it out in his head whether or not that was fair to her.

"How are your eggs?" he asked.

"How are eggs ever? Fine. It's hard to ruin eggs, you know?"

The other people in Loving's only diner were staring at her cello case propped beside their table. A summer tour meant concerns about horrors like wood warping and glue softening. He knew she would expect him to go out and acclimatize the car before she brought the cello back out again. She would never have agreed to leave it sitting over the folded down seats in the back.

"Listen, I just want you to be yourself around my family, okay? I don't want you to be nervous or anything."

She gestured at the trees beyond the grimy glass of the window. "I'm more nervous about the switches all over the place here."

"You should be," he said in a teasingly ominous tone. "And won't it be embarrassing when I head out after dinner to cut one and call you into the woodshed?"

"Oh my God! Do not do that!"

He laughed at her very real alarm. "I won't. Jesus, Caressa. My family doesn't know anything about the kinky stuff. So ixnay on the inkskray if you catch my meaning."

"You're the one who brought up the switch thing."

"Oh, I'm switching your bottom," he said, leaning close to her under the curious eyes of Loving's citizens. "I'm just going to do it where no one else will be able to hear your screams, moans, and begging."

"I don't beg," she shot back under her breath.

"Ha! You beg every night. You beg for cock until you're hoarse, you little slut."

Caressa cracked up and Kyle laughed too. She could be so genuinely fun when she let her guard down. They passed the rest of the trip to Kyle's parent's home in similar good humor. His parents greeted her warmly and she did the same. He wondered how she saw them. His father was a tree surgeon, a little on the rugged side, and his mother a soft-spoken housewife with a Texas-sized physique—and heart.

She clasped Caressa into a welcoming hug and he saw Caressa stiffen but then respond, hugging her back in kind. They were led to separate rooms on the second floor. Kyle, to his own old room, and Caressa to the room of one of his now-married sisters. Being Spur, word had gotten around in a few short hours about his return, and family and friends were already arriving for a hastily-thrown-together barbeque.

Within an hour, Kyle's brothers and their wives, his sisters and their husbands, young nieces and nephews and well-meaning friends all descended on his parents' five-acre property. Even old Great-Grandma Winchell made an appearance, agreeing to be wheeled out onto the porch from her ground floor room in the back.

Kyle accepted their excitement and affection, but still felt self-conscious. He would always be the big time Hollywood boy in their eyes. Jeremy Gray himself had come to Spur a year or so after Kyle had started working for him. That had shut down the town completely. A few weeks later, Kyle had learned that Jeremy paid off his parents' mortgage. There had also been a huge new playground built for the kids of Spur right near the center of town, aptly named Gray Park. Kyle had told Jeremy once, in passing, that kids had nowhere to play in Spur, that he'd played in abandoned buildings and train tracks as a young child. When he'd learned about the mortgage and the playground, he'd begun to view his powerful boss as someone akin to a God.

A fickle God though. Jeremy Gray had had his moments, just as his current employer did. But not tonight. As darkness fell and his parents' guests milled in the backyard to shoot the shit and drink beer under the stars, his mother prevailed on Caressa to play for them.

He thought she might refuse, citing shyness, or the evening Texas humidity, but she had him bring out her cello and sat beside the birdfeeder in a weather-beaten chair. She played a few orchestral pieces, looking acutely self-conscious at the silent stares. They weren't mean stares though, but admiring ones. There were no cellists he knew of in Spur, but one of his father's friends was a fiddler and he went right home to get his instrument. Another man went for a trumpet. A friend of his sister's had her guitar in the back of her car.

Thus began a singular exercise in existential dissonance. Caressa Gallo, world-renowned cellist, was playing at an impromptu Spur hoedown, and she didn't miss a beat. He realized with no small amazement that Caressa could play just about anything on her cello—to include songs she didn't even know. She accompanied the musicians of Spur on familiar songs and songs he could tell she'd never heard before. Country ballads and local traditional songs, even a rollicking polka. People laughed and danced and the music went on and on, long past the time he would have thought her too tired. His great-grandma even responded, clapping her bony hands and smiling crookedly.

Kyle stared at Caressa from his place beside the porch, petrified by the depth of his love for her. Love, admiration, and awe at her effortless talent. So many people had spoken to him of angels, heaven, and Caressa's "God-given" talent, and Kyle had shrugged it all off as pretty phrases. But now, under the Texas sky, amidst darkness and laughter, full bellies and joyful dancing, he saw God in her.

She could play anything. Every note in the world was hers, right there for the taking. She could produce any note like a card trick. *Ta-da.* Her fingers and that cello in cahoots with her, tucked between her knees. He realized in a flash of understanding that he never truly could come between her and that instrument. He could watch though, as he was now, and bask in the wonder of what she was.

She looked up and over at him, found him in the darkness somehow. She must have seen what he was thinking. It must have been clearly written on his face, because she looked shaken. Soon after she deferred to the other musicians and excused herself, citing exhaustion. He helped her carry her cello inside and stow it in her room upstairs so it would be safe from any guests coming in and out. He looked at her, tired and lovely, and knew he was in the employ of another God. First Jeremy and now her, glowing slick with the sweat of a bonafide Texas country party.

His mother wouldn't be in for a while, until every last guest had departed, and so Kyle stripped Caressa naked with trembling hands and fucked her there against the wall of his sister's room. She clung to him, licking him, biting his neck as their sweaty bodies slid together and his unsheathed cock impaled her. She wrapped her legs around him and he held her ass cheeks hard, squeezing them and lifting her up and then down again.

Each time he slipped inside, his whole body shook from the maelstrom inside him, the pleasure building into a monument of desire. *I love you. I love you. I love you.* A boyfriend was nothing, mere child's play. He was a worshipper, a disciple. He was a zealot at the altar, holding a miracle in his hands.

* * * * *

Kyle woke the next morning with a start, reaching out for her. She was gone. He'd had some alarming dream about forests and thunderstorms. He'd lost Caressa, and he woke up grasping for her, his heart pounding fast and hard until he remembered he was in his parents' house. He'd had to tuck her into bed last night, after they'd fucked and showered together. Even in the shower he hadn't been able to resist her, kissing and finger-fucking her while warm water sluiced over them.

Afterward, when he delivered her to her own room, he'd stayed and kissed her for almost an hour more, tasting the sweetness of her lips and reveling in her response to him. The smell of his mother's favored lavender soap had clashed with the sharp tang of dying fires outside, and that deeper scent of desire. He hadn't been able to leave her until he heard his mother puttering around noisily in the hallway. His mom wasn't a fool—she would know that Kyle and Caressa were lovers. She was just obstinate about old-fashioned morality. *Not in my house.*

He sat up now and stretched in his narrow twin bed. His room had changed a little since he'd occupied it, but not much. He'd changed a lot more. He smiled at the old baseball and football trophies his mother couldn't seem to part with, and the worn blue quilt that still graced his bed. He hit the bathroom and peeked into Caressa's room to find her still fast asleep with the shades drawn. His phone rang and he pulled the door shut quietly, taking the call back in his own room.

"Jeremy! I was just thinking of you. How are you?"

"I'm good. Where in the world are you right now with that cellist of yours?"

"Believe it or not, we're in Spur."

"Good old Spur."

"They still talk about you here. Every time I come home."

"That's why I do things, you know. For attention."

Kyle smiled. "Yeah. I always suspected that."

"You're headed to Europe soon, aren't you? I thought you told me August?"

"Yes, we go from Spur to London by way of Dallas in a couple days. Where are you? Still want to take in one of her performances?"

"We definitely do. Is she coming to Paris?"

"You're in Paris?"

"Just for a couple weeks, and then we're back to the States."

"We head to Paris after London. How about tickets for next Friday? It's Caressa's birthday, and we're planning a private dinner party after the concert."

"For a party, I'll make it work." Jeremy laughed. Then he added, "Nell will be with me."

Kyle could still read Jeremy's tone, even over a cell phone. "Yeah, Jeremy…it's okay. It would be great to see her again. How's motherhood treating her?"

"Jesus, I don't know who to adore more now, her or little Rhiannon. They're both doing great. You know Nell. She took to motherhood like a champ."

"What about you? Holding up?"

Jeremy made a soft noise. "I love being a dad. The love part is a lot easier than I thought it would be. Even when she's wailing, shitting in diapers, the bad stuff. She's impossible not to love. But it's a big responsibility. Keeping her safe."

"You've got people on it, I'm sure."

"Even so, it's a constant worry. You know, the fans. The papers and paps. But it's worth it in the end. I wouldn't give her back for the world."

Jeremy had thought the same thoughts about Nell when he'd first met her. Kyle wondered if he even made the connection. "Everything will be fine, Jeremy."

"Oh yeah, I know. You'll have to meet the little bug while you're in Paris. She's her mother's daughter. She has all this wispy red hair."

"You guys should bring her along to the party. If she gets tired, I think the hotel we're staying at will have sitters. I can check into it—"

"Kyle, you don't have to work for me anymore. My people will handle everything."

Kyle stopped, feeling foolish. Of course Jeremy had new staff now, probably an army of nannies, although Nell didn't strike him as the nanny type. Probably one nanny and an army of baby bodyguards. Kyle wanted to see Nell again more out of curiosity than anything else. He was curious about seeing her as a mother…and curious to see if he was really as "over" her as he felt.

"So what about you and this lovely cellist? Still making beautiful music together? I assume things are pretty serious if you brought her to Spur."

"We're working things out," Kyle said cautiously. "You know how it is. She's really focused on the tour right now. Her music. But yeah, we're having a lot of fun." He stopped, thinking of last night. Thinking of the thoughts going through his mind every time he looked at her. *Fun* seemed like a crude belittlement of what they had. "God, I'm crazy about her," he admitted at last. "I'm barely holding on to my sanity. But for now, I'm going at her pace."

"That's all you can do sometimes. In the meantime, keep having fun, for fuck's sake. It can't hurt. Sober fun though. Still sober?"

"Yeah, Jeremy."

"One hundred percent?"

"One hundred percent, Master," Kyle said sardonically, to laughter on the other end of the line. "Speaking of which...Jeremy...about the party. It's just a vanilla thing. I won't be able to...you know...me and Caressa are pretty...monogamous at the moment."

"Oh." Kyle heard bemusement and not offense, fortunately. "Yeah, Nell and I actually don't do the group sex thing anymore." Kyle heard the pause on the other line, could almost see the dashing smile when he followed up with, "Not often anyway. I'm a father now, you know? Time to grow up a little."

It was Kyle's turn to chuckle. "Uh huh. I'll believe it when I see it."

"Ha. I never claimed to be anything other than I am. I'm only human, but a good woman can make you aspire to something more." Kyle heard a baby's cry in the background, and Nell's soft voice saying something unintelligible. "Look, I've gotta go. I'll catch up with you in Paris. In the meantime," he said in a lower voice, "don't give up. I have a feeling this one is worth the fight."

Chapter Eleven:
Float

Caressa woke up under the light, crisp sheets, a whirring ceiling fan turning over the bed, sending down a light breeze. She stretched and looked around the country room. Sheer lilac ruffled curtains swayed in the breeze from the fan, and the sun shone through from outside. She felt utterly relaxed, which sort of alarmed her. She noted her cello sitting safely in the corner, but a quick search of her memory reassured her that she really did have nothing to do for a couple days except skulk around Kyle's hometown. Over the subtle hum of the fan she began to make out other sounds. Pots and pans in the kitchen, Kyle's mom's soft voice and his great-grandma's gruffer one. She heard men's voices outside.

After one more luxurious stretch, she reluctantly climbed from the bed to get dressed and look out the window. Kyle and his younger brothers were putting the yard back to rights after last night's festivities. Texans really knew how to party—the people in this rural town anyway. At its peak the gathering must have reached two hundred people, which Kyle informed her was about a fifth of Spur's population.

Kyle looked up at the window then, spotting her, and motioned her down. She brushed her teeth and tried unsuccessfully to do something with her hair. She hadn't brought any elastics and the Texas humidity had turned her hair from buoyantly curly to nightmarishly frizzed-out. She finally tucked what she could behind her ears and went downstairs and out onto the porch. Three lanky, muscular men stopped and greeted her, only one of whom was Kyle. Wow, something in the water out this way. Both his brothers were as ridiculously gorgeous as Kyle was. Kyle smirked at her, probably realizing the thoughts behind her assessing stare.

"Eaten breakfast yet?" he asked.

"No, S-- Um. No. Not yet." She remembered now that he hadn't drunk at all last night, even when everyone else was beer-soaked. Sobriety. That was probably why he looked just a bit more dapper than his brothers after all.

"Go on inside. My mom likes to cook breakfast every morning. She'll make you whatever you want."

"I'll wait for you."

"Don't be shy. She doesn't bite. Great-Grandma, sometimes, but not my mom." His brothers laughed in agreement. "We're going to be another half-hour or so and then I'll have to shower so…go eat." She still hesitated, but then he shot her a look she couldn't pretend to misunderstand. *Obey me. Or else.*

She turned and headed back inside to the kitchen. Lucky for him, she liked obeying his orders. Most of the time. When she didn't, she just stayed away from him. She was actually pretty hungry. She'd been so busy playing the night before she hadn't taken much time to eat the ribs and burgers and other array of foods spread out at the party. In the kitchen, Kyle's mom sat her down and extracted an order of eggs and bacon from her. While Mrs. Winchell—Melanie—busied herself at the stove, Kyle's great-grandma stared openly at her.

"Sleep good there, missy?" she asked so suddenly and loudly that Caressa jumped.

She nodded. "Oh, yes. Thank you. I slept very well. I liked the fan." Caressa stopped, feeling silly. *I liked the fan.* What kind of stupid comment was that? But Melanie went off on a short monologue about the various fans in the house and how much they saved on the cooling bills.

"I guess you learn ways to deal with the heat around here," Caressa said.

"Oh, yes. You just get used to it."

"I don't wear my skivvies when it's real hot," Great-Grandma blurted out again. She said it like *skiv-vehs*. "Lots of folks 'round here don't wear skivvies in the summer." Caressa bit her lip to keep from breaking into laughter, especially when Melanie turned around with a smothered smile to deliver a plateful of steaming food.

"I know *I* don't, Grandma," Melanie said lightly, with a furtive wink at Caressa. "Sometimes it's just better to go without."

Caressa started to eat while Melanie squeezed a fresh glass of orange juice and set it beside her plate. "Thank you," Caressa mumbled through a mouthful of biscuit. "I'm sorry I slept so late."

"Oh, that's what vacations are for. This is your vacation, isn't it? Kyle's been telling me all about you. How hard you work every day doing practice and concerts, and all that travel too. Honestly, I can't imagine how you manage it."

Caressa couldn't imagine how Melanie managed her job, feeding her family a home-cooked breakfast the morning after throwing a massive party, although she didn't say so. Melanie's home was spotless too. Caressa thought about the wreck she always made of her hotel rooms, no matter how brief the visit, and Kyle's constant efforts to keep her organized and put-together. "I don't do everything myself. Kyle helps me a lot."

Melanie sat across from her with a cup of coffee. "I'm glad to hear it. He was always a real good boy."

"Kyle?" Great-Grandma boomed out. "More trouble than a hot barrel a' monkeys, that one. Demmed if he wasn't. Don't lie to the poor girl, Melly."

"Oh, Grandma. He was mischievous, sure," she said, looking back at Caressa. "But boys are that way. I think he grew into a fine man. But mamas tend to think of all their babies as angels."

Great-Grandma muttered something under her breath, something about "more like a dee-vil" but she was smiling at the same time.

Melanie patted Caressa's hand. "I can't thank you enough for sharing your talent with us last night. That was really something special. People will be talking about that for years, I suppose. And the little children, just staring at you. I truly thank you."

"It was my pleasure. I've never been to a Texas barbeque." She'd never been to any barbeque, which she'd never admit to Kyle. But the whole experience was one she'd never forget either.

"So what kind of plans do you and Kyle have for today? He said something about taking a walk out into the woods?" Caressa thought of the switch at once, and hoped the flush rising in her cheeks didn't show too much.

"I'm not sure. This is Kyle's territory, so I'll follow him wherever he wants to take me."

"I'll pack y'all a picnic lunch so you can take as much time as you like to go out and about. It's hot, but the woods will be shady. And I think tonight he plans to take you to Burger's Pond."

"Ooh, that will be nice," Great-Grandma exclaimed in that loud, abrupt way of hers. "Burger's Pond is a nice place. So special. Specially for loveybirds."

"What's at Burger's Pond?" Caressa asked.

Melanie smiled warmly. "I'll not tell you. A nice surprising place though, this time of year. You'll like it. You can't come to Spur without visiting Burger's at least once."

* * * * *

As Melanie promised, they set out into the shady woods armed with a picnic basket of Texas delicacies, mainly leftovers from the party, but Caressa was glad to have a second shot at them. There was also lots of sweet tea and water, and a few other things Caressa watched Kyle stuff in his backpack. Lube, butt plug. Cuffs. A little knife for cutting a switch. A large blanket and a small towel. Hm.

She tried not to fixate on it too much, but she knew their trip into the forest was for a very specific reason, which was Caressa getting her ass whipped and her holes fucked. She wasn't worried about that part— quite the contrary—her *skivvies* were already wet. She only hoped these woods were as remote and uninhabited as they seemed to be.

They trekked down a well-worn path that got narrower as they followed it, then branched off into an even narrower offshoot. The woods were quiet and shady, and there was no other sign of life, so Caressa relaxed a bit more. Eventually they came to a split rail fence and Kyle guided her off the path and along the fence line until they reached a small clearing. He put down the picnic basket and spread the blanket out over the dirt floor and jutting roots.

"Hungry?"

Something in his voice made her deliciously wary. "A little, yes."

"Well, you better eat first, because you won't feel like eating after. Take off your clothes and fold them up in a pile next to the basket. Then kneel here with your hands in your lap," he said, patting the middle of the fleece blanket.

Caressa swallowed all the questions that flew to her mind. It was obvious from the tone of his voice that it was time to obey. "Yes, Sir."

She undressed as gracefully as she could while hopping around on the pine needles and acorns under her now-bare feet. When she knelt on the blanket he wordlessly took her hands from her lap and cuffed them together behind her back.

"Good girl," he said, tapping one shamelessly erect nipple. She could already tell she would never survive this. She was soaked between the legs, already throbbing just from the cool, controlled way he was looking at her. She lowered her eyes, watching him lay out the food, for himself only. He began to eat, and every so often fed her bites of sandwich and cole slaw, fruit salad and sips of tea. He thrust pieces of buttered roll into her mouth, and she ached to catch and suck his fingers.

He knew it, allowing her only the most teasing touch. What would he do after they finished eating? The fun thing about playing with Kyle is that she never really knew until he began.

At last he started packing the food away again. He gave her another long drink and then rose with the towel he'd packed, going over to the fence. He walked along it, running his hand across the top, pressing down on it. When he put the towel across a section of the top rail, she started to shake.

He returned to the blanket and put a hand on the back of her neck, forcing her forward, up onto her knees and then into a bowed-down position. She heard him rustling in the bag again, preparing the butt plug, and then felt the cold lube against her ass. The pain was always acute as the plug slid in, but when it was seated, she never felt anything but arousal.

"You like that, don't you? When I fill your little asshole?"

"Yes, Sir."

He pulled her up again by the cuffs on her wrists, tilting her head back for a deep, passionate kiss that left her breathless, and then he was helping her up and guiding her to the fence.

"Come on, girl. Up and over."

He helped her climb up until she straddled the rail. It was high enough that the balls of her feet barely reached the ground, and she shifted, trying to find her balance without the use of her arms. The rounded wood pressed against her mons, and she panicked for a moment, trying to brace her feet on the second rail to relieve some of the pressure. That only threw off her balance and she put her feet back on the ground in capitulation, clenching on the plug in her bottom.

Through all of this, Kyle only watched, no doubt enjoying her predicament. He let her go when she was more or less settled, if settled meant teetering with a plugged ass on a narrow piece of wood that was already biting into her pussy. She shifted again, fighting the discomfort. It wasn't unbearable…yet. The unbearable thing was how wet her pussy was, and the humiliating spot she'd leave behind on the towel when their game was done.

But she wasn't going to think about that now. Kyle had wandered off into the woods behind her—purposely she was sure, so she would have to turn around on the unforgiving fence rail to see him. Looking for switches. With a tiny moan she turned forward again, hearing the twist and pull of wood when he ostensibly found one to his liking. He wandered back into her line of sight, peeling the little shoots off a long, whippy branch. She bit her lip and inched forward on the rail, trying to find some relief for her engorged clit. Oh God…oh God, she was so horny—

She almost fell forward, but he was close enough to catch her by the arm. "Bad girl," he snapped, and then he brought the switch down on her bottom, offered up and rendered immobile by the solid rail.

"Owwww…" She cried out, suddenly not nearly as horny. She couldn't rub the fiery stripe and she couldn't do anything to evade another one. She gazed at Kyle with pleading eyes. "I'm sorry, Sir."

"If you would pay less attention to trying to rub one out on that fence and more attention to me, I wouldn't have to worry so much about you falling."

"If you uncuffed my hands we could both worry less," she muttered. And then "Owwww…" as he whipped her again. *Ow.* Damn, switches were vicious. She sucked in a deep breath, wanting to pull away from his grasp on her arm, but knowing she'd fall if she did so. "Please. That hurts, Sir."

"It does, doesn't it? You're going to have a sore bottom for the trip back to Dallas. You'll probably squirm all the way over the Atlantic, just the way you're squirming now."

Caressa sobbed softly and shifted on the rail, wanting to hump it into oblivion at the same time she wanted to run away screaming. "I'll definitely never, ever call you an asswipe again."

"Damn right." He laid another stripe across her bottom with the switch, right over the toy in her ass.

"Oh, God. Please! Ow, Kyle! Sir! That fucking hurts."

"I miss the gag."

Caressa laughed and then yelped in protest as he hit her again. Her ass felt like it was on fire. "Please, Sir!" His only answer was to hold her arm harder and really start whipping her in earnest.

She danced on the rail, horny but tortured, as her bottom was subjected to blow after blow. She tried to process the stinging stripes at the same time her clit rubbed against the towel and her pussy ached to be filled. No matter how violently she struggled, he held her, and when he finally stopped she was pressed against his side, her tears flowing into the soft cotton of his tee shirt.

She felt wrung out from within, and her ass seemed to throb in concert with her racing, thudding heart. He took her face in rough hands and thrust his tongue in her mouth. She kissed him back, still half-sobbing, sucking on his lips and rubbing her face against his. He pulled back and licked up one cheek, then the other, gentling her, soothing her.

"Shhh..." he whispered, reaching back to squeeze her sensitive cheeks. She cried out again and humped against the rail, shameless with need now. With a muttered expletive, he lifted her off the fence and rearranged her, bending her over the same towel, so she could feel her own wet juices against her pelvis. He ripped open his shorts and thrust into her pussy with them still bunched around his hips.

She groaned at his sudden, rough invasion. His thick cock battered against the anal plug from within and Caressa felt unbearably full and helpless. Arousal surged all over her body, from her tingling clit to her sensitive breasts and thighs, down to her toes. Her ass ached as her pussy was ruthlessly taken. She loved being used by him this way. Being conquered.

Her hands were still bound, her ass cheeks were still sore, and his pounding strokes subdued her into his mindless vessel. *Hurt me. Take me. Do whatever you want to me. I'm yours.* Still, his hands grasped her hips, protecting her from being battered against the wood, and one slipped down to slide over her slick clit until she thought she would die. A shimmering shivery feeling grew and expanded between her thighs, up to her full asshole. The pain and pleasure melded into one excruciating song, and then she heard him urging her on. "Come for me. Come for me, Caressa."

The insistence in his words and his magical touch tipped her over the edge and she reached a dazzling, clenching climax that left her limp and sagging against the rail. He came at the same time, lifting her feet from the ground as he surged into her. With some small functioning part of her brain, she worried for a moment that the rail might break right down the center. But no, the fence was as reliable and strong as him. Kyle was nuzzling against the side of her neck now, dropping kisses down to her shoulder and over her back. He gently unfastened the leather cuffs and helped her up, holding her tight until she regained her balance. She pressed against him, wanting to sob as he ran whispering fingertip caresses over her ass.

They collapsed on the blanket and she clung to him, slowly coming down from whatever high he'd led her to. His fingers trailed up and down her back, and they drowsed for a long time. She was still plugged, but she didn't mind it. It was like some continuing submission to him, some intimate mark of ownership she was happy to bear.

Finally he rose to get the towel and help her clean up and dress, and still he didn't let her remove it. "I want you to walk all the way back plugged like that, with your ass aching and sore. Do you know why?"

"Because you like to torment me?"

"Guess again," he chuckled, bending to pick up the switch and twirl it between his fingers. "And guess well."

"Because you love me?" she said, eyeing the whippy implement.

"Damn right."

* * * * *

Caressa didn't want to nap, but she was exhausted, so Kyle made her. He said he had a little work to get done anyway, plans in Europe to check on, emails to write. He had a few things left to set up for her birthday party, and some friends who needed tickets to one of the Paris performances.

And then there were his plans for tonight, for this "surprising" Burger's Pond. So she slept, or tried to, shifting on her sore ass cheeks and trying not to get turned on all over again in her small country room with the frilly curtains.

Kyle told her that Burger's Pond wasn't really any good until dusk, so Caressa had plenty of time to spend with his family, including Great-Grandma Winchell, who seemed to have taken a liking to her. After a long, jovial dinner with his family during which he obviously enjoyed watching her squirming and shifting, Kyle finally managed to steal her away.

They made the hike to Burger's Pond in twenty minutes or so while Kyle told her funny stories about his childhood. She still hadn't quite pinned down how many brothers and sisters he actually had. It was all made more complicated by the fact that the people of Spur often called each other "brother" and "sister" even when they weren't related. She finally gave up stressing about it when they arrived at an open field and Kyle pulled her through the knee-high grasses.

"Come on, it's almost time," he said. "This way."

Time for what? She hesitated but she followed. God, she trusted him. She hoped he was worthy of that trust, because she was steadily losing the ability to deny him anything at all. He led her down a low rise to a cluster of trees, and then they passed through a protected clearing to a still country pond. "Look," he said.

He didn't have to say "look". Caressa stared into the small grotto-like meadow, at dancing flickering lights, thousands of them. For a moment she thought of fairies and make-believe. Miracles. A universe of brilliant pinpoints flitting and blinking among the trees and reflected in the surface of the water.

"Wh—What is doing that?"

"Lightning bugs. Fireflies."

Of course. She immediately felt unbalanced by such a pedestrian explanation. Oh, fireflies. But this was fireflies *extraordinaire*. She still couldn't really put into words the way the beautiful display affected her.

He led her deeper into the woods beside the pond, over to a boulder he said he used to sit on as a child. He pulled her into his lap and they looked out at the display. The darker it got, the more fireflies appeared, until the whole world seemed lit up with their brilliant, fleeting light.

"It's amazing. How many do you think there are?"

"A hundred thousand, maybe? I don't know. They peak in August, but they're like this all spring and summer. They cluster here. No one knows why."

"I wish I could take a picture. I wish I had a camera so I could save this."

"I've tried taking pictures before, but you can't really capture it. The lights aren't bright enough or something." A bug blinked close to her head and he caught it in his hand, and held it in front of her eyes. A moment later the bug lit up, nature's sorcery in the cage of his elegant fingers. "Do you want to hold it?"

"Yes." Her voice felt tight, like the wonder of this whole secluded pond was lodged in her throat. He gently transferred the small black bug into her palm and she closed her fingers around it.

"Careful," he said. "Hold it loosely. Don't crush it."

She peeked through the small gaps she'd left in her fingers, holding her hand close to her eyes. "It got away."

"Wait," he said, and then the world lit up in her fingers. She opened her hand without meaning to and the insect flew off in a blur of tiny wings.

"Oh."

"Do you want me to catch you another one?"

"No." She hated that she was about to cry. She hated that he would know it.

"Caressa? What's wrong?"

She buried her face in her hands, still seeing the blinking lights behind her closed lids. "Nothing."

He pulled her closer, which only made her cry harder. "Tell me what's wrong. This afternoon?"

"No. I'm just… This is really…"

She snuck a look at him, dashing away unwanted tears. "This is really cool, Kyle," she said, forcing a smile.

It was an excruciating moment for her. She didn't mean to be crying. She didn't want Kyle to freak out about it. She fluttered a hand in front of her eyes, not wanting the worried concern in his gaze. "Just ignore me. Please. This is just…"

"Hey, let's go swimming," he suggested. "It's fun to swim in the dark with the fireflies everywhere."

"Swimming?" She laughed, glad for something else to talk about. "How are we going to swim? I don't have a suit."

"You don't use suits in Spur, honey," he said with a smile.

"But it's dark. How can you see what's in the water?"

"You don't need to see in the water. It's just a small pond, rainwater. No sharks in there. Minnows maybe, but they don't bite too hard."

He was pulling her up now, tugging her toward the shore. She dug in her heels. "I don't want to, Kyle. How deep is it?"

He stopped, looking at her with his hands on his hips. "You can't swim, can you?" It was that look again, that reproachful disbelieving look that made her want to scream. "You can't swim, right? No time for swimming between cello practice and getting ready for more cello practice."

"Just don't, Kyle. I don't want to swim anyway—"

"How much of your life are you seriously going to sacrifice in the name of this music of yours?"

He said music like an epithet, like a swear word. She glared back at him. "Sacrifice? Swimming in a dirty pond in the middle of nowhere? Some fucking sacrifice."

"Why do you do it, Caressa? Just explain it to me. Why does it come before everything else?"

"It doesn't!"

"It does! There's a whole big world out there. This earth is spinning and time is going. You're turning twenty-one next week and your life has been *this big*." He held his hand in front of her face, his fingers spread a scant inch apart. "There's so much more to life, don't you get that? Look!" he yelled, waving his arm around. "One hundred thousand fireflies, Caressa! A million! Do you even know what you're missing?"

"Yes," she shrieked. "Yes, I know! What do you want me to do? I have a gift. I'm not going to throw it away because you think I should be…whatever. Going fucking shopping. Catching fireflies. Eating god-damned biscuits with your great-grandma. All of this was a fucking set up, wasn't it?"

She started to stalk across the field, the grass whipping at her knees. She turned back, pushing at him when he followed her. "You wanted to bring me out here just to shove this in my face. Everything I'm missing. Well, you're an asshole." It was a punishment word. She didn't care. "You're a jerk, you're a stupid country hick who doesn't understand anything about music. You say you love me but you're not even trying to understand—"

He took her arms and pinned them at her sides. "And you're a stupid city girl who doesn't even understand why you're still playing. Tell me why, Caressa. That's all I'm asking." He nuzzled against the tears on her cheek, his chest rising and falling in deep breaths against hers as he held her close. "Just tell me so I can understand."

She took a deep, shuddering breath. "I just don't feel like I can stop. Not yet. Can't you let me figure this out for myself? Can't you give me more time?"

He sighed, looking grieved. He ran a thumb down her damp cheek. "But life is so short, Caressa. Look at Jacqueline du Pré."

"I'm not her. I'm Caressa Gallo. You have to let me write my own story. In this, you do."

He stepped away from her, in a wrenching movement that she felt as a physical pain. "I didn't bring you here as some ploy, Caressa. To make some point. I just thought you would enjoy it."

She took her own deep breath and reached for his hand. "I'm sorry I said those things. I didn't mean them. I flipped out."

After a moment, he drew her hand to his lips and kissed her fingers softly, the very tips, like he was praying. He finally looked up at her with a rueful sigh. "My little madwoman. As your tantrums go, that was pretty mild." She laughed weakly, letting him pull her back into his arms. He cupped her face in his hands and kissed her gently. "I'll forgive you on one condition."

"What?"

"Come back to the pond with me. Let me teach you how to swim."

She followed him back down the rise, only to find twice as many fireflies clustered in the trees. She let him undress her and pull her into the water. The pond was black now, the only light in the darkness coming from the bugs and the half moon. The bottom was smooth, uneven stone, so she didn't sink into it as she'd feared. She still clutched him as he drew her deeper.

"It's scary out here," she said. "I can't see what's down there."

"I know. You'll be okay."

He held her as she kicked her feet in the water and attempted a pathetic kind of dog paddle. "I'm not real coordinated."

"You're doing fine. The important thing is just getting comfortable in the water and learning what to do with your hands and feet. And understanding that you're not going to drown. Nothing dire is going to happen to you, as long as you don't panic. You can always float if worse comes to worse."

He slid a hand under her back and lifted her up in the water. She resisted and he shook his head at her. "Relax. Let me hold you. I'm going to show you how to float."

He made her put her head back and lie straight and still. "Let the water hold you. Just let go and be a lilypad on the surface. The water will hold you from beneath."

Caressa smiled a little, trying to be a lilypad. To her surprise, she found the water did hold her. She took slow, deep breaths, feeling her arms and legs bobbing on the surface, her entire torso buoyed up by the blackness underneath. Her breasts were small silver mounds in the light of the moon. "I'm not even holding you now, Cara. You're doing it yourself. You feel it?"

She nodded, laughing softly. "Yeah."

"Now come back down in the water and try to do it yourself. As long as you know how to float, you'll do pretty well for yourself. You'll keep your head above the surface, anyway. You'll be able to breathe."

Caressa lifted her feet from the rocky bottom and lay back in the water. She flailed for a moment, but then she pulled her tummy up to the surface and relaxed her shoulders back into the water. Above her a few stray fireflies still blinked their intermittent, tiny blinks, like faraway stars. *You'll keep your head above the surface anyway. You'll be able to breathe.* It was the most she could ask for. She smiled over at Kyle. "I did it."

She felt his hands in her hair, separating the curls where they floated on the surface. "I knew you could."

She looked over at his bare chest, and the moon shining on the water reflected a scar on the right side. "What's this from?" she asked, grabbing onto his shoulders and running a finger over the reddened ridge.

"My unrequited love. I got shot."

"What? Okay, wait. Explain."

"It's a long story, Caressa."

She hopped in the water beside him, practicing some of the moves he'd taught her. "The night is young, and the fireflies are still out. Tell me what happened."

He hesitated, but then he said, "You remember, I used to work for a movie star."

"Yeah, Denise told me his name once. I can't remember. James? Jethro?"

Kyle snorted. "Jeremy. He's a pretty big movie star. Anyway, one of the things I did as Jeremy's assistant was…well…find him girlfriends. Women to date. He was a little too famous to go out and make passes at women in a bar or whatever."

"That's kind of creepy."

Kyle laughed. "Honestly, it was really creepy, but he was a good guy, so I did what I could for him. Anyway, I found him this girl."

"The girl you were in love with."

"Not right away. I fell for her over weeks…months. A lot of stuff went on."

"She was cheating on him with you?"

"No. Well, it's hard to explain, but I can't really tell you the specifics because I signed a confidentiality agreement."

"Ooh la la. It must have been pretty depraved stuff. If you had to sign a confidentiality agreement."

He looked at her. "I signed one to work with you."

"Did you? I didn't ask you to."

"A lot of people are running around behind the scenes keeping the Caressa Express on the rails. Your lawyer required it. My agency's lawyers would have required it too, if yours hadn't."

"Oh." She digested that interesting fact, feeling kind of foolish. Well, at least she didn't have to worry about him blabbing about her finer meltdowns in some tell-all book someday.

"Anyway, one of Jeremy's deranged fans—"

"He had more than one?"

"Unfortunately, yes. But are you going to let me tell this story?"

Caressa made a lip-zipping motion and wrapped her legs around his hips, letting him hold her in the water.

"Any*way*…this deranged woman showed up at his girlfriend's hotel room to kill her. I tried to take her gun away and she shot me in the chest. Or maybe I shot myself. It was hard to say in the heat of the moment."

Caressa was flabbergasted. "God, you really might have died."

"I might have. It was eight centimeters from my heart, they told me. But I was actually fine. I was only in the hospital a few days. *She* died. The crazy woman," he added soberly. "I had to shoot her."

She gazed into his eyes, saddened to see the shadow crossing over his face. "I'm sorry. But that wasn't your fault. You were a hero."

"I guess."

She ran her fingers across a small blemish above the bullet scar. "What's this from?"

He cringed. "I had her name tattooed there afterward." Caressa giggled softly, mostly from the beleaguered look on his face. "I know, embarrassing. Having it taken off was one of the best things I did in rehab." He shook his head. "I don't know why I got so crazy over her."

"Maybe because you saved her. That has to create a special bond between people."

He stared at her a long time. "I don't know if it really works that way. But you know what, Caressa? I hardly think of her anymore."

Caressa couldn't quite hold his gaze, it was so intense. "Because of me?" she asked quietly.

He didn't reply, only drew her through the black water to the shore. He laid her on the edge of the pond with her head resting on the damp grass and covered her with his body. She shivered, looking up at the moon, letting him love her and warm her.

The fireflies had gone, lights shuttered for the night, but she knew she'd always remember that light shining out from her fingers, and the blinking above her as she floated under a Texas moon. *Oh, Kyle, Kyle.* His cock was pure bliss, and she arched her hips up to feel him spread and fill her. His hair tickled against her cheek and she licked his neck, tracing the straining tendons. She clutched at his back as he slid deep inside her, lapping against her like the dark, dark water.

"Thank you for teaching me how to float," she whispered, but she knew he didn't hear.

Chapter Twelve:
Fighting

She got on the plane to London without a blip. He'd worried about the flight change issue but she seemed to have forgotten it completely. Or perhaps she was only distracted. Their sojourn to Spur had left both of them with a lot to think about. She slept now as they flew across the ocean, one hand clasped in his, the other resting against her cello case. He searched his conscience again. No, he really did *not* want to make her stop playing. He just didn't want her to miss out on other things.

Like making a life with you, his conscience chided. Damn conscience. It never shut up. And she was still riddled with anxiety. When she didn't practice, she fretted. When she had a less than perfect show, she suffered. When reviews weren't one hundred percent raves, she shut down for hours after reading them. He didn't want to make her quit playing, he just wanted her to realize that if she *did* want to quit, or just pull back a little, it would be okay.

He was determined to make it okay. He would be there for her, because he couldn't *not* be there for her. He would fend off Denise and all the music mavens who'd come after her, begging her to reconsider. He'd make her smile, make her laugh all day. He'd see to it that she never paced back and forth the length of a dressing room again, but instead played in ways that made her joyful. If that meant playing three hundred concerts a year, so be it. But maybe it meant playing smaller concerts or only a few concerts a year…whatever it took to make the stress and anxiety go away.

"I like London," she said drowsily beside him.

He leaned to kiss her on the forehead as she stirred against his side. "I didn't know you were up. There's still an hour or so to go. Sleep some more if you want to."

"I might wear my red gown tomorrow."

"There's another meet-and-greet afterward."

"You told me that yesterday."

"Well, I'm never sure you're listening," he chuckled. "London should be cooler than Texas anyway. Then we're on to Paris for your birthday."

"Are there going to be French pastries at my party?"

"You're gonna be swimming in them."

"French champagne?"

He frowned. "Maybe."

"I'm going to be twenty-one, remember? Old enough to legally drink."

"Don't remind me."

She laughed softly and leaned her head on his shoulder. "Will there be brie at my party? And baguettes?"

"I'll give you a big, hard baguette a little later, *ma petite*."

He pinched the inside of her thigh, enjoying her little squeak. She was in high spirits the rest of the flight and all the way to the London hotel, and then the cloak of duty and stress seemed to smother her again.

Kyle ended up having to give Denise the report on their trip to Spur when Caressa shut herself in her room to practice. By the time he and Denise strong-armed her out to dinner, she was nearing hysteria over how unprepared she was and how badly she was going to bomb at the

Royal Festival Hall. Kyle hauled her into the bedroom as soon as they returned to the hotel suite, intent on shutting down her tantrum before it started.

"Caressa, I'm telling you right now, don't even start this."

"I'm not prepared. I should have practiced more last week."

"If you aren't prepared by now—Jesus. The tour's over in less than a month, you realize."

"You don't—" She stopped the words at his warning glare.

"Listen here," he said, emphasizing every word. "I do not want you to stress about this. Yes, we're in Europe now. You did fine in the States and Canada. You'll do fine here. Snap out of it."

She stayed in her room that night, and he tried not to be offended by it. She was better the next day, but worse the following. She had a meltdown at a media event, bursting into tears when a hapless reporter likened her to Jacqueline du Pré. "She died, and I'm the one who didn't die," she yelled. "Do your research!"

He held her in the car afterward while she sobbed on his shoulder, trying to gauge where the moodiness was coming from. "Cara. Sweet pea. Is it only that the tour is ending soon?"

"I don't know," she sobbed.

"You know, I'm not going to leave when it's over. When my contract with you is up." He chuckled softly. "Not that we've been adhering to the contract guidelines anyway. But we'll be back in New York together. We can go wherever you want from here."

"I don't want to go anywhere," she said petulantly.

"Well, you'll have to go somewhere." He tried to kiss her but she shied away from him. They rode the rest of the way to the hotel in brittle silence, a silence that loomed too much in the following days. Kyle ached to reach for her, but she was armored again. He gave what support she would accept and spend his nights alone, not trusting himself to go to her.

It wasn't until the first morning in Paris that she finally crept into his room, her face pale and her eyes red from tears. She crawled into bed with him and buried her face against his neck and begged for forgiveness. He did the only thing he could think to do, which was forgive her. She pressed against him and kissed him and he responded even though he'd told himself he was done with it. That she was a hopeless case. A lost cause. He'd already nearly killed himself over one lost cause. He wouldn't do it again.

But he would. He did. He took her wrists in his fingers and squeezed them until she whimpered, and then he rolled on top of her and pinned her down with his cock. That, at least, he could do.

She moaned and tried to reach for him, and in the end he let her wrap her arms around him and leave bleeding scratches on his back. A short rest, not even twenty minutes, and he was inside her again, seeking her heat and the wildness that entranced him.

He grew rougher, pulling her tangled hair as he forced her up on top of him. They traded slaps as he sought to pin her wrists again and she fought to stay free of him, all the while riding furiously on his cock. After she came in a rolling, bucking movement, he grasped her breasts and tumbled her over, falling on top of her so her breath left her in a rush. He had a thousand things to say to her, and yet nothing to say to her, so he just fucked her until he emptied himself with a shuddering groan. She was crying when he looked at her, silent rivers of tears.

"Don't. Please don't cry, Cara. I can't stand this."

"I'm sorry."

"Did I hurt you? I didn't mean to."

"No, I'm just *sorry*," she sobbed. "I'm sorry, I'm sorry. I'm sorry I'm this way. I really love you. I just... I just..."

The words were like skewers. *I just... I just...* "It's okay, Caressa," he said, shushing her with a kiss. He brushed her hair back from her face and gently stroked the breast he'd squeezed earlier. "Don't worry about it right now. Just know I love you too, okay? And I'm here for you, wherever things end up."

She nodded, sniffling. He pulled her closer, savoring the deeply-missed moments of her surrender. "It's your birthday, sweet pea," he whispered against her ear. "Happy twenty-one."

He went out later while she was practicing to buy a present for her. The one he'd gotten her wouldn't work anymore. The one he was planning to get her probably wouldn't go over too well either, but he found it anyway at a kiosk outside a Metro station. He bought a silver bag and tissue paper to wrap it in. By the time he got back it was almost time for an early dinner before the concert.

Jeremy called him and they made plans to meet backstage afterward and then travel back to the hotel for Caressa's party. Kyle was strangely nervous about seeing Jeremy again, and not just because Nell would be with him. It had been about a year since Jeremy had shaken him out of bed and made him get his shit together. Unfortunately, aside from maintaining staunch sobriety, Kyle wasn't sure he'd done much to better himself.

Backstage in the dressing room, Caressa looked lovely in the ivory gown she'd first worn in Cincinnati. It still took his breath away. Her hair was down, a wild mass of brunette curls like a mane, and her lips were painted a dark crimson. She looked a thousand years old, and yet a little girl. Twenty-one, such a young age. Denise was putting on a diamond pendant necklace she'd bought Caressa for her birthday—with Caressa's own money. Kyle couldn't judge though. Caressa was still paying him too, for all he did—and didn't—do for her. He wasn't sure anymore if it was a fair arrangement.

Caressa paced a little, but mostly she stood still and looked beautiful. He told her so, in as equivocal a voice as he could. *You look beautiful, Caressa.* Meanwhile, he added in his mind, *I loved fucking you today. Why won't you look at me like you did at Burger's Pond? What happened?* But no answers were forthcoming from that pretty-doll face.

Kyle watched from the wings as she took to the stage and mesmerized yet another audience. Paris at her feet. Tomorrow he'd take her to the top of the Eiffel Tower and let her look out at the city she'd charmed. Lit up at night, it would almost be like the fireflies.

There had to be a way for them. There had to be a way to win her over. He peered out at the spellbound audience, and saw Jeremy and Nell in the second row. Good tickets. At least he could still do something right. They were watching Caressa with the same expression as everyone else, with awestruck, rapt attention. When Caressa played it was so hard to look away. He knew. By now, he knew every note of these concerts by heart.

Afterward he stayed backstage to look after her cello. The conductor drew him into a conversation, enthusing about Caressa's performance in rat-a-tat broken English. By the time Kyle arrived at the backstage lounge, Jeremy and Nell were already there with several members of the orchestra. Jeremy was deep in conversation with Caressa back in a corner.

Kyle couldn't see Caressa's face, but Jeremy seemed delighted by her. He still looked the same. Broad shoulders, short blond hair. Those mesmerizing eyes. Kyle stuffed down jealousy and simply enjoyed the sight of the two most talented people he knew making one another's acquaintance.

Then Kyle felt a tentative hand on his elbow and turned to find himself face-to-face with Nell. She was wearing a Grecian-style pale green gown and a spectacular emerald necklace. She looked as fresh and angelic as ever, even after the things he'd done to her, the things Jeremy had done to her in darker days. He pushed those thoughts away also.

"Hi, Kyle," she said with a genuinely warm smile.

"Hi, Nell." He lifted his hands, at a loss for words for a moment. "You look amazing. Happy. I'm so glad."

"You look good too. The concert was wonderful. Thanks for getting us tickets."

"You're most welcome." In the tense silence, they both swung and looked at Jeremy, still chattering away with Caressa. Kyle chuckled softly. "You know what's really funny? She has no idea who's talking to her. No idea how famous he is."

"I think that's why he's enjoying her so much," Nell said, laughing. "Look at him. What do you think they're talking about? You, maybe. Jeremy told me you two were…"

Something in his face must have made her stop. He shrugged and forced a half-smile. "We're trying to work things out. She's been really

stressed with the tour and everything. You know how it is. But yeah…"
He nodded, then shrugged again. "I don't know."

Nell's luminous green eyes searched his face. "Oh, Kyle."

He didn't reply, didn't need to. They used to fight and battle. Jesus, how he'd hated her and loved her, but in the end, they had this. Understanding. She took his hand down at his side, squeezed it very gently. "Everything will work out. Things have to work out for you. Otherwise the universe makes no sense. Does she love you too?"

"I think so. At least I've got that going for me this time." He mentally kicked himself for that indirect jab. He looked back at Nell, squeezing her hand harder and then pulling his away. "I'll always love you, you know. Just because of all we went through. But I know you were never meant for me. I just hope… I always hope that you're happy, wherever you are with him."

"I'm so happy, Kyle. And I hate to see you hurting, but at least it's not over me anymore." She was teasing him, now, while his heart was laid bare to her.

"You always had a nasty streak, you know."

"I fully admit that." She gazed in Caressa and Jeremy's direction. "She's looking over here at you, Kyle. And it's a really nice look. Come on, introduce me to her."

They met Jeremy and Caressa in the center of the room. Jeremy hugged him, clapping him on the back, and then pulled away to straighten Kyle's tie. "Looking pretty snazzy and important, young man."

"I try. I'll never live up to you," Kyle answered with a smirk, giving Jeremy's bespoke tux the once-over.

They fell into easy conversation, as if it hadn't been a year since they'd seen each other. Caressa listened, and Kyle could tell when understanding dawned from the assessing look she turned on Nell beside her.

Yes. She was the one. But she can't compete with you.

* * * * *

"So he was your old boss? He's the big movie star guy?"

Caressa really wanted to ask about the other one, Nell, but she couldn't bring her voice to frame the question without sounding jealous or insane.

Kyle looked over at her in the darkness of the hired car. "I can't believe you've never seen any of his movies. Yes, he's a big star."

"Why didn't you tell me that's who he was? He just said he was some friend of yours."

"He is a friend of mine."

Caressa crossed her arms over her chest. Denise was sitting on the other side of her, staring out the window.

"Have you seen his movies, Aunt Denise?"

"Some of them, yes. A little violent for my tastes."

Violent? Probably not as violent as what I feel like doing to that chick Nell. She and Jeremy were coming to the party later with their baby. Awesome. Her twenty-first birthday was going to get overshadowed by a movie star, the woman Kyle was obsessed with, and their cute-as-a-button baby, no doubt. As soon as she got there, Caressa was going to start swilling champagne for all she was worth.

Damn him. Since Spur, it had been impossible for her to keep her mind on her work. It had been difficult all along, but now it was just…torture. But she knew the price of being with him, *really* being with him, and the price wasn't something she could afford. She hated that he still stayed with her, but she couldn't find the strength to send him away. But perhaps now…

She wanted to scratch the redhead's eyes out. And then Kyle's when she was finished. She'd seen the way they'd talked together when they thought she wasn't looking, the way they looked at each other like they shared some special secret.

"You okay?" Kyle asked, taking her hand on the seat and squeezing it. "What did you think of Jeremy? What were you guys talking about?"

"Where to get pizza in Paris. We were talking about food and how bad we were at speaking French. He said the concert was good."

"It was. How did you think it went?"

She shrugged. "Okay." *I'm still going to get wasted at this damn party.*

Kyle and Aunt Denise had invited all one hundred and fifty of the members and administrators of the Orchestre de Paris, and the hotel reception room was already filling with tuxedos and black concert gowns. True to Kyle's word there were tables of pastries, pâté, French bread and wine, and a large American-style birthday cake in the shape of a cello. Nice touch.

Caressa grabbed some champagne from a table and lingered around the pastry table for a while, fielding birthday wishes and polite compliments. Her face was starting to hurt from smiling by the time they cut the cake and sang Happy Birthday in English and French. Through all this she followed Kyle around with her gaze whenever he wasn't hovering over her. He spent some time cuddling the Gray's baby girl, who was disgustingly cute.

"Are you enjoying the party, Caressa?"

Caressa spun around mid-stare to find her aunt beside her. She was looking a little flushed from drink as she took Caressa's arm and gave her an awkward hug.

"It's wonderful. Thanks for setting it all up."

"Kyle did most of it. A party in Paris for my little girl. I'm so proud of you, you know."

Aunt Denise held her tighter and Caressa felt a sudden tickling in her throat, like she might just start crying. Like a dam was about to burst. "I'll remember this forever, Aunt Denise. I wouldn't have wanted to spend my birthday any other way."

"Do you mean that?" her aunt asked. Caressa wanted to get away, to find a private place to hide, but her aunt was still looking at her with those bleary, half-drunk eyes. "Tell me something, Caressa. Be honest. You do enjoy this, don't you? You're not doing this for me? Or for…for your mom and dad?"

Oh God. "No, Aunt Denise. Of course not. Has Kyle been pscychoanalyzing you too? Jesus." But as she said it she suddenly wondered just who she *was* doing it for. Like a lightning flash at the top of a thirty-five story building, the question flashed and burned in her mind. Why did she really do this? For attention? For approval? She put down her empty champagne glass and picked up another as Kyle slid a look at her from across the room. *Yes, I'm getting plastered. Deal with it.*

"Denise, I have to pee," she muttered, taking off across the room. Kyle cut her off by the door.

"How much are you drinking?"

"It's my party. I'll drink as much as I want. All I have to do is stumble upstairs later. I have to pee," she said, pulling away. He let her go and she ran into the bathroom with her champagne glass still in hand.

She ditched it on the sink and hid in a stall, pulling her voluminous skirts up around her waist and trying not to fall off balance as she yanked down her panties. She needed an assistant skirt holder, she thought to herself. She banged out of the stall and reclaimed her glass, smiling wide at the woman who'd just come in. Caressa couldn't place her in the orchestra. Tympani maybe? Drums? Maybe she should become a drummer. Beat on drums and dance around. It had to be easy to do that right.

"Excuse me." She pushed around the woman when she looked like she might talk to her, and then Kyle took her under the arm outside the door and led her to a chair beside the cake table.

"Some people have brought presents, Caressa," he said in a voice that she understood to mean, *Sit your ass down here and open your presents.*

She parked herself in the chair and swallowed a protest when he made off with her nearly-full glass. There was a plaque of appreciation from the French orchestra, something she needed like a hole in her head, but she smiled and made a fuss over it before passing it to Kyle. There were a few bottles of wine from individual musicians, and a collection of gift cards to local sights and restaurants. As if she had the time or inclination to go out and gad about town like a tourist. It was like something Kyle would make her do. Jeremy and Nell got her an illustrated book about famous cellos and cello makers. It was actually a pretty cool gift. Had Kyle told them about her fascination with the great makers, with her own priceless Peresson? She thanked them, and thanked Aunt Denise for the earrings she'd bought her to match the pendant she already had on. Then Kyle handed her a silver bag with iridescent tissue paper. She knew this one was from him.

What had he gotten her? The room was so quiet now. Some of the guests had already gone but most were arrayed around her chair and she suddenly felt intensely nervous. Her fingers shook as she parted the tissue to pull out a small, plain bound book. It had the words *Les Horaires du RER, Metro, Train et TGV/Eurostar* on the cover. She flipped the book open and realized like a punch to the gut what she was looking at. Her world went red.

"Train schedules, Kyle? Really?" She stood without thinking and threw it at him—and missed. She wanted it back so she could rip it to shreds in front of his face. He just stared at her, with reproach and longing. It enraged her. She forgot about everyone watching and started yelling at him. "Enough! Enough already! I get it. Do you think I'm stupid? Do you think I don't understand what you keep trying to say over and over and *over*!"

He shook his head a little, but she was beyond stopping and shutting the fuck up.

"I hate you! I hate you for this. I hate you for all of this. You think you're saving me? Knight in shining armor? Well, I don't want to be saved. It doesn't make you special and it doesn't make me love you. I don't want you to save me and get some fucking tattoo of my name on your chest. Don't you understand that?" Her voice climbed in volume, to a hysterical scream. "Is that clear enough for you? You can take your fucking book of train schedules and—"

A shrill wail and the cry of an infant pierced the silence with the echoes of her tirade still bouncing off the walls.

Caressa broke off and ran. She heard Denise call after her but she only ran faster. She could hear the baby wailing still, and she ran like wolves were at her heels. He would come after her and she couldn't bear that. She would fight him if she had to, to keep him away. Train schedules, God.

She sobbed all the way up the elevator and down the hall to the suite, then realized she didn't have a key. She slumped against the door and buried her face in her hands. Denise came shortly afterward and hugged her until Caressa's chest started to ache from the sheer weight of her tears.

* * * * *

Kyle sat at the bar, staring down at the bubbles in his seltzer water. God, he needed a real drink. A stiff one. But he couldn't do that now. That would be pointless, complete destruction. There had been enough destruction tonight.

He didn't know why he'd decided to give her the book of train schedules. Spite? Love? Desperation? It had been one of their first real conversations, when she'd told him about Moeran and the train schedules, one of the first times she'd really opened up to him. But too late, he remembered that conversation ending the same way. Furious shrieks and screaming.

"I hoped I wouldn't find you here."

He turned at the deep familiar voice, hushed now in the nearly-deserted hotel barroom. "Don't worry. I'm not drinking. Yet."

Jeremy sat beside him, signaling the waiter to bring him the same thing Kyle had.

"How's Rhiannon?"

"She's fine. Nell got her calmed down pretty quickly. Poor thing was tired anyway."

The waiter brought the drink and Jeremy asked for lemon in passable French. The lemon was dispatched to the table and Jeremy squeezed it into his glass before he looked back at Kyle.

"These books. Always getting us men in trouble. You couldn't buy her something else? Flowers or something?"

Kyle frowned. "I wasn't trying to make trouble. I was trying to get through to her. I was trying to send her a message."

"Well," Jeremy said with a sigh. "From what I saw, she got your message. She just didn't like it very much."

Kyle looked over at Jeremy's drink. Jeremy hated seltzer. He was only drinking it because of him. Those were the kinds of things friends did for each other, to protect one another. Not wrapping up books of train schedules to make a point.

"She was right. I've pushed her and pushed her. She's right to be angry."

"Pushed her?" Jeremy fiddled with a stack of coasters. "You should have just stepped up the beatings a tad."

Kyle laughed. "That's your answer for everything."

"I know. But it works."

Kyle looked back at the bubbles in his glass, swirling them around with a fingertip. "So what do I do now?"

"You're asking me? I'm the fuck up. You're the one with a steady head on his shoulders."

"You're the one in a healthy relationship with a wonderful woman and a beautiful baby."

"Love prevails."

"Love only prevailed for you because I interfered. On several occasions."

"I've been trying to return the favor."

Kyle fell silent at his words. It was true that Jeremy had helped him numerous times, but in this instance… He gave Jeremy a desperate look.

"You're the famous one. Can't you give me any insight into what she's feeling? Why she plays when she's so unhappy?"

Jeremy thought for a while. "I'm not sure I can give you any insight. I mean, she's not famous like I'm famous. I act for petty reasons. For attention and the fawning fans. I act because I'm an egotistical jackass. I assume she doesn't play for same reasons?"

Kyle didn't even have to think about it. "No. Music is like a vocation to her. An almost…religious experience."

"Hm. See, matters of faith and religion can be very personal. And very mysterious. I think you may have to face the fact that you may never understand."

You don't understand. You don't understand. Kyle's mouth curved into a rueful grin. Jeremy was a jackass, but he could find insight at the most unexpected moments.

"You know, Kyle, there are a lot of things people do that I don't understand. But that doesn't mean I have a right to make them do things differently. That's something I've learned in my advancing years."

"You're turning into a regular sage."

"Thank you. Are you feeling any better?"

"A little. I'm going to go up soon. You don't have to sit down here with me. I'm not even tempted to take a drink."

"I'm glad to hear it. Oh, and…thank you for letting go of Nell. She worried about you for so long. I think it was nice for her to see today that you really are over her."

"What all have you told her?"

"Not everything. Not much. I kept your secrets. I didn't tell her about the tattoo, because that was just creepy," he said, rolling his eyes. "But she's a sensitive woman. I think she knew a lot that she never talked about. More than either of us will probably ever know."

Kyle saw a cell phone come out at a table nearby, watched the furtive clicking of the camera. From old habit he subtly angled himself to block Jeremy from the personal intrusion. Jeremy noticed and gave a resigned smile. "It's okay. Don't worry about it. Part of the job. Anyway, we're back to Boston tomorrow. But if you need anything…"

"Thanks, Jeremy. You know, thank you for everything. Really." *Everything.* His job. His sobriety. Even Caressa in a way. Jeremy had taken a country boy from Spur and brought him over a circuitous route to this five-star Paris hotel, and sat with him as he drowned his sorrows in a glass of seltzer water.

"You're welcome," Jeremy said with an easy smile. "And you want my best opinion? Give her some space and let her think about things."

Kyle knew it was wise advice, but it would be really hard for him to do.

Chapter Thirteen:
In Concert

Caressa woke up in her aunt's bed, where she'd cried herself to sleep the night before. Her aunt wasn't there though. Caressa could hear the shower going. Damn the fucking hotel suite. She didn't want to go out in the main room in case she ran into him, but she felt sick and hungry, and all her stuff was in her room. She went in Denise's bathroom to pee. God, all that champagne. She'd slept fitfully and she felt like crap. She rubbed a spot off the steamed-up mirror to find she had bags under her red, swollen eyes. Happy twenty-first birthday. She didn't look a day over eighty-two.

She went back out and lay on the bed to wait for Denise to finish in the shower. Her aunt came out a few moments later, toweling off her hair. She smiled at Caressa.

"How did you sleep?"

"Terribly."

Caressa turned away as her aunt started to dress. Aunt Denise was only in her mid-forties, but she too looked older than she really was.

Caressa never really considered all her aunt might have given up to support her music career. A husband? Kids? A life out in the suburbs? The idea depressed her. Caressa picked at one of her toenails and thought about how bad she had to shave her legs.

"So what are you going to do today?"

She looked back up at her aunt, considering her open-ended question. Did she mean it in a general, "what's-your-schedule" kind of way, or was she talking about…

Ugh. The way she'd left the party. She was going to have to face Kyle eventually. Aunt Denise came to sit beside her on the bed.

"He would probably like a chance to talk to you, honey. I know he wasn't trying to hurt you. He planned that big party for you—"

"So what?" she said in surly voice. "I don't know why you don't just let him go now. Why are we still paying him? The tour's almost over."

"He's helpful to have along. He does a million little things for you that you probably don't even realize."

Caressa snorted and glared over at her. "Why are you taking his side now? I thought you didn't like him."

"There are no sides here. I just think we should hold onto him until we finish out the tour. It's just a couple more weeks, Caressa. Do you really begrudge him the money?"

"I don't care about the money." Caressa propped her head on her knee. "It's just…he kind of… I don't know. I don't need him anymore. I really don't. I realized that last night. It's like I'm putting myself through this drama and trauma that I don't really need. I wish you would just fire him. This morning."

Aunt Denise looked at her a long moment, then shrugged. "I think that's a little harsh, but you're the boss. But he's *your* employee, so if you want to fire him, you do it. Don't put it on me." Then she got up and went out into the other room before Caressa could think of a suitable retort.

Well, fine. She would do it then. It had to be done or she'd never survive until Rome. She opened the door and stalked through the main room to her bedroom. He was sitting there, waiting silently on the couch. Damn him. She threw on some clothes, trying to ignore the mess she'd already made of her luggage. *He does a million little things for you that you probably don't even realize.* Kyle always cleaned up her messes, but she was pretty sure she could do it herself. She had done everything herself before he came along and started in with his kisses and caresses. His orders and stern, scary looks. Those fingers.

She opened the door before she could psych herself out of it. "Can you come in here, Kyle? I have to talk to you."

She didn't need him. She didn't need the sex and the control. She didn't need the disapproval, goddamn it. He walked into the room in his jeans and tee shirt and stopped just inside the door. She couldn't even face him. She looked out the window, trying to think how to begin, but he spoke first.

"So, I suppose you either want me to pummel you back into submission, or leave."

"I want you to leave."

He stood still and silent, and she felt blood fill her face, rushing through her veins in a panicky drumbeat.

"I'm tired of being treated like a child. I'm not a child."

"I'm happy to hear you say that."

"I'm not saying it to make you happy. I'm saying it because that's how I feel. I don't want to do this anymore, and I don't need your approval."

"No, you don't."

"I want you to leave. I'm tired of being bossed around by you."

"Maybe you just feel that way right now."

"No."

"Because for a long time I felt like you really enjoyed being with me. In and out of the bedroom. I thought we made a good couple. You were happy."

She wanted to deny it, but she couldn't. She turned from the window, from the blinding light of the sunny Paris morning. "If you wanted me to be happy, you'd let me be myself. You would accept me for what I am. A musician."

"I accept you as a musician, Caressa."

Ugh, his voice was so steady, not shaky like hers. He rested his hands on his hips, staring at her. She wanted to run to him and kneel at his feet, but she couldn't. She couldn't give everything up. "Look, I'll keep paying you for the last two weeks," she said. "If that's what you're worried about."

He moved then. He moved so fast and so threateningly that she backed up to the wall to get away from him.

"Money, Caressa? You think I'm worried about *money*? You can have every fucking red cent of the money you paid me. I don't want it." He pinned her against the wall, waving a finger in her face. "You can send me away, and I'll go, but let's be clear about two things. Number one, I was never here for the money. Not from the moment I heard you play that first time—"

"You see?" she cried out, pushing against his chest. "It's the music! All I am is the music! Even *you* admit it. Would you even love me without it?"

"Number two," he said, talking over her. "Number two, Caressa. I love you no matter what. Music or no music. So let's just be clear about those two things before you send me on my way."

She turned her face to the wall, defeated. He was lying. Love? He threw that word around an awful lot. He thought he'd been hopelessly in love with that Nell girl. He'd even tattooed her name on his chest. "It's not love," she said to the wall in a flat monotone. "It's just more bullet-wound-hero-bullshit."

That did it. He slammed his hands against the wall on either side of her head, and then he left.

* * * * *

"Caressa?" Aunt Denise stuck her head in the door of her room. "Hadn't you better practice? We have a photo shoot for the big Berlin write-up at two today."

Oh yeah, they were in Berlin now. Caressa couldn't keep track. She hated Europe. Hopping from city to city on dirty little flights, listening to a bunch of gibberish languages she didn't understand. The days were dragging and there was still Budapest and Rome to go.

She definitely was going to practice. Practicing was a good thing. She looked again at the package on the desk.

"Haven't you opened it yet?" her aunt asked.

"Why don't *you* open it?"

Denise put her hands on her ample hips. "Why don't *you* open it, since he sent it for *you*?"

Caressa tuned her out. She wasn't up for fighting lately. She was vaguely aware of Denise taking up the package and opening it while Caressa played an aimless, sliding run of notes. She lifted her bow from the strings with a dissonant squeak. "Just give it to me."

Her aunt shoved the box into her hands and stood waiting. Caressa glared at her. "Fine, Aunt Denise. I'll open it. But you might want to leave first. It's probably anthrax or something."

Denise threw up her hands in exasperation and turned to go. Caressa considered the box on her lap. It had been sent from Paris ahead to this hotel. Where was he now? Probably back in New York, moving on with his life, hopefully. She was happy to be moving on with hers.

Actually, she was doing just fine on her own. Kyle had taught her a lot of useful skills in their time together. She was more organized then she'd ever been. Her suitcase was a vision of orderliness. He would have been amazed to see it. She was pretty damn proud of herself.

She was getting better at other things too. She hadn't had a meltdown—not even a small one—since he'd left. That might have been because a lot of her spirit left with him. But it was for the best. She really believed that. She was doing her best work now that he was gone, playing flawless concerts. She was acting like a grown-up. She had to. He wasn't there to break her falls anymore.

She snapped open the tape and lifted the manila wrapping from the rectangular item. If it was another book of train schedules, she'd fly to New York herself to shove it up his ass. She ripped off the bubble wrap to find it wasn't a book at all, but a framed photograph.

She had to look at it a moment to figure it out. She recognized the grassy edge of the pond finally, and the line of trees among all the little pin dots of light.

There was a note she opened with shaking fingers. He hadn't written much. *Dear Caressa*, it read. *I hope you're doing well. This is the gift I originally meant to give you for your birthday. Please...I don't mean for this to make you mad. It's just that you said you wished you had a picture, and I told you there wasn't any way to take one, but I found someone who knew how to do it with some kind of prolonged exposure technique. So it can actually be done. I miss you. Kyle.*

She put the photo and note back on the desk and picked up her cello. *So it* can *actually be done.* She knew exactly what he meant her to understand from those words, from his brief note.

He never gave up, she thought ruefully. The photo was pretty though, the blurry lights scattered around like fallen stars in the forest. Maybe if he'd given her that instead of the train schedule, he'd still be here with her today. Making her laugh, cleaning up her messes. Holding her and making her world so much bigger than the music, so much more than practice and concerts. If he was here, he'd be kissing her and pulling her to the floor. He always knew how to make moments like that. She plinked out a series of treble notes that reminded her of fireflies blinking. Her world was a bleak, dark forest without him.

She looked down and saw a piece of paper on the floor that must have fallen out of Kyle's package. She leaned down and picked it up. It was a check for all the money she'd paid him, down to the penny, undoubtedly. She tore it into tiny pieces and then went and crawled into bed.

* * * * *

Kyle had hoped to hear from her after he sent the photo. Perhaps it was too little, too late. Her concerto—and the sorely missed music of her voice—still echoed in his mind all the time. He was still in Europe, still following her around. Did she think he wouldn't? And tonight—there was no way he could have missed this last performance. She was leaving a wake of adoring fans behind, Caressa of the striking gowns and the lovely scarlet lips, and the constellation of wild curls around her head. He was one of them.

There had been no evidence of a black elastic in weeks now. She truly seemed to have come into her own. She was playing with a greater, more skilled intensity than she ever had. The fact that this new, improved Caressa had appeared only after he left smarted somewhat. Perhaps she'd been right all along. Perhaps he *had* been bad for her.

Still, he didn't begrudge her her success. He was proud of her, and he'd always wanted what was best for her. He looked down at his watch, anxious for the concert to begin. It was past time. But then, this was Rome, where people often moved at their own maddening pace.

The longer the audience waited, the louder the murmuring grew. Kyle looked ahead at the heavy velvet curtain, and imagined he could hear the orchestra growing restless backstage. Then, over the swishing of the silk dress of the woman shifting beside him, beneath the rustle of programs opening and closing, he heard it like some haunting undertone.

His body was in motion before his mind had even decided to act. He unfolded his long legs from the cramped balcony seat and inched by the elderly couple beside him. He took the balcony stairs to the main level and then to the left aisle. Everyone watched him as he stalked toward the stage, mostly because there was nothing else to watch.

He said a few terse words to the usher, gesturing to make up for his lack of Italian. A moment later he was through the stage door and walking down the hall. He didn't even know what he'd said to the usher. He wasn't sure if he'd been granted egress because of his words, or because of the impetus behind them. The usher probably realized if he hadn't let him through, Kyle would have simply pushed him aside.

He followed the sound of her screaming down the white, sterile hallway until he reached the door with the "Caressa Gallo" sign. He pushed it open and took in the scene with the quick facility of someone who'd lived through it many times. He noted the impatient conductor, the mousy stagehand, the harried aunt, and two men in suits he assumed were theater personnel.

And behind them all, huddled in the back with her cello bow waving like a weapon, he saw Caressa herself. His wild girl, backed into a corner. He frowned as he noticed one of the suited-up men squeezing her forearm. Denise was wiping away frustrated tears, and Caressa was melting down in her own inimitable way.

"No. *No!*" she screamed. "I can't do it. I won't go out there until this is taken care of. This is my reputation as a musician—"

"Caressa, honey—" Her aunt begged.

"No, it's not in tune! I swear to fucking God—"

The conductor shook his head. "It is in tune. Be reasonable, Miss Gallo. I checked it." He spoke to her loudly, trying to capture her attention, but she wasn't listening, wasn't hearing a word. Kyle recognized the look on her face. He had seen it before. He knew all she heard at the moment was the terrifying pounding of her heart and the sound of the earth opening to swallow her whole.

"I can't! I won't play! The tone is off. How can you ask me to do this?"

The circle around her closed tighter, scolding, cajoling. They didn't even notice Kyle until he started pushing them out of the way. Then Caressa was in his arms, the warm, living shape of her. With one hand he pried the shredded bow from her fingers and handed it to Denise. Caressa went silent and stared in shock as he pulled her close, turning his body to block the others from her.

He could feel her shaking against him—pure, wild terror in a silk gown. She only fought him a moment before she slumped against him. He cradled her head against the lapel of his tux, not caring that her tears would probably ruin it.

"Shh. That's my girl," he said. He put his hand against her cheek and held her tighter, whispering in her ear. "I'm here now. Caressa. Shh. Be a good girl." He felt her sucking in breath, and her hand clutched spasmodically at his arm. He made soft, sibilant sounds against her temple until he felt her gasping breaths slow.

He pulled away to look at her. The others—the conductor, Aunt Denise, the theater people—had retreated to the other side of the room. It was just him and her, and a theater of waiting people. A lifetime of accomplishment—and deep, paralyzing fear.

"Miss Gallo, please," the conductor pleaded. "We must know if you will fulfill your obligations. The audience—"

"She'll play," Kyle said. "Tell them there's been a short delay."

At Kyle's look, the rest of them left. He looked down at Caressa in consternation. "You will play, won't you? You didn't endure this entire tour to blow off the last night."

"What are you doing here?" she asked in a trembling voice.

"Like all these other people, Cara, I came here to see you finish this thing."

She closed her eyes, leaning against his chest again. "I can't. You were right, Kyle. I don't know why I'm doing this. I just want to be left alone. I just want the music. That's all."

Kyle stroked her hair. "You have the music, Caressa. You *are* the music. The rest of them are just spectators. Cara, you're those fireflies at Burger's Pond. Something special. Something amazing. You make people's hearts beat faster, you make their mouths drop open. You're the only one who can do what they're waiting out there for you to do."

"I don't know…"

He squeezed her tighter, his cheek brushing against her ear. "You're the only one, baby. It has to be you. If you don't pull it together and walk out on that stage and play that concerto, it ceases to exist as only you can create it."

"I cease to exist," she whispered on a sob.

"No, that's not true. You know that's not true. You and I will still be here, no matter what."

"You left me."

"You sent me away, you maniacal diva."

Caressa laughed softly, a wondrous sound to his ears. "Why did you come back?" she asked.

Kyle made an impatient noise. "I never left, and I'm not going anywhere anytime soon." He cupped her chin and tipped her face up, pinning her with his gaze. "We have things to talk about, and plenty of time to talk about them. But right now, there are fifteen hundred people out there waiting for you to show them something they've never seen. Something unforgettable. One hundred thousand fireflies. You're the only one who can do it."

"I can't do it."

"That's a lie."

"I don't want to do it," she insisted. "I don't."

"If I believed that for one second, I would carry you out of here. But I don't believe you. You need to do this. You need to finish this and have a place to stop, at least for a while. After this, you and I are going to take a vacation somewhere and we're not bringing the cello. We're going to go somewhere, just you and me, and the only person you're going to need to please there is you. Caressa. Do you understand? You've done enough. You've satisfied everyone. It's time to get some distance and find out what Caressa needs and what Caressa wants. The cello will be here when you get back. Okay?"

"Well…" She sniffled. "I guess. But what about pleasing you?"

He smirked at her, running a hand over the intricate embroidery of her dress. "You can do that too, if you choose. Let's see how it goes."

"Okay," she said. She drew in a deep breath, and he saw her steel herself. "But…I guess I'll need a new bow."

A fellow musician produced a spare bow and there was a scramble to the wings. Kyle brushed back her hair and wiped the last of the sheen of tears from her face.

"I'm so proud of you," he whispered. "Go out there and enjoy every second of this."

She nodded, squeezing his hand in her cold fingers. The venue was in disorganization and the stagehand who was supposed to carry her cello onstage was nowhere to be found. In the end, it was Kyle who followed his lover onto the stage carrying her precious Peresson. As she arranged herself in her upholstered chair, Kyle looked out of the corner of his eye into the glare of lights and the sea of shining faces. Even for him, who had seen so much and done so much, the massive-scale scrutiny was daunting.

He looked away, focusing on his lover at his side. She reached for the cello and he passed it to her by its long, slender neck. Her hands shook just a little. Only his eyes could have detected those tiny tremors, but they moved him. She settled the instrument between her knees and looked up at him with a brave, conspiratorial smile. *Oh, Caressa, my God. That I ever thought I could live apart from you.* He had to leave her though, for this. The welcoming applause was dying out and his cello-carrying duties were discharged. On impulse he took her hand before he turned to go, bowing over it with what he hoped was a dashing kiss.

He received more than a few speculative stares as he started back to his balcony seat, but then Caressa began to play and all eyes were on her. If any of her fear or hysteria remained, she didn't show it. Her playing was a victory, a triumph. A swan song? Perhaps. Or perhaps not. They would worry about that later.

For now, Kyle let himself sink down into the melodies, those lovely melodies that were just one part of the wonderful whole that was Caressa. *My God, those knees of hers.* He wanted to be between them, clasped between them just like her cello. He should have been the one with the strings drawn vertically down his chest, and the f-holes on either hip. Well, no f-holes. But he'd never really been the conductor, any more than she'd ever really been his to play.

* * * * *

There was a reception after the show to celebrate the last night of her tour, and Kyle made her go to it since the Italians had so graciously thrown it for her. But Caressa had wanted to celebrate something else, and in an entirely different way than wine and pasta. Kyle seemed to know exactly how eager she was to be alone with him, but he insisted she fulfill her duties as the guest of honor before he would let her go.

There were music critics there she recognized, and notable music and cello patrons, all of them effusive in praising her accomplishments on the tour. Kyle stood beside her through all these conversations, silent eye candy. No one probably suspected how many times it almost all came tumbling down around her, or how instrumental the man standing at her side had been.

At last the crowds thinned and they made their escape, leaving Aunt Denise at the suite with hugs and reminders of the flight back to New York the following morning. Kyle switched his ticket in the cab on the way to his hotel so they could fly back together. Caressa watched his fingers on the phone, and the casual way he sat back and loosened his tie as they inched through city traffic. It was all she could do not to crawl into his lap, but she made herself sit still and quiet while he talked to a ticket agent in pretty good Italian.

He was so *good* at everything. She was good at one thing, but it didn't make her happy. Not the way she was currently doing it anyway. She'd take a break, take time to think. Take time to enjoy life and then find out what place music was going to have in her life. But it couldn't be everything. It couldn't rule over her. Not anymore.

"Okay?" he asked when he was through, squeezing her hand and looking down at her.

"Yeah," she said. "I think I'm okay."

As soon as they got to Kyle's hotel room, they both stripped, but stood apart as if to gather their defenses. Caressa eyed him from across the darkened hotel room, gawking at the beauty of his masculine virility. "So," she asked in the silence, "where are you going to take me?"

Kyle cast a lascivious look from the top of her head down her entire nude body to her feet. "Tonight…or later? I know where I'm taking you tonight," he said in a voice that thrilled her. "But the other… We'll talk about it some other time when I can think more clearly." He smiled at her. "Come here. You've been away from me for too long."

She bit her lip, moving toward him. She breathed in the still-familiar scent of him as he clutched her close.

"Hmm," he growled softly in her ear. "You've been a pretty bad girl."

"I'm always a bad girl," Caressa said. "You still said you loved me. I'm holding you to that."

"If we can just get the meltdowns down to once a month or so, I think I could eke out some tender feelings for you."

She pulled away with a protesting giggle, but he wouldn't let her move an inch. He kissed her—a demanding, skillful kiss that reminded her of all the things she loved about him. One hand tightened on her waist while the other grasped the back of her neck, angling her face so he could kiss her deeper still. The force of it stole her breath and had her groping for his engorged cock nestled between them. As soon as she started stroking him, he pulled away and ordered her to the bed, collapsing on top of her and nudging her thighs wide open with his knees.

"God, I'd like to make this last longer," he said. "But you really make things difficult sometimes."

"I'm sorry," she said, wiggling under him as he nudged at her slick opening.

"I don't think you are, but I'll punish you for it later, so it's okay."

Her laughter cut off in a moan as he lifted her legs over his shoulders and fell forward, filling her to the hilt. His cock stretched her open and slid deep, so she felt him in every place and every nerve. She reached for him and they grappled until he caught her hands, pressing them to the pillows over her head.

"Be a good girl," he whispered, twisting his hips to rock her in a wonderful, sensual friction. The stern endearment sent the ache between her legs into full throb. She clenched her fists over her head, determined to be the best girl in the history of civilization. He gazed down at her, grasping her by the waist to control her frantic jerky attempts to meet his thrusts.

"Kyle, Kyle…" She sighed as his hands slid up to cup her breasts. She arched into his touch, then shuddered as his fingers closed on her nipples with unrelenting pressure. As the pain built she tried to pull away even as the brutal ache caused a flood of slickness to her pussy. He fucked her harder, lifting her from the bed. He twined his fingers with hers and nudged her arms up to wrap around him as he released her legs.

They nestled together, belly to belly, so close she could feel each breath he took from the tickling slide of his chest hair against her still-sensitive nipples. He slid his hand down the back of her bottom as she clung to him, and he lifted her for each pounding stroke. She began to jerk her legs, seeking that final release that would join them together in that magical avalanche of pleasure. He ground his hips against hers so he slid across her clit, teasing her higher and higher. She clutched at him, squeezing a handful of his hair, and let go.

She knew she would never fall. He always caught her. He held her as her world disconnected into nothing but animal awareness and the unyielding pressure of him between her legs. She felt him tense and growl against her ear, going still in her, seated as deeply as he could manage. "Oh, God. Caressa…"

She laughed out loud, surprising herself, and surprising him too, since he looked down with a question in his eyes. She didn't know why she laughed with that wild, abrupt laugh except that she was just so happy. It had burst from somewhere deep inside her, some new place illuminating out of the darkness.

She laughed again and realized she was crying as hard as she was laughing. She pressed her face to his neck, embarrassed. She could feel the wetness of her tears and smell their faint, salty scent mingle with the sensual aroma of his aftershave. Her fingers slowly unwound from his hair as he nuzzled against her forehead and dropped a kiss on her nose.

"Okay, sweet pea?"

"I need you, Kyle." She blurted out the words through more uncontrolled laughter and tears. She wanted to explain to him just how *much*, but she was helpless to do it. She wanted to explain what he meant to her, with his strong arms and his quiet, reassuring voice. His faith and his unwavering focus. But in the end, all she could do was hiccough and repeat herself twice more. "I need you. I need you."

"You have me, Cara. I'm right here, I'm still inside you," he said, shifting his hips so she felt the delicious tease of his still-hard member. "If you tell me you can't feel me there, you might just hurt my feelings."

She giggled softly. There was a line of gold expanding at the edge of the darkness that had threatened her so long. Daybreak. Or sunset.

Her fingers tightened on his arms around her, the arms that promised to keep her happy and safe. Through her bleary, tearful eyes her world snapped into focus as his voice rumbled and his thumb stroked her cheek. "Where do you want me to take you now, Caressa? Anywhere."

She thought a moment. "First I want to go back to Spur. To Burger's Pond. Are the fireflies still there?"

"They may be. If not, there's always next year."

Next year. Years and years. They had so much time to see and do beautiful things together. She would go with him to Spur and catch fireflies for herself this time, and peek at them as they lit up a tiny world inside her fingers. That had been her once, trapped in a cage of her own making. Now she would have a whole forest of delights to flit around in.

"Are you sure I can't bring my cello?" she teased.

His look was priceless. Pure exasperation.

"You're lucky I love you so much, Caressa Gallo," he whispered as he gathered her close.

Epilogue
One year later

Kyle paced back and forth across the porch, going over a sizable mental checklist. Jeremy sprawled in a creaky rocking chair nearby, looking more wilted than Kyle could ever remember seeing him. A glass of Great-Grandma Winchell's special sweet tea dangled from Jeremy's hand, the icy drink sweating in the August Texas heat.

"You might have picked a cooler day to get married," Jeremy said, arresting Kyle's pacing with a leg stuck out in front of his path.

"We had to do it now, you know. The fireflies." Kyle rolled his eyes at Jeremy's long-suffering expression. "You'll live. Forgive me if I don't have much sympathy for you. I'm getting *married*."

Jeremy laughed and leaned forward, raising his glass in a toast so the ice inside clunked and tinkled. "Yes, you're getting married, and you couldn't be happier. So sit down and relax. Take off your organizer hat for just one day. You're like some kind of..." He searched for a suitably insulting word. "Bridezilla or something. Sit the fuck down."

Kyle collapsed in the rocking chair opposite him. "You have the ring? You're sure?"

Jeremy leaned back and shoved his hand in his lapel pocket. "I'm pretty sure I do, but hell, I'll check for the twenty-fifth time if it makes you feel better. Yeah, it's still there."

"I'm just nervous. I want this to be perfect for her. Her dream wedding."

Jeremy looked at him for a long moment. "I think her dreams have already come true. But I can understand wanting everything to be perfect."

"Did you feel like this on your wedding day? Your wedding was even bigger."

"Yeah, but I passed all the responsibility off on you and the wedding planner," he said with a laugh. "All I did was put all my energy into enjoying the day. Which is what I would suggest you do. Everything's going to go fine." He sat back and waved a hand toward the tree line. "At least you don't have fucking helicopters hovering over and paparazzi hanging from the rafters."

"If we did, I think my uncle Ray and my cousins would have had a blast shooting them down."

Jeremy narrowed his eyes. "I think I remember your uncle Ray."

"He's kind of hard to forget, once you've met him."

Kyle closed his eyes and tried to stop obsessing, but there had been so much planning to do. His mother, aunts, and sisters had been cooking for a week now, and a grandiose five-tier wedding cake had just been delivered from Dallas. All this in addition to the hospitable contributions of neighbors and friends, none of whom would ever come to a Spur wedding without food and spirits in hand. The reception tables over in Burger's Field were undoubtedly groaning under the weight of the feast.

The house was full of gifts, from the overly-generous cash tributes of Jeremy and some of Kyle's other show business friends, down to the burnt-orange and green pot holders Great-Grandma had painstakingly knitted and presented to a tearful Caressa the night before.

Caressa. Kyle loved her so much he ached with it, and he never loved her more than when she was here in Spur. He would gaze at her in abject adoration as she chatted with his loopy Great-Grandma, or rocked in companiable silence with his mom on the porch. Caressa was as comfortable here now as she was sitting in front of a full orchestra, which she still did—on a slightly less frenetic performance schedule. As for meltdowns, he couldn't remember the last time she'd had one.

No, he was the one in meltdown mode now. Caressa asked for a Spur wedding and Kyle had been happy to oblige, electing himself head wedding planner. Now she was off relaxing and getting dressed with her aunt while he was sweating the details in his tux on the porch.

"It'll cool off when the sun goes down," Kyle said, as Jeremy swiped his tea glass across his forehead. He followed Jeremy's gaze to Nell and little Rhiannon under the big oak tree. The active toddler was barreling around with an army of other kids under the shady shelter, and their laughter carried up to the house.

"God, it's nice here, Kyle," Jeremy said. "It's a fine day for a wedding."

"Oh! The cello! The cellist—"

"Is already down by the pond, ready to play the wedding march. Relax, Kyle. It's all done."

The men were silent for a moment, their chairs creaking in the late afternoon heat. Then Jeremy looked at Kyle with a curious tilt to his brow.

"So what's next for Kyle Winchell? Somehow I imagine you're not going to want to put in personal assistant hours anymore. Not with *la Caressa* waiting for you back home."

Kyle smiled. "Yeah. I've been thinking about what to do next. I might just devote myself completely to *la Caressa*'s happiness. I could plan a much better tour than that dolt who worked on the last one."

Jeremy looked meditative, rocking with one leg lazily propped on the other. "There's nothing more precious to an artist than a true, trusted partner and friend. If the only job you do is being there for her…" He glanced up again at Nell with a brooding expression. "Being someone who loves her as she is, whether she's on top or slowly sliding down into obscurity…that will be your most important job. It doesn't pay well, but…" Jeremy was rarely serious, but he was now. "Kyle, it's the most important job you could do for her, you know?"

Kyle was touched, as he always was when Jeremy spoke from the heart. He looked at his former employer with an equal level of gravity. "I'll always be that friend to you too, Jeremy."

"I know," he said, making another big show of mopping the perspiration off his forehead. He flashed Kyle his trademark dashing grin. "Why the hell else would I be sweating my ass off in Texas at this time of year?"

* * * * *

The clearing above Burger's Pond had been transformed into a wedding wonderland. The knee-high grass had been razed and a series of tents erected to hold all the food, guests, and bands so people could dance. The biggest tent held the cake and the bride and groom's table. It seemed all of Spur had congregated there, socializing and waiting for the wedding to begin.

Kyle saw faces he hadn't seen in years, and other faces that were endearingly familiar. He chased Rhiannon and made her scream with laughter while Nell followed, chastising Kyle for winding her up right before the ceremony. Great-Grandma Winchell was holding court by the dessert buffet, yelling orders about the best way to arrange the gelatin molds. His mom was serene as ever, kissing cheeks and distributing hugs to all the guests as if she hadn't spent the entire past week slaving in the kitchen.

Just at dusk Jeremy came to him. "They're ready."

They're ready. They're ready. Word spread through the waiting guests and they departed in one big group down the hill to Burger's Pond. Kyle took his place at the edge of the water beside the reverend, the same man who'd sermoned him to walk a straight path when he was a child. For what it was worth, Kyle thought he hadn't walked a very straight path in life. But if it brought him here, it could only be good.

Jeremy stood at his shoulder, patting his lapel to reassure him one last time that, yes, he had the ring close and ready. The sea of loved, familiar faces stood around in a semi-circle, and then the circle parted, and Caressa was coming toward him on her aunt's arm. She wore a simple, sleeveless white gown and a broad, contented smile. Her wild hair fell loose across her shoulders and down her back. She clutched a handful of impatiens from his mother's garden, peaches and pinks to match her blush. His lovely spitfire. God. For a moment he almost wept at the picture she made. She was so beautiful, so beautiful…

He was saved from the ignominy of shedding manly tears when Great-Grandma boomed "Ain't she purtyful?" loud enough to be heard over the strains of the cello's wedding march. Everyone laughed, and Caressa's eyes fixed on his, and then he couldn't think of anything but the beauty of her smile. Like most men, he'd never daydreamed about his perfect wedding, but he knew this was it. This day, this hour. This minute, as Denise placed Caressa's hand in his.

They made public vows, none they hadn't already whispered to each other long ago. *I'll love you forever. I'll live to make you happy, because you make me so happy too.* Then, as Jeremy handed him the ring to slip onto her finger, the first *ooh* sounded in the gathering dusk.

Kyle could see the blinking from the corner of his eye. A few children broke from their parents to run closer to the pond, eager to take in the burgeoning, flickering display. Caressa looked too, then back at him with a crooked, happy smile. Kyle didn't have to turn and look. All the wonder he needed was there, right there in front of him.

As the voices of the assembled guests rose and the spectacle of the fireflies drew their attention, Kyle took Caressa's chin in his hand and sealed their vows with a kiss.

* * * * *

When Caressa had asked for a Spur wedding, she'd never imagined how lovely it would actually be. They stayed down at the pond until the fireflies were nearly blinked out, stealing kisses between the congratulations of their guests. Once the reception line was done, she gave up on pomp and circumstance and ran after the fireflies with the children, managing to catch a good number, even hampered by her long silk gown. Kyle just watched her, shaking his head in mock disapproval until he gave up and joined her. Then they sat to rest on his favorite boulder, just watching the creatures flit and blink around them.

Caressa nestled back against her new husband and took his hand. "Thank you," she said.

"You're certainly welcome," he murmured, kissing the top of her head. "But for what?"

She squeezed his fingers, tracing the contours of his platinum wedding band. "For everything. For this day. For loving me. Mostly for putting up with me when no one else would have had the patience."

His other hand drifted up the side of her bodice to furtively stroke the underside of her breasts. "It wasn't only patience that sustained me through the difficult times, I have to admit."

She laughed, snuggling closer to him. "Whatever it was, I'm glad. And now we're married. I almost can't believe it."

"Not having second thoughts already?"

She looked up at the last of the fireflies, the blinks growing lighter and more intermittent. "No, not second thoughts. Only one thought. How much I love you." Her stomach growled in the still darkness. "Oh, yeah. And how hungry I am."

Kyle pulled her up and they made their way through the field to the reception tents. People were eating and drinking, calling out congratulations. Jeremy Gray winked at her, and his wife waved from his side. Now that Caressa had gotten to know Nell, she didn't hate her anymore, even though she'd probably never get over the fact that her husband had once tattooed her name on his chest.

When he managed to draw her away, Kyle led her to the cake table, and Caressa giggled over the tiny cellist and conductor up on top of the massive white confection.

"I suppose that's you," she said, pointing to the pompous-looking, tuxedoed figurine.

"Yes, with my orchestra of one," he replied, poking her in the side. "Mom looked everywhere for those to put on top of the cake, so don't knock them in front of her."

"I think they're awesome. Look, I even have brown hair. Where did she find them?"

"It's probably better not to ask."

As if on cue, Melanie Winchell swept up to the couple and enfolded them in a joint hug. "Oh, my dears," she drawled. "Could it have been any more beautiful? Did y'all steal some kisses before the fireflies blinked off?" Caressa blushed as her new mother-in-law hugged her once more and moved back into the fray of guests. She turned the other way to see her Aunt Denise being twirled around the dance floor by one of Kyle's brothers.

She soon found herself swept up in the noise and jubilant dancing too. She danced with every one of Kyle's relatives, and twice with Jeremy, who still seemed like a down-to-earth guy no matter how famous he was. She got some wedding night pointers from Great-Grandma Winchell that made her toes curl, and then to her relief, Kyle pulled her away and led her to another, quieter tent. Guests relaxed and chatted in muted tones as a string quartet played. Caressa noticed the cellist from the ceremony in the corner with his instrument propped against his leg. Kyle led her over with a strange, secretive smile on his face.

"Caressa, allow me to introduce David Gordon. He flew here all the way from Denmark, where he plays with the Copenhagen Orchestra."

Caressa thanked the dark-haired, middle-aged musician for coming to play at the wedding, but she was a little confused that Kyle hadn't just hired a more local cellist. *Copenhagen?* Mr. Gordon complimented Caressa effusively, explaining that he'd seen her play in her last tour through Europe. Then Kyle gestured toward the man's cello. "Mr. Gordon plays a Peresson too. This particular one is on loan to him." He paused. "It belonged to Jacqueline, Cara."

Caressa blinked, then blinked again. *David Gordon. Copenhagen Orchestra.* Now she remembered the name, and the shock of Kyle's surprise hit her.

"Oh, Kyle." It was all she could think to say. She reached for the instrument, tracing lightly down the side of the fingerboard. "Oh, Kyle. Really? *Really?*" And then: "Please, may I play it? Please?"

At first she played with the quartet, and then, as spectators filled the room, the quartet dispersed, leaving only Caressa and the new-old cello she cradled between her knees. The cello surprised her, its tone close and yet not exactly alike to her own instrument. She became acquainted with it as an hour passed, and then another. She played for Jacqueline, gone too soon, and for love and taking chances. For passion and fear, and longing. For twinkling, blinking bugs, orange potholders and happy children. For storms and for shelter.

For Kyle.

Later, he took the cello from her and passed it back. He took her hand and led her away from the smiling crowds to his childhood home, to his bedroom. The fan above the bed made its own whirring music as they undressed and lay down together on the narrow mattress. She reached out for him, shaky and shivery with bliss.

"Play me now, Kyle," she whispered, covering his face with feather-soft sweet kisses.

"Yes," he said. His fingers trailed up her stomach to her breasts, tracing invisible strings. "Any song you want."

They started with a lilting ballad, and progressed to a fiery appassionato. After a rest, they created a sweeping waltz, and some time later, a noisy hornpipe.

When the sun came up they were still playing. They had so many songs to play together, and a lifetime to do it. *Accarezzévole.* Sweeps and scales of shimmering, harmonious notes.

A Final Note

I owe a great debt of thanks to musical artists in the creation of this story. I first heard Stephin Merritt's song *100,000 Fireflies* in 1992 when a band called Superchunk covered it. I later heard The Magnetic Field's original 1991 version and liked it even better. It contains a particular lyric I love: *"I'm afraid of the dark without you close to me."* That line—and the image of all those fireflies—blinked in my mind for almost two decades before resulting in this book. Perhaps you will give Merritt's song a listen.

Spur, Texas is a real town—with beautiful sunsets, I'm told—and Burger's Pond, while fictional, was named for Donald Ray Burger, a Houston attorney who spearheaded a project to bring fireflies back to Texas. At his site you can read people's reports of firefly "sightings" all over the United States dating from the early nineties up until the time of this writing. Jacqueline du Pré, the cellist Caressa admires, was also real person, and her cello recordings and videos are worth a listen too.

Finally, if you have not read my book *Comfort Object*, I hope you will. It's a prequel to *Caressa's Knees*, and tells Jeremy and Nell's mythic love story. Many thanks to Miri, the fan of *Comfort Object* who convinced me that Kyle needed his own story. Without her prompting, I'm sure this story would never have been written. Thanks also to Audrey, my tireless editor, who's been with me from the start of this adventure.

I end this book with a wish: that all desperate people, no matter their place or situation, eventually find respite from their storms, whatever they may be.

Caressa's Knees

About the Author

Annabel Joseph writes emotionally intense stories about the romance of dominance and submission. She has published erotic fiction with Ellora's Cave, Loose Id, and her own indie imprint, Scarlet Rose Press. You can learn more about her books, read reviews, and find contact information at **http://annabeljoseph.wordpress.com**.

CPSIA information can be obtained at www.ICGtesting.com
Printed in the USA
LVOW13s1818170713

343352LV00008B/900/P